T0051231

CASH MONEY CONTENT

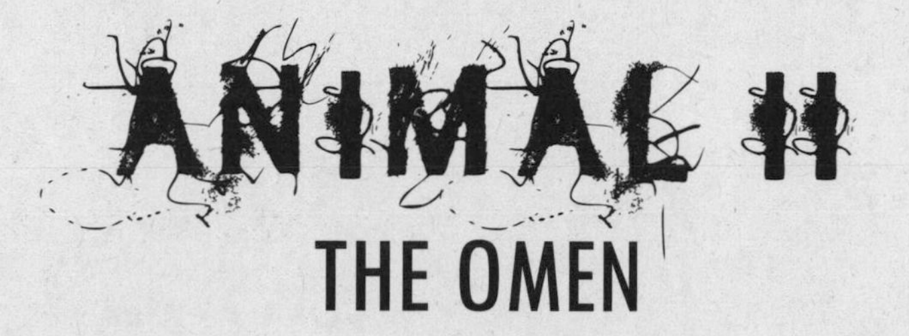

THE OMEN

K'WAN

ANIMAL 2

Any similarity to persons living or dead is purely coincidental.

First Trade Paperback Edition: November 2013

Cover Design: Baja Ukweli

www.CashMoneyContent.com

Library of Congress Control Number: 2013950119

ISBN: 978-1-936399-29-1 pbk
ISBN: 978-1-936399-30-7 ebook

21 20 19 18

Printed in the United States

"Dedicated to my mother, who constantly watches over me and guides these gifted hands. Love you Brenda.

My wife, Charlotte, and my children Alexandria, Nijaa and Star, who all gave so much of themselves as I was writing this novel. When I retreated to the furthest corners of my head to produce Animal II they held things together in the real world. We suffer together and prosper together, such is the make up of who we are. My love for you guys is unconditional. #TEAMFOYE above all."

Kwan

PROLOGUE

IF YOU ASKED ANYONE ABOUT RICK JENKINS, most of them would likely have the same opinion of him: a liar, a cheat, a scum bag and all around loser. That had been the story of his life, losing, at least until recently.

Rick was a grifter who made his money playing the con game. His most recent scam was bogus apartment rentals. He would run ads on sites like Craigslist claiming to be a Realtor for a luxury apartment complex. He had a buddy who worked in maintenance at the complex, so gaining access to empty apartments for showing was easy. Rick would even go as far as giving people their keys in exchange for cash up front. By the time the renters tried to move in and realized they'd been duped, Rick was long gone. He had managed to scam ten people before management finally got hip to the scheme.

Of all the people Rick had scammed with the phony apartments, there was only one he felt kind of bad about. She was a young chick with a hard-luck story to tell that tugged at Rick's heartstrings. She was fresh out of the hospital after a near-death assault and looking to move out of the neighborhood it happened in. Rick was going to turn her away, until she offered to pay him three months' rent in advance. Greed got the best of him, and Rick took the poor girl's money and got ghost.

Since Rick had a little money saved up, he decided to give the bogus rental con a break and take some time to enjoy himself. This night, he had gotten up with some of his buddies and hit the town. Toward the end of the night, they had stumbled upon a dice game. Rick saw it as easy pickings. By the time he'd left the dice game, he was five grand richer. He could've probably left with double that if he'd lingered around long enough, but he didn't want to press his luck. It would only be a matter of time before someone caught on to the fact that he was switching the dice.

Rick had said good-bye to his friends and hello to a money-hungry young smut who'd attached herself to him at the dice game. Rick couldn't wait to get her back to the motel he'd been staying at and see how far she was willing to go in the name of a dollar. It took less than five minutes after they arrived for her to show him. She was on Rick like a cheap suit. The girl had just taken all of him into her mouth when the door came crashing open.

It was dark, and the person standing in the doorway had a high-powered flashlight which he kept pointed at Rick's eyes. Rick moved to get up, but the distinct sound of a hammer being cocked froze him. "I'm gonna need you to stay right where you are, my nigga," a masculine voice said from behind the glare of the flashlight.

"Man, I don't know what this is about, but—" Rick began,

but his words were cut off when the flashlight collided with the side of his head.

"If you shut the fuck up, I'll tell you," the man with the flashlight said. The light turned to the girl, who was cowering at the foot of the bed. "Leave. Don't get your clothes, don't get your purse. Just get the fuck out. If you look back, I'm going to kill you. Do you understand?" The girl didn't even answer. She just bolted from the room. "Like I was saying." The light went back to Rick. "You know, I respect a nigga trying to get money, legal or illegal, but what I don't respect is a fucking parasite. Worms like you ain't got the balls to grind for it, so you take it from hardworking people. The thing you never take into account is that there are people in the world who got love for the folks you robbing, like my peoples you took for her bread."

"My dude, I don't know you or your peoples," Rick said. He was racking his brain trying to think who he might've wronged enough for them to want him dead. The list was too long for him to even fathom.

Suddenly, the room was filled with light. Rick's vision was blurred, but when it cleared, he found himself staring down the barrel of a large .357 being held by someone familiar. "I know you. I saw you at the dice game."

"If you knew me, then you'd have gotten out of town the minute you saw me instead of sticking around," the gunman said.

"Fam, if this is about the money I won at the dice game, then you can have it." Rick scooped his jeans off the floor and held them out to the gunman. "Everything is in there except what I spent on the cab to get here with shorty."

The gunman slapped Rick's jeans from his hands. "Nigga, this ain't about what you won at the dice game. It's about you being more careful of whom you steal from. My home girl trusted you, and you did her dirty, and now you gotta make it right."

Rick was scared shitless. He had no idea if the man was going to kill him or just kick his ass and rob him, but he wasn't ready to gamble on the mercy of strangers. In a last-ditch attempt to save his skin, Rick lunged for the gun. The gunman moved off reflex when he pulled the trigger. The powerful slug hit Rick high in the chest and carried him sailing over the bed and crashing into the corner.

"Dumb, just fucking dumb." The gunman shook his head. "I just came to get the money you beat my home girl for, and you've turned it into something else."

"Please!" Rick gasped as he bled out onto the motel carpet.

The gunman placed the .357 over Rick's head. "I didn't plan on killing you, but you've changed that plan. I'm not a complete scum bag, though." He moved the barrel from Rick's head to his heart. "I'll make it so that your people can bury you with an open casket," he promised, and pulled the trigger.

The gunman walked down the motel hallway, counting the money he'd taken from Rick. With his dice game's winnings coupled with the money he already had on him, it came to just under six grand. He wasn't sure if that would cover what she had lost to the scam artist, but it would have to do. He'd already gone further than he planned to.

As he passed the front desk, the clerk sat with her face buried in a magazine, trying her best to act like she didn't see him.

The gunman tapped the .357 to get her attention. Nervously, she looked up. The gunman peeled off ten hundred-dollar bills and slid them across the desk with a gloved hand. "This should hold you for a week or so while you're looking for another gig. I think you've outgrown this place," he said, before slipping from the motel and disappearing into the night.

UNFINISHED BUSINESS

"A man who would betray his friends is the lowest form of human being. His death should reflect that. I don't just want his life, Priest. I want that rat fuck's cheese-stained tongue!"

—SHAI CLARK

ONE

FOR A LONG FEW MOMENTS, ALL WAS silent in the church. Kahllah leaned against the wall closest to the raised stage, which had once been graced by some of the most beautiful voices in Harlem. A strand of her silky black hair blew across her face from the breeze seeping in through the cracked stained-glass window. Kahllah pushed the hair from her face and once again thought about cutting it. She was a beautiful girl, with flawless sun-baked skin and rosy lips that always seemed to be pouting. She was the picture of the girl you wanted to take home to meet your mother, until your eyes landed on the big black gun dangling from her hand. Her dark brown eyes took in the scene unfolding before her but revealed nothing. She watched it with the enthusiasm of a blind person at a silent movie.

Gucci, however, was a bit easier to read. She sat in the front pew, with a worried expression on her face. She had lost a bit of weight from her long stay in the hospital, and her hair was badly in need of a perm. She wasn't exactly the curvaceous vixen she'd been, but she was a far cry from the empty shell they'd wheeled into surgery almost a month before. While out partying with friends, Gucci had been the recipient of a bullet meant for someone else. While she lay in the hospital, teetering between life and death, mass murder was being committed on the streets of New York in her name. Her lover was merciless in his vengeance, but it was the same all-too-consuming lust for revenge that had inevitably doomed both of them and brought them to the dark place, unsure if they would live or die. A few feet away from Gucci sat her heart. The man who had died as her protector and been resurrected as her dark horseman.

Animal had been sitting stone-still on the army cot for what seemed like an eternity. His head was lowered and spills of dark black curls fell around his chocolate face. His dark eyes were downcast, locked on the object in his trembling hands. It was a picture of Animal when he was a baby, with his mother and his biological father. Every so often, he would look from the picture to the man who had handed it to him and shake his head. There was no denying the resemblance. This couldn't be!

The man in the picture, Priest, loomed over Animal, dressed in black priest's robes, thumbing the gold rosary through his fingers. Priest was a hard-faced man with a clean-shaven head and a stubbly salt-and-pepper beard. The black patch he wore over his eye made him look more like a mercenary than a man of the cloth, but he was actually both. For many years, Priest had walked the path of the righteous, until tragedy caused him to stray. When God abandoned Priest, he abandoned God, and so began his slow walk to damnation. Priest was a reputed assassin, personal executioner for the Clark family, but he was also Animal's father. The revelation had stunned everyone in attendance, but none seemed more shocked than Animal.

Animal's eyes stayed fixed on the picture. It had been years since he had laid eyes on the woman who had brought him into the world and even longer since she had looked like she did in the picture. Animal's mother, Marie, had been beautiful in her day. She was a mix of black and Hispanic, with dark curly hair and pretty bowed lips, which she had passed on to her youngest son. She was the object of desire for many men but had eventually given herself to a cancerous young punk named Eddie. Things had already been hard on them when Animal's biological father left, but they became worse when Eddie came into the picture. The years spent with his stepfather were a living hell for Animal, and he was made to suffer all forms of mental and physical abuse. One of Eddie's favorite methods of disciplining Animal when he was upset was locking him naked in a dog cage and starving him for days at a time. Animal would lie awake on the cage floor some nights and dream of killing Eddie for making his mother suffer, then killing his real father for abandoning them. Years later, the debt between him and Eddie would be settled in blood, but he had unfinished business with the man standing before him now.

"There is no shame in showing emotions. It's a spiritual release when we're in pain," Priest said. "You must have a million and one thoughts running through your head and none of them pleasant ones."

Animal hadn't even realized he was crying, until a teardrop splashed on the tattered photograph. He wiped his face with the back of his hand and turned his red-rimmed eyes to Priest. His voice was heavy with emotion when he spoke. "Why?"

Priest cocked his head to the side as if he didn't understand the question.

Animal placed the picture neatly on the cot next to him and gave Priest his undivided attention. "I lay awake many nights thinking of what I would do or say if I ever met my biological father. A bunch of scenarios played out in my head, but in all of them, I would always ask why. Why leave your little boy to face the evils of the world all by himself? This is what I said I'd ask my daddy, right before I killed him."

Before the threat could even register in Priest's head, Animal lunged at him. The older man was caught off-guard, so the first two punches landed square on his chin and staggered him. When Animal faked high, Priest reflexively covered his face, leaving his gut exposed to the next punch his son threw. Priest was doubled over in pain, so Animal tried to finish him with a kick to the face, but the chain clasped around his ankle threw his aim off. He launched another punch, but Priest was ready. He grabbed Animal by the arm and, with a twist, dislocated it from his shoulder. For good measure, he swept Animal's legs and put him on his ass. When Animal tried to get back up, Priest stomped on his injured shoulder.

Priest squatted down beside Animal, who was rolling around on the ground, clutching his shoulder. "I ain't some punk-ass gun boy who shits his pants every time he sees them shiny grilles of yours, Tayshawn. I've been doing this since before I shot you outta my nut sack. You're good, son, but I'm still better." Priest grabbed Animal by the back of his shirt and helped him to the cot.

"Fuck off me." Animal jerked away from him. His arm was throbbing, and he couldn't feel his fingers.

"You got a lot of fire in you, boy, and that's a good thing. You're gonna need it for this shit you plan on pursuing," Priest said.

"And what do you know about my plans, old head?" Animal asked.

"I know that you got a fire burning in your belly that's eating you up a chunk at a time. A wise man would've taken the pass and high-tailed it to greener pastures, but the men in our family aren't known for their smarts, we're known for our need to hurt people. You might look like your mother, but it's my demons that live in your heart."

Animal chuckled. "Listen to you, trying to sound all fatherly and shit, like you give a fuck about what's in my heart. Let's be clear, I lay no claim to you or anybody else from your side of the gene pool. I ain't yo son, the gutter spit me out. I was birthed by a drug whore and raised by the streets. Where the fuck do you come in?"

"There's that rage again," Priest said.

Animal stood and got nose-to-nose with Priest, but the older man didn't even flinch. "You have no idea what rage is until you've been violated to the point where you feel subhuman."

"The good Lord places obstacles in front of us as tests of our faith. From the most faithful to even the wretched, we are all tested. To reach the kingdom of heaven, we must first brave the fires of hell," Priest said.

"So says your fake biblical ass," Animal said, mocking him. "You know, I actually think this is kinda funny, the priest who fathered the omen. My birth was a sure sign of things that would come to pass. For as much grief as I've brought into the world, I can't even say that I blame you for cutting out on me."

Priest sighed. "If only you understood the whole story."

"The way I see it, there ain't much to understand. You were just another bitch-ass nigga who was afraid to take care of his responsibilities," Animal said venomously.

Priest felt his hand twitch, but he fought back the urge to knock Animal's head off his shoulders. "Tayshawn, you can either keep acting like a spoiled-ass kid with a chip on his shoulders or get your head back in the game and act like you want to live through this. I'm trying to help you."

"I don't want your help!" Animal spit.

"What you want and what you need are two different things, Tayshawn, but all roads lead to your ultimate goal: Shai Clark. If you move wrong this time, I doubt if there'll be another resurrection. Kahllah." He turned to her.

"Yes, Father?"

"Take them upstairs to the place we've prepared for them. Tend to Animal's injury, let him shower, and give him the fresh clothes I left. I need him ready to travel by the time I come back from my meeting," Priest told her. After issuing some last-minute instructions, he pulled Gucci to the side. "For all that you've gone through with and for him, I take it you love my son?"

"I don't think whether I love your son or not is the question. I've been in his life longer than you have," Gucci said with a hint of attitude. Flashes of the older her were coming back.

Priest's bowed lips cracked into a half grin. "A bit of fire in the soul is a good thing, but don't let that fire get so big that it burns you. My ties are to Tayshawn, not you. As far as I'm concerned, your life serves as nothing more than a distraction to the grand scheme. The only reason there are two empty graves in that scrap yard instead of one is that I know my son cares about you, and your passing would no doubt leave him irreparably broken. You don't have to like me, but you will respect me. Are we clear?"

"Crystal," Gucci said, but she'd taken some of the bass out of her voice.

"When I return, my son and I are going for a little ride so we can have a long-overdue talk. Kahllah will tend to your needs in our absence," Priest told her.

"Where are you taking him?" Gucci asked.

"That isn't your concern. What you should be focused on is helping me persuade him to do the right thing so that you may both walk away from this with your lives."

"I can try, but Animal has his own mind. Once it's set, it's hard to change," Gucci said honestly.

"You'll do more than try, for your own sake. There are a great many things in motion which neither you nor Tayshawn totally understand. Things that have been years in the making, and we will not see them ruined because my son couldn't control his emotions. I am tolerant, but Kahllah is not, and there's no doubt in my mind that she won't hesitate to hurt you to control him," Priest warned, and left the church for his meeting.

THE MEETING WAS SET TO TAKE PLACE at a truck stop off the New Jersey Turnpike, just over the George Washington Bridge. It was early in the afternoon, so the parking lot was busy with cars coming and going. The tall black man in the priest's robes drew more than a few stares as he crossed the lot, headed to the diner. A trooper, who was coming out of the diner, stopped to hold the door for the holy man.

"Bless you, my son." Priest gave him a phony smile and stepped into the diner. The man he had come to see wasn't hard to find. His was the only booth flanked by minions who looked every bit of the hired guns they were, dressed in off-the-rack suits and wearing sunglasses indoors. The man they were protecting sat at the rear of the booth, facing the door. He was dressed in a white collared shirt, with a salmon-colored blazer and blue jeans. He was joined by two other people. A woman, who had her back to him, and a young light-skinned man with dusty brown hair. When the man in the salmon blazer spotted Priest, he motioned for him to come over.

"Thanks for coming." Shai Clark stood and greeted Priest with a handshake and a smile. He was a handsome man, with a baby face and joyful eyes. Shai looked more like a college kid than a ruthless crime boss who controlled the New York City underworld.

"You call, and I come, that's the way it works, right?" Priest said with a smirk. "I thought this was a private meeting." He glanced from the young man to the woman at the table. She was older than Priest but had the body of a woman half her age. Her skin was smooth and dark, in contrast to her silver hair, which she wore up in an elegant bun. The green skirt suit she wore fit her body perfectly, no doubt tailored to fit. Around her neck, she wore a string of white pearls. When her dark eyes glanced up at Priest, her red-painted lips parted into a smile that said she had a secret that she couldn't wait to tell. For all intents and purposes, she was the picture of someone's loving grandmother, but those who knew her knew better.

"No worries. This is a friend of ours. I'd like to introduce you to—"

"Who in the underworld doesn't know Machine Gun Ma Savage?" Priest cut him off.

Ma smiled, showing off two perfect rows of white teeth, one capped by a gold crown. "Machine Gun Ma is only for niggers I plan on killing or nosy reporters. It's just Ma to my friends. Are we friends these days, or do you still wanna lock ass over that lil' misunderstanding we had back in 1982, Tay?"

Priest stiffened at her use of a name he had buried when he first donned the black robe. "I prefer Priest, and yes, I'd say we're friends these days, Ma. The past is the past."

"That's good to know, because you never can tell with members of y'all's clan. I swear I could never figure out how a bunch of muthafuckas as pretty as you all are could be so deadly. I'm still holding on to the hope that one of my boys gets accepted into your little club." Ma gave him a wink.

Shai was surprised. "You two know each other." He looked from Priest to Ma Savage.

Ma cackled. "Of course we do. Me and old Priest got history, don't we?"

"Indeed we do," Priest said in a less-than-pleasant tone.

"Ma, is this the old nigga you always going on about?" The light-skinned young man spoke up. "Shit, he don't look like much to me."

Ma Savage slapped him upside the head with her purse. "You mind your damn manners, Bug Savage. Excuse my youngest boy. Sometimes he lets his ass speak for his mouth. How you been, Priest?"

"I've been better, but I'm alive, so I can't complain," Priest said with a shrug. "How're the kids?"

"Still ornery as ever. Big John is finishing up a dime in a fed joint somewhere in Illinois, so Dickey and Maxine have been handling the business. I got no idea where Mad Dog is these days. He comes and goes as he sees fit, and most of the time, he's got the law a few steps behind him."

"Same old Mad Dog." Priest shook his head. Even as a kid, Mad Dog had been the wildest of the Savage boys. He had no understanding of right or wrong. He was like an animal and moved off instincts rather than rational thought. "And Killer?" he asked of the forth-oldest Savage boy.

"Killer goes by Keith these days," Ma told him. "My delusional son has abandoned his evil ways and is working for the other side now. He just graduated law school. Can you imagine a Savage working on the wrong side of the damn law? His daddy is probably turning over in his grave right now over that blasphemous shit!" She spit on the floor, drawing some less-than-pleasant stares from the people eating at the next table. "I don't bother with him, but he speaks to Maxine and Dickey pretty regularly. Outside of that, he keeps his distance, and that's fine by me. Whether I pushed 'em out my pussy or not, I got no care or no time for ungrateful kids. You know how many muthafuckas I done shot to keep food in his prissy-ass mouth, and this is how he repays me, by leaving his poor old mom and siblings to fend for themselves while he's out trying to save a world that don't wanna be saved? He prances around rubbing shoulders with his new white friends, like his last name ain't Savage same as the rest of us. Let's see how friendly them crackers would be if they knew his education was paid for with blood money." She cackled. "A walking contradiction, that Killer is."

Priest nodded in understanding. "He always was a bit different from the rest." He reflected on the man formerly known as Killer. Keith had always been the quiet one, who kept his head buried in books. He was docile in contrast to his brothers, but when provoked, he was one of the most dangerous of the Savage boys.

Ma placed her hand on the light-skinned young man's shoulder. "And of course, you met my youngest, Fire Bug. We call him Bug for short."

Priest studied the young man. He didn't look to be much older than sixteen or seventeen. "Don't tell me you're thinking about getting into the family business, too?"

"I'm the future of the family business," Bug said proudly.

Ma hit him in the head with the purse again. "You ain't the future of shit just yet, Bug Savage. My word is still law in the Savage household. Now, why don't you take your pyromaniac ass outside and try not to set anything on fire while we're in here finishing up our business?"

"But Ma—" Bug began, but Ma's glare cut his words off. "A'ight." He got up from the booth. "It was nice meeting you, Mr. Clark. And we'll make sure that business gets handled for you." He shook Shai's hand. On his way out, he looked up at Priest. His lips parted as if he wanted to say something, but he wisely kept his mouth closed and kept walking.

"You'll have to excuse him," Ma began once Bug had gone. "He's the baby, so I keep him close to me, but unfortunately, he's picked up some bad habits, same as the rest of my boys. Bug's smart like Keith and got more heart than Mad Dog did at his age. I can't count how many times I tried to turn Bug off to this lifestyle, but he's got that Savage blood in him. If he insists on playing the game, all I can do is show him how to win."

"Sometimes all we can do is make sure they're the best at what they do, even if it isn't right," Priest agreed.

"Right on." Ma nodded. "How's that pretty boy of yours?"

Priest felt his heart skip but didn't miss a beat when he answered. "Dead. He was killed a while back."

"I'm sorry to hear that," Ma said sincerely. "You know, I always hoped that he and Maxine would hook up one day. That marriage there would make our families mighty damn powerful out here."

"I never knew you had a kid, Priest," Shai interrupted.

"That's because you were probably too young to remember.

You boys spent some time together while your fathers were talking business," Priest said with a wink.

Shai thought back. Poppa had never allowed very many around his children, so Shai's play dates were few and far between. He vaguely remembered during one of Priest's late night visits to the Clark estate there having been a kid with him. The reason it stuck out was one of the very few times that Poppa had allowed him to stay up late, eating candy and watching movies. Shai didn't remember much about the kid other than the fact that he had very sad eyes. Poppa had taught him from an early age how to read people's eyes to get a sense of who they were, and it was obvious, even to young Shai that the little boy with Priest had been through some terrible things. With a father like Priest, it was no wonder. Shai had shared his toys with the boy and it seemed to cheer him up, but the sadness in his eyes remained. Shai wanted to ask Priest how the boy had died, but the question would've been disrespectful, especially in front of outsiders, so he didn't press it further.

"Let me get going, before Bug gets restless and tries to set something on fire. It was good seeing you." Ma gave Priest a hug. "Shai"—she turned to him—"don't you worry none about that piece of business, either. My Fire Bug is disrespectful and a little anxious, but he's good at what he does."

"You know your word is as good as gold, Ma. Thanks for meeting with me, and take care." Shai gave her a hug.

"All right, now, and give my regards to Tommy Gunz." Ma waved and left the diner.

Priest waited until he had watched Ma and Bug get into their SUV and pull off before speaking. "If you're meeting with the Savage family, it could only mean somebody is about to die.

If you're meeting with *Ma* Savage, it must be somebody important. Is everything OK, Shai?"

"Yeah, everything is good, Priest. Sit down." Shai motioned toward the seat Ma had just vacated. Once Priest was seated, Shai sat back down. He leaned in to whisper so that only Priest could hear what he was about to say. "I needed to make someone vanish, but it had to be done by someone who has no affiliation with me or this family. So I outsourced."

Priest felt slighted by the fact that Shai hadn't come to him to take the contract, but he didn't show it. "Where's your shadow?"

"Swann? In the streets with it, like he always is. A few of our people got hit up on some bullshit. I swear these lil' niggaz are forgetting their places."

"Any idea who did the deed?" Priest asked.

"From the viciousness of the hit, I'd say it was Animal, but we all know he's dead, right?" Shai watched Priest's face for a reaction.

"Dead and stinking," Priest lied with a straight face.

Shai nodded in approval. "Word on the streets is that it was one of King James's people. You know he's got all these little niggaz thinking they're superheroes."

"Speaking of King James, when are you finally gonna put that rabid dog to sleep?" Priest asked, happy to change the subject.

"That nigga on borrowed time. When I take him out, I wanna do it in grand style for the whole hood to see. They gonna respect the Clark name," Shai declared.

"Shai, let me tell you a story. Years ago, there was another little nigga with a chip on his shoulder named K-Dawg. Like

King James, he had big ideas, too. Everybody ignored K-Dawg, because his crew was too small to pose a legitimate threat, but they realized their errors when K-Dawg and his crew staged a mutiny and whacked out several of the old bosses. They damn near took over this whole city, because they were underestimated. If you want my advice, I'd say let me put King James to sleep for you immediately."

"I hear you, Priest, but I didn't call you out here for your advice. I need your services," Shai told him. "A friend of ours has called in a favor."

Priest didn't need Shai to speak the name to know whom he meant. A friend of *ours* meant Mr. Gee, a.k.a. Gee-Gee, acting boss of the Cissero crime family. He had been a business associate of Poppa Clark's, and when the mantle was passed to Shai, he kept the lines of business open, albeit grudgingly. "And what is it that our little balding friend wants?"

Shai gave a look around as if he expected someone to be eavesdropping. "There's this smuggler, they call him the Little Guy. He's connected to just about every crime faction in the United States and a few outside the country. His connections with the unions make him the man you see if you want something moved from point A to point B with no questions asked. From drugs to immigrant whores, he can move it. The Little Guy was the darling of all the crime families until the dumb fuck got himself pinched in some slum-ass motel room for kicking the shit out of a junkie whore and in possession of enough blow to cater a small party. It ain't looking good for him, and our friends are concerned about what the Little Guy might be willing to do for his freedom."

"How much does he know?" Priest asked.

"He knows enough to topple the whole house of cards. The Little Guy has shaken some very important hands."

Priest clasped his hands in front of him on the table and thumbed his gold rosary while he weighed the situation. "Can you remind me again why we give a fuck about some snitch turning state's on the Italians? The last time I checked, none of those pasta-eating bastards were Clarks."

"Italians aren't the only ones the Little Guy has dirt on," Shai said.

Priest didn't need to ask who else the Little Guy had dirt on. The look on Shai's face said it all. "What happened to cleaning up the Clark backyard and not creating new legal troubles?"

"I didn't create this problem, Priest. I inherited it. The Little Guy's arrangement with the Clarks goes back to before I was born, so I kept doing business with him when I took over," Shai explained.

"You don't have to say any more. I'll take care of it, Shai. Dead men tell no tales." Priest said. He stood to leave, but Shai had some parting instructions.

"A man who would betray his friends is the lowest form of human being. His death should reflect that. I don't just want his life, Priest. I want that rat fuck's cheese-stained tongue!"

THREE

ABOVE THE CHURCH WAS A SMALL KITCHENETTE apartment. It was sparsely furnished, with only a sofa bed, a radio, and a wooden table with a laptop resting on it. The paint was peeling, and the carpet smelled slightly like mold. It was a far cry from their house in Houston, but Animal and Gucci would have to make do, seeing as how it would be their new home until Priest said otherwise.

Animal had finally calmed down enough for Kahllah to free him and reset his arm. Popping it back into place hurt more than when Priest had dislocated it. Kahllah had expected Animal to try to escape, but he didn't. He was still angry, but he stewed in silence. When Kahllah looked into his eyes, he seemed drained. Not so much physically tired, but his soul seemed drained. He moved as if he was in a daze, while she handed him some fresh clothes and directed him to the bathroom where he could clean himself up a bit.

While Animal showered, Gucci and Kahllah sized each other up from opposite sides of the room. Gucci wasn't sure how to feel about Kahllah. When Priest had first brought them there, it was Kahllah who tended her wounds and tried to comfort her while they waited for Animal to regain consciousness. It was almost like they were girlfriends, but her demeanor changed whenever Priest was around. She became withdrawn and cold, more like a solider. She didn't understand what kind of strange hold Priest had on the girl or how she played into everything.

"For as long as I've known Animal, he never mentioned having a sister," Gucci said, breaking the silence.

"Because he didn't know about me," Kahllah replied.

"But you knew about him?" Gucci asked.

Kahllah weighed it before responding. "Not at first. I only learned of Animal when he made the news a few years back for killing all those people. Since then, Priest and I have been watching him from a distance, measuring him to see if he was worthy."

"Worthy of what?" Gucci asked.

"That's none of your concern," Kahllah said.

"If you've been watching him all these years, I'm sure you know what he's been through. Why not come to him sooner?" Gucci asked.

"For the same reason a man sees a woman being abused by her husband on the street but keeps walking. It wasn't my business," Kahllah explained.

Gucci's facial expression betrayed the disgust in her heart at Kahllah's statement. "Not your business? That's your brother!"

"Tayshawn and I are siblings in name only," Kahllah said.

Gucci was confused. "But I heard Priest refer to you as his daughter, so I thought––"

"No, he's Animal's biological father, not mine. My parents

were killed when I was very young, and Priest adopted me, so to speak. He's responsible for the woman I am today."

Gucci shook her head. "This is some country we live in, where decent folks can't adopt kids, but they give little girls to killers."

Kahllah laughed. "Don't be so quick to pat your government on the back and condemn my father until you know the whole story. I was born just outside East Kalimantan, Indonesia, to a dirt-poor family. My mother was a native, my father a black man from the States. I never got to know either of them very well. Cancer took my mom when I was six, and a burglar took my dad when I was nine. For the next few years, I wandered the countryside, stealing when I could and starving when I couldn't. I thought starvation was the worst pain imaginable, until I found myself passed through a network of slave traders. Do you know what slave traders do to pretty young virgins? Sometimes they would go one at a time, and other times they would have their way with me in groups. They call it conditioning, but rape by any other name is still rape. They broke me, body and soul."

"I'm sorry," Gucci said sincerely.

"Don't be sorry for me, Gucci. Be sorry for the little girls who weren't fortunate enough to make it out. I offer up a prayer for them every morning."

"So Priest bought you?" Gucci asked.

"No, he *took* me. I had been purchased by a man and taken to Africa, where he kept me as a servant and sometimes a bed-mate. To this day, I shudder when I think of the things he did to me. Fortunately for me, the man who owned me had offended a very powerful man. For his offense, the man sent Priest to claim my owner's life. Priest killed my owner's family and everyone else who was in the house at the time, but he spared me. To this day, I don't know why, and I don't care. All I know is that he took me out of that hell and gave me a home, an education, and a purpose. He was my salvation."

Gucci shook her head. "I never would've thought a man like Priest was capable of compassion."

"Some might say the same thing about Animal," Kahllah countered. "They are both murderers, are they not? Yet we love them unconditionally, because, unlike those who fear them, we know that death is not the sum total of who they are. They are lovers, fathers, sons, and protectors."

"I can't argue with you there, because Animal has risked everything to keep me safe," Gucci admitted.

"Yes, he has. Now, my question for you is, what are you prepared to do to keep him safe?" Kahllah asked.

"Anything," Gucci said confidently. Animal was her heart.

"It's easy to say it when it's just the two of us having girl talk, but what happens when you have to prove it? What do you do when his enemies are scratching at the door, and the only choices are to kill or be killed?"

"I do whatever it takes," Gucci said.

Kahllah regarded her for a few moments. She stood up and removed the gun from the holster clasped to the back of her pants and cocked the slide. Gucci watched nervously as Kahllah handed her the gun.

"What's this all about?" Gucci asked.

"Shoot me," Kahllah told her, shoving the gun into her hands.

"Kahllah, I ain't playing this sick little game with you," Gucci said.

"It ain't no game, Gucci. Shoot me," Kahllah repeated.

"Look, I'm not--"

"Gucci." Kahllah drew a blade from her bra and popped it open. "One of two things is going to happen. You're going to shoot me, or I'm going to cut your fucking throat."

Gucci studied Kahllah's face to see if she was serious. She was. When Gucci took too long to make up her mind, Kahllah moved in on her with the blade. Gucci raised the gun, finger hesitating on the trigger. She didn't want to kill Kahllah, but she didn't want to die, either. When it was clear to her that Kahllah intended on making good with her threat, Gucci pulled the trigger. Nothing happened.

Kahllah slapped Gucci's hand, sending the gun flying in the air. She fluidly moved behind Gucci and threw her into a choke hold, catching the gun with her free hand. She flicked the lever on the side of the pistol and dug the barrel into Gucci's cheek. "If I was one of Shai Clark's shooters, you'd be dead, all because you didn't know to take the safety off first," she whispered in Gucci's ear.

Gucci shoved Kahllah off her and spun in anger. "What the hell is your problem?"

"My problem is that you don't understand the seriousness of your situation. I don't know if you've been paying attention or not, but Animal isn't going to let this thing with Shai go, and that's your fault!"

"Animal is pressing the issue because he doesn't want to leave his friends in harm's way. You can't put this on me!"

"The hell I can't. My sucker-for-love-ass little brother came out of hiding because of *you*." She jabbed her finger at Gucci's chest. "He went at Shai Clark because of what happened to *you*."

She jabbed her again. "And he's likely going to die because he loves *you.*" Her voice was heavy with emotion. Although they had only met twice, she had been watching Animal for years and felt an attachment to him.

"You act like I asked for this to happen!" Gucci shouted. Kahllah's words cut her because of the truth in them. "I know I'm the cause of all this, but it's out of my hands. What am I supposed to do, Kahllah?"

Kahllah turned the gun, butt first, and shoved it into Gucci's chest, forcing her to take it. "When my brother's enemies come for him, be more than just a pretty fucking face."

"What's going on?" Animal's voice startled both of the girls. Neither of them had heard him come out of the bathroom. He was shirtless, wearing a pair of black fatigue pants and construction Timberlands, which were untied. The clothes were courtesy of Priest. He didn't know his son, but he sure knew his style. Animal's mop of curly hair was wet and hung down around his bare shoulders in tangled strands.

Kahllah's eyes lingered on his chest a second longer than she intended, before answering, "Just having some girl talk."

"With a pistol?" Animal asked, looking back and forth between them suspiciously.

"Don't worry, I'm not gonna hurt your little girlfriend, unless her hand calls for it," Kahllah told Animal.

"She's a bit more than a girlfriend, and you'd do well to keep that in mind." Animal turned his attention to Gucci. "You good, ma?"

"Yeah, I'm fine, baby. Kahllah was just schooling me about firearms in case I ever needed to pop off," Gucci said, holding the gun up like she was posing for an album cover.

Animal took the gun from her hand. "Guns are dangerous, and you don't need to be fucking with them. Leave the artillery to me." Animal gave the gun back to Kahllah. "She ain't 'bout this life, and I'm not gonna force her into it."

Kahllah spun the gun on her finger, before returning it to the holster expertly. "Wrong. You brought her into this life as soon as you started whacking people in her name, so don't cry foul now, lover boy."

"I ain't crying foul, I'm just saying I wanna do everything I can to keep Gucci out of harm's way," Animal said.

"Bullshit." Kahllah mock-coughed. "If that were the case, then you'd accept the blessing Priest has bestowed on you and vanish with her. You could ride off into the sunset, yet you chose to plunge head-first into a fire, after having already been burned twice. All for what, because you want to try and save a bunch of knuckleheads who'll likely be dead by next summer anyhow? Priest always praises you for being intelligent, but I think you're an idiot."

"I don't care what you think, nor do I expect a mercenary to understand loyalty," Animal spat.

Kahllah smirked. "I understand loyalty far better than you ever will. When I took the vow, I pledged to put the will of my father and my Lord before all others, including myself. I have forsaken life and love to serve God, as my father has directed."

Animal looked at her as if she had lost her mind. "So you mean to say that Priest has convinced you that murdering people is God's will?" He shook his head. "I know I'm a little fucked up in the head, but you're on another planet with it."

"Animal, you will never understand, because you've not received the word," Kahllah said seriously, "You haven't been shown the light. While people like you pop bottles with rapists and killers, I smite them. Do I get paid for the bodies I drop? Absolutely, because praises for doing what must be done don't pay bills. You call me a mercenary, but I am much more than that. I am the antidote to the sickness that has corrupted our society. I am the Black Lotus amongst the weeds."

Animal saw the passionate look in Kahllah's eyes when she spoke. It was as if Priest was speaking but through her lips. Obviously, he had been conditioning her from an early age. He had raised her with one purpose: taking lives. Animal tried to imagine what it would be like if their roles had been reversed, with him being nurtured by the killer instead of a base-head mother, and reasoned that he had gotten the better end of the deal than Kahllah. Animal had been through more than his share of hardships, but he at least had free will. Kahllah belonged to Priest, mind and body.

"You don't get it." Animal turned to walk away, and Kahllah appeared in front of him, blocking his path.

"Oh, but I do get it, Animal. You're an honorable man, and I respect that about you, but there is no honor in suicide. The world thinking you're *really* dead this time is the only thing you've got to your advantage. It puts the element of surprise on your side. Shai Clark isn't some street punk; he's the king of this city. Rushing back into the battle head-first will unquestionably be the death of you, and all this will have been for nothing."

"So, I leave Ashanti and Zo to the dogs after they tried to help me?" Animal asked.

"Not at all, but going at Shai with guns blazing isn't going to help anyone," Kahllah said.

"Which is what I've been trying to tell him." Priest appeared in the doorway. He had traded his robes for a black suit, white shirt, and black tie. "My wayward son is determined to see either the light or the darkness. I hope by the time we return from our little outing, I'll be able to show him the light."

"Whatever, nigga," Animal said, pulling the thick black hoodie over his head. He turned to Gucci. "You gonna be OK here with her?" He nodded at Kahllah.

"I'll be fine, you just hurry back." Gucci kissed him on the lips.

"Don't worry, I'll take care of her, Animal," Kahllah promised.

"I'm going to hold you to that," Animal told her.

"My word is my bond." Kahllah placed her hand over her heart dramatically.

"Kahllah will keep your lady safe," Priest assured him. "Now, let's go. We have a lot to cover, and time is not our friend."

"So where are we going?" Animal asked.

"To a funeral," Priest told him with a knowing smirk, and walked out.

Reluctantly, Animal followed Priest.

When he got to the door of the apartment, Kahllah called after him. "While you're gone, I'll check in on your comrade Ashanti. I know you're worried," she told him.

Animal smiled. "Thanks for that, Kahllah. I wonder what the little homie is up to."

Kahllah shook her head. "Knowing him, probably mischief, as usual."

FOUR

ASHANTI SAT IN THE PASSENGER SEAT OF the rental car, watching the block from behind hooded eyes. Every so often, he would take a toke of the blunt pinched between his fingers. The weed was primo, so good that it stung his nostrils every time he blew smoke through them. When his finger grazed his lip, he noticed that it was damp. His palms were sweating. He set the blunt in the ashtray and wiped his hands on his pants. No sooner had he dried them than they started sweating again. That was a bad sign.

"I should've stayed on the block," Ashanti mumbled to himself. He had been thinking it for the past few hours, but that was the first time he'd said it aloud. Ashanti didn't know why he had allowed himself to be persuaded to go out that night, other than he needed some action in his life. He'd been sitting around for days, and it was driving him nuts. It had been a rough time for Ashanti. He had lost some friends and gained some enemies, with the scale being tipped toward the latter. His test scores during his first few semesters at the University of the Streets had elevated him from the status of mischievous kid to recognized shooter, and his name was ringing in the hood. Ashanti would bang on anything if the price was right or the offense serious enough, and everybody knew it.

Ashanti had become the poster child for the abused and unwanted, and those who felt his pain flocked to him like he was the Oliver Twist of the projects. King James currently had the hood on smash and therefore held sway over the present, but Ashanti controlled the future and not everybody was comfortable with that.

For as many disciples who had rallied to Ashanti, there were two knuckleheads he had a special love for, Cain and Abel. Zo-Pound didn't particularly care for the two brothers, because they were young, wild, and in a rush to die, but these were the qualities that made Ashanti love them. Like him, they were broken children whom the world had thrown away.

Cain and Abel were a set of twins who were identical in appearance but like night and day in personality. As kids, Abel was always the happy and outgoing twin, while Cain was bitter and quiet. He was the kind of kid who took pleasure in torturing and killing stray cats. It had been apparent since Cain was a child that he was damaged goods, and a freak accident would make him just as ugly on the outside as he was on the inside. The twins were playing with their mother's crack pipe, imitating what they saw in their home, when Cain decided to put a lighter to the pipe. The glass exploded in his face, scarring him and nearly blinding him in his right eye. Fearful of catching a Child Services case, their mother treated him at home, plucking the glass out of his face with a pair of old tweezers and cleaning the wound with Johnnie Walker Red whiskey. After patching her handiwork up with a wad of napkins and some tape, their mother laughed and told Cain, "Now you wear the mark, just like your namesake."

Abel tapped Ashanti's arm. He was behind the wheel. "Blood, you hear me talking to you? I asked if you fucking with this," he extended the pint of Hennessy he'd been sipping from.

Ashanti took the bottle and turned it up to his lips. The brown liquor burned when it first touched his tongue, but within a few seconds, his taste buds had gone numb, and the drink flowed smoothly. He tried to hand the bottle to Cain, who was in the backseat, but he declined.

"I'm good," Cain said in a raspy whisper. He was tugging at the strings of his hoodie to the point where it almost completely engulfed his face. All you could see was his eyes and his long braids spilling out. He always wore hoodies because he was self-conscious about his scar.

Cain's silence unnerved Ashanti. He'd known Cain long enough to recognize the calm before the storm. He was ready to get it popping, and before long, it wouldn't matter who he got at. He was an adrenaline junkie and needed to get his fix regularly.

"Why we still just sitting here like this instead of going in and handling our business?" Abel asked. He was generally the more docile of the brothers, but he tended to get agitated when Cain did. It was some twin shit.

"Because it's not time to go in yet," Ashanti told him. He picked the blunt back up and fished around in his pocket for a light. Before he could find one, Cain was leaning over the seat with a Bic in his hand.

Cain sparked the lighter and lit the blunt for Ashanti. While the flame danced under the charred cigar, Cain whispered in Ashanti's ear. "My nigga, I know what you're thinking. On the hood, I'll be mindful of any kids in the spot, but everything else is food. I'm starving, Blood. Let a nigga eat before I lose it," his voice was almost pleading.

"We move when I say we move," Ashanti said through the smoke. A few seconds later, the door to the barbershop they'd been watching came open. A woman stepped out, leading her little boy by the hand. He was smiling and eating the lollipop he'd gotten for being a good boy during his first haircut. When she and her son disappeared down the block, Ashanti addressed his crew. "Now we can go in."

"About fucking time," Cain said, chambering a round into the big Glock in his hand.

The small bell hanging above the door of the barbershop announced Ashanti when he entered. There were three barber chairs lined up. The first and the third had men sitting in them getting haircuts, and in the second sat a gray-haired old barber, reading a newspaper. He glanced up at Ashanti, then went back to his paper.

In the chair farthest from the door, a man sat getting a shape-up and talking to the barber who was taking care of him. He was light-skinned, with a thin mustache and curly hair. He couldn't have been more than twenty, if he was a day. One of his manicured hands rested on the arm of the barber's chair, and you could see the flawless diamond pinkie ring poking out. It was obvious from his appearance that he was handling. He glanced up at Ashanti in the reflection of the mirror, and for a moment, their eyes met. Ashanti turned away like he was afraid. Seeing that the young boy didn't want any sauce, the man in the chair went back to his conversation with the barber.

"Like I was saying, the bitch got the nerve to come back talking about she ain't made but two hundred. I knew off top she was lying," the man in the chair said.

"So what'd you do next, Percy?" The barber loved it when Pretty Percy came to the shop. Not only was he an excellent tipper, but he always had a funny story to tell.

"I did what any sporting nigga would've done, stripped that ho butt-ass naked and checked her until I found the bread she was trying to hold out on," Percy said.

"And where was she hiding it?" the barber asked.

"In her pussy!" Percy told him, and they both burst out laughing.

"You boys need haircuts?" the barber at the first chair asked.

"Nah, no cuts for us today, fam. As a matter of fact, why don't y'all take an early lunch?" Cain said, flipping the sign on the door from Open to Closed.

Sensing something was off, the man with the pinkie ring who had been getting the shape-up slipped his hand under the smock that was protecting his clothes from the falling hair. Before his hand could reemerge, Abel was on him, pointing a sawed-off shotgun.

"What you reaching for, my nigga?" Abel moved in on him and stuck his hand under the smock. He came out holding a 9mm. "Now, what was you planning on doing with this?"

"If you boys are looking to rob us, I'm afraid you won't find much. Business has been kinda slow lately," the old man who had been reading the paper said.

Ashanti patted the old man on the shoulder. "No worries, old-timer. I got love for the working man. I just wanna holla at Pretty Percy right quick. Why don't you all take a walk and come back in about ten minutes?" he told the barbers and the few men who were waiting to get their haircuts. The patrons quickly filed out of the barbershop.

"Fuck y'all want with me?" Percy asked. He was trying to hide the nervousness in his voice, but the sweat on his forehead gave him away.

Abel swung from behind him and slapped Percy in the mouth. "Speak when spoken to, nigga!"

"Why don't y'all leave Percy alone? He ain't done nothing to y'all," the old man said, speaking up.

Ashanti shot the old man a cold look. "Don't test the boundaries of my kindness, old head. Take a fucking walk."

"Come on, Pops." The two barbers ushered Pops toward the door. They knew trouble when they saw it and wanted no part of the three wild young teens.

"Godless creatures. Just Godless," Pops said as he passed.

"You got that right, muthafucka." Cain kicked Pops in the ass, causing him to stumble on his way out. "And while you're outside calling the police, tell them to make sure to bring a cleanup crew, too. You're gonna need it when we're done."

When only the four of them remained, Ashanti addressed the man known as Percy. "What's popping, slime?"

"You tell me. Y'all the ones with the guns," Percy said.

"We just wanna rap with you for a taste," Ashanti told him with a sinister grin.

"Look, shorty, you're about to make a huge mistake. I'm Pretty Percy. I got some powerful friends who might not take it so well if something happens to me," he said, trying to intimidate Ashanti. It didn't work.

Ashanti slapped Percy so hard that blood shot from his lips and splattered on the mirror. "Miss me with that tough-guy shit. You ain't a gangster, you a pimp. I know just who your friends are, and that's exactly why I'm here." Ashanti turned to Cain and Abel. "Why don't y'all make sure old Percy here sits still while we're having our little chat?"

Abel held Percy at gunpoint while Cain gathered the straps hanging from the chairs that they used to sharpen the razors and tied Percy down. Ashanti removed a pair of the barber's shears that had been resting in the cleaning solution and approached Percy.

"Getting back to your powerful friends . . . I need some information on Swann," Ashanti said.

Percy faked ignorance. "Who?"

"Wrong answer." Ashanti stabbed him in the leg with the shears. Percy howled in pain, but Cain shoved a brush full of shaving cream into his mouth to silence him. "How the fuck is he supposed to answer me if you choke him?" Ashanti asked Cain.

Cain shrugged. "I'll bet he's used to talking with cream in his mouth. Ain't that right, Percy?" He slapped him on the cheek playfully.

"Knock it off." Ashanti nudged Cain out of the way. He removed the brush from Percy's mouth. "We really gonna play this game?"

"I keep trying to tell you—" Percy's statement turned into a shriek of pain when Ashanti stuck the shear in his other leg.

Ashanti drew his gun. "Percy, it's in your best interest to stop insulting my intelligence."

"I don't know shit!" Percy insisted.

Ashanti sighed. "OK, you wanna go about this the hard way, huh?" He shoved the gun into Percy's mouth. "Word around town is that you like to suck big black shit in your spare time, so I'm gonna give you something to suck on." He pushed the pistol to the back of Percy's throat. "When this nuts, ain't gonna be no joy juice on this floor, only your brains."

Tears sprang to Percy's eyes. He shook his head back and forth, with his lips still wrapped around the gun.

"You feel like talking now?" Ashanti asked. When Percy nodded, he removed the gun but kept it level with Percy's face.

"OK, I know Swann. I run whores, and in exchange for protection on the street, I kick Swann back a taste," Percy admitted.

"How does a bitch pimp bitches?" Abel asked. He looked genuinely confused.

"Fuck you!" Percy spat.

"Fuck me? Nah, fuck you." Abel aimed the sawed-off at Percy's face. "I'll blow those dick-sucking lips off your face, pussy!"

"Cool the fuck out." Ashanti pushed him away. "As you can see"—he turned back to Percy—"my lil' one is ready to rock you, scrams, and I just might let him, unless you tell me everything you know about Swann, including where he lays his head."

"I don't know," Percy said.

Ashanti slapped him. "Percy, you must think I picked your name out of a hat. Nigga, I been laying on you for weeks, and I know that there's more going on between you and Swann than just you paying for protection. You're Swann's play nephew. No relation, but he's been looking out for you since you were a kid. There are a lot of nasty rumors floating around about the nature of your relationship, but it ain't my place to judge. I just want to know where I can put my hands on this nigga. Now, tell me something good, Percy."

"I can't betray my family," Percy said, his voice just above a whisper.

"You can, and you will," Ashanti assured him.

"Man, Swann is crazy. You don't know what he'll do to me if I talk," Percy said in a frightened tone.

"And you must not know what we'll do to you if you don't," Abel said.

"Ashanti, kick back and let me have a go at it." Cain put his gun into his waistband and tightened the leather gloves on his hands. He went to one of the drawers that held the barbers' tools and pulled it out of the counter. Cain dumped the contents of the drawer onto Percy's lap so that he could get a good look at the instruments. From the pile he selected a razor that was sharpened to a fine edge. "Dig this," he whispered in Percy's ear. "One way or another, you're gonna spill your guts before we leave here."

His brother, Abel, locked the front door and watched through the window for police, while Ashanti got comfortable in one of the barber's chairs and listened to the sounds of Percy's screaming.

Ashanti had to admit, had Cain chosen a path other than the streets, he probably could've been a master butcher. He started with the razor and then moved to anything and everything in the shop that had a sharp edge to it. Just as he'd promised, Percy had spilled his guts, literally and figuratively. By the time he was done talking, Ashanti was dizzy with information. He had only come to Percy to get a location but had gotten much more than he expected. It was true what they said about what's done in the dark eventually comes to the light.

Pretty Percy wasn't very pretty anymore once Cain was done with him. His body was slumped in the chair, motionless. The only way Ashanti knew that he was still alive was by the gurgling sound coming from him.

"Damn, that was some heavy shit," Abel said to Ashanti. He was still shaking his head in disbelief.

"Heavy like a boulder, my nigga," Ashanti agreed.

"You gonna run this to King James?" Abel asked.

Ashanti thought on it for a long moment. "After a time, I will. For right now, I just wanna marinate on it. Keep it to yourself until I say otherwise, ya heard?"

"You know it ain't going no further than us," Abel assured him.

"Let's get gone," Ashanti said. "Yo, Cain. We gotta go—" His words froze in his throat. Cain was straddling the barber chair and Percy's body. "What the fuck are you doing?"

Cain turned so that they could see his handiwork. In one hand, he held the bloody razor, and in the other, the skin from Percy's face. He held the flesh up over his own face like a mask. "Halloween is coming, and this year, I wanted to dress up as a bitch-ass nigga." Cain laughed hysterically.

Ashanti, Cain, and Abel went back to Ashanti's crib to regroup after the hit. They took turns taking showers and changing clothes. Cain's clothes were bloody, so they poured bleach over them and tied them in a plastic bag. When they went back out, they'd find somewhere to burn them.

When Ashanti came out of the shower, Cain and Abel were sitting on his couch playing Xbox on his big screen. They looked so innocent, more like the kids they were than the killers the hood had made them. Ashanti was proud of his little recruits. They had been hanging tough for a while, but this had been their first actual murder mission together. They had to be tested before letting them in fully, and they had passed with flying colors. If Animal were there, he'd have been proud of Ashanti for picking them to add to his little family.

Thinking about his comrade brought a smile to Ashanti's face. When Animal had come back into the picture, it had been like a sign for Ashanti. Seeing his teacher and best friend reminded him of what a real nigga was supposed to move like.

It inspired him to carry on the tradition of getting money and making bitch niggaz suffer. Losing Animal for a second time hurt worse than the first, but it sparked something in Ashanti. He would ride until they laid him to rest on a cold sidewalk, just as his mentor had.

"Y'all niggaz cut that video game off, and let's hit the streets. We got business to attend to," Ashanti told him.

"Chill, we in the third quarter," Abel said, still flicking the joystick.

Ashanti turned the game off. "I said, let's go. You, too, Dr. Lecter." He tossed Cain the bag of clothes.

"A'ight, let's gather up the straps and dip," Abel said.

"Nah, we don't all need to be holding since we gonna be together. It's easier to beat one gun case than three, feel me?" Ashanti told him.

"If we only taking one, I'm gonna hold it," Cain said.

Ashanti looked at him as if he'd lost his mind. "After that shit you pulled in the barbershop, it might be a while before I let you hold a weapon around me. And I hope you got rid of that nasty-ass skin mask."

Cain got quiet.

"Blood, are you fucking serious? Man, get rid of that shit," Ashanti ordered.

Cain mumbled something under his breath before taking the plastic ziplock bag from his pocket that held the bloody skin. He put it into the bag with the clothes and stormed out of the apartment, the bag thrown over his shoulder.

"What the fuck is wrong with that nigga?" Ashanti asked Abel.

Abel shrugged. "Cain is just different."

The three amigos found a quiet alley to set their little fire. Cain squirted lighter fluid all over the bag and the trash can they'd thrown the clothes in.

"Be easy with that shit," Ashanti said, noticing Cain splashing the walls.

Cain ignored him and fished around in his pocket for some matches. After tossing the match into the can, he stepped back and watched as the fire slowly built. The fire wasn't burning fast enough for him, so Cain decided to speed up the process. Before anyone could stop him, he threw the entire container of lighter fluid into the can. A small explosion rattled the trash can and probably woke up the entire neighborhood.

"What the hell is going on down there?" someone shouted from one of the windows. They looked up and saw an older lady leaning out of the window. When her eyes landed on the flaming garbage can, she shrieked, "Lord Jesus, it's a fire! I'm calling the police!"

"Oh, shit!" Ashanti said, and took off running.

They darted up the block, laughing and cracking jokes as if they hadn't just almost burned down an entire apartment building. Ashanti was irritated with Cain for throwing the lighter fluid into the flames, but he had to admit it was funny as hell. They were all scared shitless.

They had just turned the corner when there was the sound of tires screeching. Ashanti dived out of the way seconds before the brown Buick jumped the curb, but Cain wasn't so lucky. He bounced off the hood and landed in the street, dazed and in a world of pain. Two men jumped from the car, one black and one Hispanic. Abel made a beeline across the street, but Ashanti and Cain got snatched up.

"Look what we got here," Detective Alvarez said with a smug grin, yanking Ashanti off the ground by his arm. He was a tall Hispanic man who wore his hair cut in a low Caesar. He made up half of the duo known on the streets as the Minority Report. They were hard-nosed cops who were known to use dirty tactics to make cases stick.

"Somebody left their trash lying in the street." Detective Brown pulled Cain to his feet and gave him a rough shake. He was a short black man, with a stocky build and a box-cut Afro that he'd had since the eighties. He was the more serious of the two detectives.

"Damn, I think you broke my leg, blood!" Cain yelped.

"Fuck yo leg, lil' nigga." Detective Brown shoved him against the car and began patting him down. Luckily, they'd agreed to only bring one gun out, and Abel was long gone with that. "Where'd your friend rush off to, pretty boy?"

"Up your ass," Cain spat.

"Oh, you a funny guy, huh?" Brown kneed him in his injured leg but had a firm grip on the back of his neck so he couldn't fall. "I got a few jokes of my own."

"What you want with us, now, fam?" Ashanti asked Alvarez, as he was frisked.

"Same thing we always want, to put your deranged little ass in prison until you're old and gray," Alvarez said.

"Ain't worked out for you too well yet."

Alvarez shoved Ashanti. "You've been lucky until now, Ashanti, but shit birds like you always slip eventually. You see what happened to ya man Animal? He slipped and got his wig split."

"Ain't you got no respect for the dead?" Ashanti asked.

"Fuck no, especially not a murdering piece of shit like Animal. He almost got me and my partner killed. My only regret is that I wasn't the one to put the bullet in the back of his head. But that's OK, because you're following right in his footsteps, so I'll be able to put a bullet in the back of your head instead."

"Nigga—" Ashanti tried to spin but froze when he felt the gun on his cheek.

"What?" Alvarez barked, pushing the barrel deeper into his face. "You wanna break bad, lil' one? Go ahead, pop off. I would like nothing more than to put your brains on the hood of this car. Say something!"

Ashanti remained silent.

"This one is clean, partner," Detective Brown said to break the tension.

"See? We ain't got nothing, so why don't you let us go?" Ashanti said to Alvarez.

Alvarez was pissed. He just knew that Ashanti would have his gun on him like always, and he'd be able to start building a solid case against him. Frustrated, he made one more search of Ashanti's pocket and found something. "Well, look what we got here." He held up the hundred-dollar bag of weed. "Looks like you're going downtown after all."

Ashanti was shocked. "What? You gonna take me in for a bag of weed? Come on, Detective Alvarez, we supposed to be better than that."

"The law is the law, shit bird," Alvarez said gleefully.

"What about this one?" Brown asked, nodding to Cain.

Alvarez thought on it for a moment. "Fuck it, we'll split the bag of weed up between them when we get in the car and book them both for possession."

"This is some bullshit," Cain said while being handcuffed.

"Thank your mentor, Ashanti, for the heat you guys are catching," Brown whispered to Cain as he shoved him into the car.

"Alvarez, I used to have some respect for you, but this is some low shit. You know collaring me for anything less than a murder is a discredit to both our reputations," Ashanti said.

"I'll take my victories where I can get them. You have the right to remain silent . . ."

SURVIVAL OF THE FIT

"I'm trying to kill him, and he's trying to stop me from killing him. That ain't beef, that's fact."

—Animal

"WHERE ARE YOU TAKING ME?" ANIMAL ASKED, noticing the signs welcoming them to Rye, New York.

"I told you, to a funeral. I figured on the way, we could have some time to talk," Priest told him, watching the road.

Animal gave him a comical look. "What do we possibly have to talk about?"

"Animal, beneath all that Buster Bad Ass shit you keep kicking, I'm sure you're at least curious about our history," Priest said.

"Our history is pretty clear. You fucked my crackhead mother and then cut out, same as every other nigga she ever brought in the house," Animal said venomously.

"Why don't you watch your fucking mouth? Marie had her hang-ups, but she still brought you into the world. If your little ass can't show some appreciation, at least show some damn respect."

"Yes, *Father*," Animal said sarcastically.

Priest took his eye off the road to shoot Animal a look. "You make it really hard to like you, kid."

"Obviously, since not even the two people who brought me into the world wanted anything to do with me."

"You really think it was just that simple, don't you?"

Animal shrugged. "Unless you plan to convince me differently during our little outing."

Priest sighed. "Listen, Tayshawn, I know you think me and ya mom were just two fucked-up kids who brought a baby in the world that they couldn't raise, but it wasn't like that. You weren't just some popped condom or result of me forgetting to pull out. We wanted you. Your mom and I had a whole game plan."

His unexpected admission got him Animal's undivided attention.

"Your mom turned into a different person when that shit took hold of her, but she wasn't always like that. She used to be the finest thing in New York, and whenever we'd walk into a spot together, she'd turn every head in the joint," Priest reminisced. "Back then, Poppa Clark had just become boss, and I was his right-hand man. Me, him, ya mama, and his wife, June, used to run around heavy. The four of us were like family, which makes your beef with Shai so ironic. Y'all damn near kin."

"It ain't no beef. I'm trying to kill him, and he's trying to stop me from killing him. That ain't beef, that's fact," Animal said.

"Call it what you want, Animal, but it still doesn't change the fact that you're my son and he's the son of a man who was once my best friend, so your destinies are intertwined whether you like it or not," Priest told him. "Like I was saying, Poppa was the new king, and I was his right-hand man. Shit was good for us, but to keep things good, we had to put in the work. Me and Poppa were always in the streets, so your mother and June occupied their time partying and spending money. I heard things about your mother, and some of them were not so nice. I was losing my lady to the same streets I was running in, and I needed to do something to get a handle on things. It was around then I suggested we have a kid. She already had Justice from that pretty nigga she used to run with, but you would be the symbol of our union."

Animal laughed. "And what a union that turned out to be."

"Call it what you want, but in the beginning, it was pure . . . beautiful," Priest recalled. "When you were a baby, you spent more time with me than you did with your mother. You were my little soldier, and I was the happiest nigga north of 110th Street. Then a cat named Mobi came to town, and everything changed."

The name rang familiar to Animal. He could remember a few years before hearing Tech and some of the older heads talking about a dude named Mobi who was supposed to have been a real maniac. One story that stuck out was how he supposedly cut a kid's feet off for accidentally stepping on his shoes in a crowded club.

"Mobi was what you would call a man without honor," Priest continued. "Because of his family's political status, he felt like he was entitled to whatever he wanted, and what he wanted was what belonged to Poppa Clark. So we went to war. We immediately saw what kind of man we were dealing with when Mobi went to Poppa Clark's favorite little bakery and killed the baker and his wife because they refused to poison Poppa Clark's morning coffee. Nothing was off-limits to him, including family. I had to protect you at all costs."

Animal could vaguely remember flashes of him and his mother always living in different places. She would tell him it was because his father was in the military and his job required them to move around, but none of the apartments was ever outside the five boroughs.

"I tried to kick the real deal to your mom, but she was too caught up in the lifestyle to hear what I was saying, so I had no choice but to put some distance between us. For as much as it hurt me to be away from my son, I couldn't run the risk of Mobi finding out about my family and paying y'all a visit. The only sure way to keep you out of harm's way was to kill Mobi."

"Judging from the fact that you're here telling me this story, I'm gonna assume you succeeded in killing Mobi. So what stopped you from coming back for us when he was dead?" Animal wanted to know.

Priest hesitated before answering so that he could check the address he had written on a slip of paper against the dilapidated bar they'd just pulled up in front of. When he confirmed he was at the right location, he killed the engine, but he didn't get out of the car yet. There was still much to be said between him and Animal, and he needed to get it off his chest as much as his son needed to hear it.

"The feud between Mobi's crew and the Clarks went on for longer than any of us expected. It took me almost three years to finally corner him and kill him, and that came at a price. His uncle was a heavyweight in Africa. He was connected politically and had a strong hand in the streets, which made him twice as dangerous. When he found out that it was me who put the love on his nephew, he demanded compensation. Back then, the Clark family didn't have the political connections they have now, and Mobi's uncle would've crushed us like bugs. Still, Poppa Clark was my friend, and he refused to turn me over. He was ready to kick off a war that we had no chance of winning to protect me. Mobi's uncle saw this, and it gave him a newfound respect for the Clarks, so he offered a compromise."

"Which was?" Animal asked in a very interested tone.

"I was put on loan in the service of Mobi's uncle to take out one of his rivals in Africa. To settle the blood debt over Mobi's life, he demanded the life of his enemy and the lives of the enemy's family," Priest explained. "It went against my beliefs, when I still believed in anything, but I didn't have much of a choice. The children I gave quick deaths. With each dimming of their young lights, my soul became darker, more stained. I took my self-hate out on their parents and killed them in the messiest ways I could think of. I slaughtered everyone in the house, except the slave girl. She wasn't of their blood. When Mobi's uncle released me from his service and I was allowed to leave, I brought her with me."

"Kahllah," Animal said, putting the pieces together in his head.

"Yes, my little Black Lotus. It's funny how I saved her from a life of servitude and she saved me from myself." Priest chuckled. "After the things I'd seen and done in Africa, I wasn't the same person Poppa Clark had put on that plane. Everywhere I looked, I saw the faces of the children I'd murdered, and it drove me mad. I retreated into the furthest corners of my mind and had no desire to leave, but Kahllah refused to let me slip away. Even when I was at my lowest point, Kahllah never left my side."

"And what of us?" Animal asked, trying to keep his emotions in check. Listening to the pain in Priest's voice as he told the story was getting to him.

Priest blinked, and when he opened his eye it was moist. "By the time I got myself together, Marie was a washed-up base head, and the streets had you. My little boy was gone, and you were the Animal."

For a long while, Animal said nothing. He just sat in the passenger seat, weighing everything. Animal didn't know Priest very well, but he was an expert on the hearts of men, and there was too much genuine pain in Priest's voice for it to have been a lie. In a few short hours, the man claiming to be his father had told him more about his origins than his mother had in all the time he was with her. He felt like a weight had been lifted as some of the blanks in his life had finally been filled in, but the bitterness of being abandoned and abused remained.

"So what now? Are we supposed to go toss a football in the park or some shit? I can respect the position you were put in, especially being in a similar situation. I'd do everything I could to protect someone I love, even if it meant letting them go." He thought of Gucci and the constant danger she was in by being with him. "Sacrifice is sometimes a necessary evil, but that still doesn't absolve you from abandoning your responsibilities."

Priest turned to face Animal. "You still don't get it, do you? This isn't about absolution. I'll be judged by a much higher authority than you or anyone else. I don't expect you to forgive me; I just want you to understand."

Animal nodded. "One thing I still don't get is if you're so loyal to the Clarks, then why help me? And don't feed me that family shit, because we hardly know each other. What's your angle?"

"Poppa Clark is one of my oldest and dearest friends. I watched him bust his ass for decades trying to create the American dream for his kids, only to have his youngest offshoot piss it all to hell with his Hollywood shit. Shai is a good kid, but I'm not a fan of the way he's running his father's empire. Maybe a good pat on the ass is what he needs to get his head back in the game and get you out of the fire all at the same time. If we play this right, then everybody walks away with what they want. Shai gets a wake-up call, the feud is ended, and I can die knowing I helped my son when he truly needed me."

"Shai hates my guts, and I hate his. The only way he's gonna ever truly let go of the grudge is if one of us is dead," Animal said.

"Animal, death is the most effective resolution to most problems but not always the only resolution. Pay attention, and you just might learn something from your old man before it's all said and done." Priest got out of the car.

SEVEN

"I THOUGHT YOU SAID WE WERE GOING to a funeral," Animal said, once they crossed the threshold of the tavern. It was a cramped little bar that smelled of musk and alcohol.

"We are," Priest said, scanning the room. He spotted the man he was looking for, hunched over the bar, nursing a glass of something brown. "Follow me, and say nothing unless I tell you to," Priest told Animal, before making his way to the bar.

The man nursing the drink must've felt Priest approaching, because he looked up from his glass. He was a light-skinned man who looked to be about fifty, with a balding head. His eyes were beet-red, but the dried tears on his face said it wasn't from the alcohol. He had been crying.

"Ain't you afraid you might burst into flames coming in this hellhole, Father?" the old man said over his shoulder.

"I go wherever the word needs to be heard." Priest invited himself to the stool next to the old man. "How are you, Charlie?"

"Not too good," Charlie said, tossing the drink back and

motioning for the bartender to bring him another one. "I buried my wife this morning."

"I heard. You have my condolences. Nancy was a good woman," Priest said sincerely.

"Too good for a wretch like me," Charlie said. "You know, she could've had any guy in the world, but she chose me. I always asked God what made me such a lucky bastard."

"Sometimes it's senseless to question his will. Everything the most high does, he does for a reason, and the reasons aren't always for us to understand," Priest said, watching Charlie take the fresh shot down.

"Would've been nice if you could've been there to say a few words," Charlie said. "I know you take that collar about as seriously as I take my liver, but it still would've been good for show, huh? Nancy never did give up hope that you'd find your way again one day."

"I wish I had half the faith in myself as Nancy had in me." Priest raised his hand and motioned for the bartender to bring them three more shots of whatever Charlie was drinking. When she set them down, he slid one to Charlie and one to Animal and kept one. Animal stared down at the glass quizzically.

"Who's this, your new altar boy?" Charlie asked Priest.

"No, this is my son," Priest said.

Charlie turned around on his stool and gave Animal the once-over. "I ain't seen him since he was knee-high. Where you been hiding him, Priest?"

"We're estranged," Animal answered for him.

Charlie laughed. "He abandoned you, too, huh? Yeah, Priest is good at walking away from shit. Cold-blooded, that one is."

"Compassion is only a friend to a fool. When people find

places in your heart, they use them to their advantage." Priest raised his glass.

"Touché, nigga." Charlie threw his shot back. Priest sipped his. "Never known you to be much of a drinker," he said to Priest.

"I'm not, but I make allowances for special occasions." Priest took another sip.

"A special occasion, huh?" Charlie asked suspiciously.

"Yes, a home-going ceremony." Priest threw the rest of his shot back. "You ready to go, Charlie?"

Charlie stared at the empty glass. "How long we known each other, Priest?" He never took his eyes off the glass.

Priest thought on it. "Maybe thirty years now."

"Thirty-two years," Charlie corrected him. "I remember the day you got out of boot camp and they tossed you into our unit. You looked scared to death, but the minute we got out there in the combat zone, you took to it like a fish to water. Even back then, we all knew that you were BTK. Do you know what BTK is, youngster?" he asked Animal.

"No, sir," Animal said.

"BTK is a phrase we used in our platoon. When you enlist, you do so knowing that there's a possibility that you might actually see some action. None of us really wanted to be out there, but we did what we had to do in the name of survival. Then you had the BTKs. Those are the ones who can be knee-deep in a blood bath and don't bat an eye. They thrived on the violence. These men were said to have come into the world without souls. We classified those wack jobs as BTK, born to kill."

Animal listened to Charlie's tale, and it reminded him of how he'd handled business when he was on the streets putting in work. He never showed fear or remorse; he moved like a man without a soul, BTK. He wondered if he was that way because of the circumstances he was placed in, or was it something he'd inherited from the father he'd never known?

"For as much as we'd like to hear some more of your war stories, Charlie, we've got a schedule to keep." Priest tapped his watch.

"Yeah, I know," Charlie said sadly. "Think we got time for one more?"

Priest nodded and motioned for the waitress to bring them one last round. When she set the drinks on the table, Priest picked up the tab for the drinks he'd ordered plus all the booze Charlie had consumed before he got there.

Charlie smiled. "A gentleman to the end." He threw the shot back and slammed the glass onto the table. Charlie removed his watch, his pinkie ring, and the gold crucifix hanging around his neck and placed them on the bar. "Hold on to these for me for a spell, darling. I'll come back for them later," he told the bartender.

The bartender looked from the jewelry on the bar to Charlie and his two companions. "Is everything OK?" she asked, ready to pull out the shotgun hidden under the bar or alert the police if need be. Charlie was one of her regulars, and she liked him, but she didn't care for the two strangers. From the moment they arrived, she knew they were bad business. She could smell the stench of death clinging to them from a mile away.

Charlie gave her a wink. "Everything is jus' groovy, baby." He rapped his knuckles on the bar. "All right." He turned to Priest. "Let's get this fucking show on the road."

Priest told Animal to get behind the wheel, while Charlie sat in the passenger's seat and Priest got into the back directly behind him. He directed Animal out of town and down a seldom-used dirt road. The tension in the car was so thick you could've cut it with a knife. Charlie made small talk with Animal about shit that either didn't matter or had happened long before Animal was born, anything to keep his mind off the man sitting behind him and their destination.

Animal started to ask what was going on but thought better of it. He looked up into the rearview mirror at Priest, who was staring back at him. Gone was the face of the man who had schooled him in his history and traded war stories with an old friend, replaced by the face of the hardened killer he was best known as.

"Pull over up here," Priest said from the backseat. Animal steered the car into the stand of trees Priest had directed him to. "Everybody out," Priest ordered, slipping from the backseat. Animal got out, but Charlie remained seated. He looked so terrified that Animal doubted he could move even if he wanted to. "Let's go, Charlie." Priest opened the door for him.

"I'm coming, man. Just let me get myself together." Charlie wiped the sweat from his brow with his hand. When he tried to stand, his legs gave out. Animal caught him before he could fall. "Thanks, youngster. I must've had too much to drink." Charlie mustered a phony smile.

"You never did have the head for liquor, or anything else, for that matter, Charlie. I hate the fact that you've put me in this position," Priest told him, pulling a pistol from his jacket.

"Priest, I know you salty, but we got history. It ain't gotta be like this. Just let me walk away, and I'll vanish. On my dead wife, you'll never see me again," Charlie pleaded.

"You know I can't do that, Charlie. The only reason I've waited so long to come for you was out of respect for Nancy, but she's not here anymore," Priest said.

"You want me to beg? OK." Charlie dropped to his knees. Tears began rolling down his cheeks. "I'm begging you, don't do me like this!"

Seeing Charlie on his knees groveling turned Priest's stomach. "Get the fuck up." He snatched Charlie to his feet by the front of his shirt. Charlie kept trying to collapse, but Priest wouldn't let him. "What are you doing, Charlie? Have some fucking dignity!" Priest shook him.

Animal placed a firm hand on Priest's shoulder. "Why don't you take it easy?"

Priest looked at Animal's hand as if it was something that had crawled up from the foulest gutter. "Why don't you get yo fucking hand off me before it becomes another trophy in my war room?"

"Thanks, youngster, but don't waste your breath," Charlie said. "Once the Clark executioner has been sent for you, there's only one outcome, even if it is the God Father to his only son. Ain't that right, Priest?"

Priest said nothing.

Charlie patted Animal on the cheek. "Son, unlike your daddy, you've got a heart of gold. You care about people. Hold on to that quality, youngster. The heart is the last line of defense when those demons come scratching at our souls."

Priest called to him. "Charlie."

"Keep your robe on, holy man. I'm coming," Charlie said. He turned back to Animal, and there were tears dancing in his eyes. Charlie pounded Animal's chest lightly with his fist. "No matter how many guns you got, nothing is more powerful than your heart and standing behind what you believe in versus what somebody is trying to feed you. You remember what I told you and the circumstances they were told under. You hear me?"

Animal nodded.

Charlie turned to face Priest. "I fucked up, didn't I?"

"You sure did, Charlie." Priest screwed a silencer on the gun.

"So this is what's it's come to? Three decades of friendship thrown out like yesterday's trash to make sure the faithful old hound dog doesn't fall out of his master's good graces?"

Priest didn't take the bait.

"I understand you're just doing like you're told, Priest, but you might wanna think about it. I'm still a made guy," Charlie reminded him. He had been a major player in the underworld during his days, and at one time, Charlie's name held weight.

"Charlie, this ain't the nineties. Your power on the streets dried up a long time ago. Poppa Clark was throwing you a bone when he gave you this town to run. You remain a boss in name only," Priest said.

"Call it what you want, but there are still quite a few people who got love for old Charlie. I might be old and washed up, but my son Chuck's still got a strong hand out here. When he finds out what you did to his daddy on the day we laid his mama to rest, he's gonna come for you to settle this debt," Charlie warned.

Chuck was Charlie's only son. Priest had watched him grow from a mischievous young man into a solid soldier, who was known to bust his gun. Charlie was the boss of the operation, but Chuck and his goons were the muscle.

"Chuck is a good young kid, and if he wants to live to be a good old man, he'll chalk this one up to the game and keep it moving. If he does get it in his head to come around looking for death, I'll be sure to help him find it. This I can promise you," Priest said. "You have no one to blame for this but yourself, Charlie. I connected you so that you could do for you and your family, not run off like a common thief and make me look like a poor judge of character."

Charlie shook his head. "Is that what they told you? That I ran off with the money? Figures, white men been lying on niggers for years. Priest, you know me. I ain't never stole nothing from nobody that didn't have it coming. I got tired of them Irish muthafuckas coming around here acting like they owned the joint, acting like they owned me. I took that bread to show them what time it was. It wasn't about the money, it was about my pride!"

"And your pride has brought us to this point." Priest held the gun up. "All you had to do was come to me, Charlie, and we could've worked something out. Mickey and his boys respect me."

"The same way the Clarks respect you, huh?" Charlie said slyly. "Just because I'm way up here in the sticks don't mean my ears ain't still to the streets. People are talking about Prince Shai and his lack of respect for his elders."

"How I do business with Shai Clark is no business of yours. I'm a soldier, and that's just the way it is," Priest said.

Charlie laughed. "Do you hear yourself, Priest? Me, you, and Poppa Clark started this shit, remember? The hustler, the brain, and the killer . . . three the hard way, what happened to that? What happened to the dream of us all sitting around the round table breaking bread like real OGs?"

"That dream died with Poppa Clark," Priest told him before putting a bullet in Charlie's chest. He put two more slugs in his body, mindful of his face so that his children could give him a proper funeral. Priest knelt beside Charlie's body, kissed his fingers, and touched them to Charlie's forehead. "Your debt is settled, old friend. Be with your wife now."

Priest drove back to the city. Animal was silent for most of the ride. Every so often, he would look up at Priest, who was humming along with the oldies station that was playing on the radio like he didn't have a care in the world. He was the epitome of contentment, after having just murdered one of his friends in cold blood.

"You keep cutting your eyes over here like you're thinking about either kissing me or taking a swing at me. I should hope for the latter," Priest said.

"What the fuck was that?" Animal asked.

Priest glanced out the window. "Looks like a Ford to me, though it could've been a Dodge. The bodies on those models were similar."

"I'm not talking about the car. I'm taking about that bullshit you pulled back in Rye!"

"Oh, *that*? Just a lil' business that had to be taken care of," Priest said, and went back to his humming.

"So whacking somebody you've known over three decades is just *a lil' business*? What kind of monster are you?" Animal asked heatedly.

"I'm the same kind of monster you're gonna have to become, considering the route you're going," Priest told him. "The law of the jungle is survival of the fittest, and you better damn well learn it if you plan on locking ass with Shai Clark, lil' nigga."

"Fuck what you talking about, I could never murder a comrade like that," Animal told him.

"You don't know what the fuck you'd do if your life depended on it," Priest shot back. "Charlie was my main man, but his bullshit was interfering with my plans, much like Ashanti's riding with King James is interfering with yours."

"So you trying to say I should murder Ashanti like you did Charlie to get Shai off my back?"

"No, I'm telling you not to make the same mistakes I did and find yourself in a position to have to make that choice," Priest said seriously. "Shai is a cold piece of work, and brute force ain't gonna beat him. You're gonna need to be cunning and patient."

"You said it yourself that time isn't on our side," Animal reminded him.

"Tayshawn, you don't have a reason to, but I need you to have faith in me right now. I'm going to take you back to the church so you can spend some time with your lady. I'm sure she misses you. Rest up, and I'll come back in the morning to speak more of the plan."

Animal did miss Gucci. He didn't want to sit idle and wait for Priest, but he didn't have much of a choice at the moment. "Your word don't hold that kind of weight with me just yet, but I'll fall back for the time being. Just let me be clear on something. I won't hesitate to take Shai's life if given the opportunity, whether your plan works or not."

"Fair enough," Priest agreed. "While I'm gone, I want you to think about what I said, Animal. In this world, the only person you can depend on to be stand-up at all times is you."

"I hear you, but there's an exception to every rule. I can't speak on what happened between you and Charlie, but I *can* speak on me and Ashanti. He's hard as steel. That's my brother."

EIGHT

INTERROGATION ROOM A.

"DO YOU KNOW HOW MANY TIMES I'VE dreamed of having you in this position?" Detective Alvarez asked from across the steel table. He and Ashanti were in an interrogation room at the precinct, where they had been since his arrest a few hours before.

Ashanti gave the detective his most serious stare. "Ain't you gonna say 'pause' after that statement? It sounds suspect as hell." He laughed.

"Very funny, Ashanti, but you know what'd be funnier? If I jumped across this table and slapped that grin off your face," Alvarez said in a low growl.

Ashanti looked down at the shackle that went from his right wrist to the table. "The fact that you got me cuffed to this table and still got one hand resting near your gun, just in case, says you know how I'm built. Blood, the thought of you or anybody else putting their hands on me and not getting their face torn off is laughable. What else you got for me?"

"I got life in a cage for you if you don't tell me something good," Alvarez threatened.

"Detective, I know it's a shortage of real niggaz for y'all to lock up, but it's a sad day for law enforcement when the best you can do to get me off the streets is try to build a case off a bag of weed." Ashanti laughed.

"I ain't talking about weed, dipshit. I'm talking about murder." Alvarez slid several pictures across the table to Ashanti.

Ashanti was still grinning when he leaned over to look at the pictures, but the grin quickly faded when he saw himself in one of them.

INTERROGATION ROOM B.

"Cain Collins." Detective Brown read from the folder containing Cain's rap sheet. "Grand larceny, assault, possession, grand theft auto . . . the list goes on. At seventeen, you've got a longer rap sheet than men twice your age. Your mother must be proud."

Cain simply rolled his eyes and remained silent.

"Who was the other guy that was with you, the one who ran off?"

Cain shrugged.

"The strong, silent type, huh? Funny, I'd have taken you more for the pretty boy," Brown said, taunting Cain.

Cain's muscles tensed as if he wanted to spring, but he kept his cool.

"Oh, you don't like people talking about your little beauty

mark?" Brown reached to touch Cain's scar, and he jerked away.

"Keep your fucking hands off me!" Cain spit.

"Shut up, lil' nigga. You ain't calling the shots around here. I am." Brown jumped to his feet. "Now, you keep shooting that smart mouth off, and I'm gonna knock your teeth down your throat."

Cain looked up at the detective. "Is this the part where I'm supposed to get scared? You ain't 'bout shit, toy cop!"

Brown grabbed Cain by the neck and yanked him out of the chair. "There's that big-ass mouth of yours again." He gave Cain a good shake. Cain drew his fist back to strike, but before he could follow through, Brown had his gun drawn and pointed at his temple. "Go right ahead. Give me a reason to splatter you, sucka!" Cain wisely calmed down. "That's what I thought, muthafucka." He shoved Cain back down in the chair and sat back down himself.

"What the fuck you want from me, man?" Cain asked with an attitude.

"I want you to die in the fucking gutter, but I know I ain't gonna get that, so I'll settle for a name." He slid a picture across the table to Cain.

Cain looked at the picture. "Who the fuck is that?" He faked ignorance. He didn't know the man in the picture's name, but he knew his face.

"That's the muthafucka you and your cronies put to sleep a few days ago," Brown said.

Cain looked at the officer in disbelief. "Nigga, you got me fucked up. I don't know nothing about no murder, and if I did, what the fuck makes you think I'd tell you?"

"The same reason they all tell me, son. You don't wanna grow old in prison. See, you think you're hot shit because you're running with that little scum-fuck Ashanti, but you ain't really 'bout that life. I know a killer when I see one. Ashanti, that kid is a murderer, but not you. You sweet, youngster. I can smell the sugar coming all off you."

"Fuck outta here with that shit," Cain said, trying to keep his anger in check.

"What, you mad? Like I give a fuck. If you're really mad, get your black ass up outta that chair and do something," Brown said, challenging him. Cain remained seated. "Just like I thought, pussy. Now, you can play that gangsta shit all you want, but I know your monkey ass. I see dozens of fuck-tards like you on a daily basis. Angry little piss-ants, born to less-than-shit-ass parents who were either too lazy or too dumb to use birth control, so it falls to good citizens like us to clean up their bullshit."

"You don't know shit about me," Cain spat.

"Oh, but I know enough. You're the son of a two-bit crack whore, who'd rather suck dick for a blast than make sure you ate a decent meal at night." Brown laughed mockingly.

The truth in Brown's words cut Cain like a hot knife and sent him into a rage. Without even thinking about it, he was on his feet and leaping across the table. Brown was caught by surprise, so the first blow hit him square in the chin and knocked him out of the chair.

INTERROGATION ROOM A.

"Bullshit." Ashanti slid the pictures back across the table. He had almost shit his pants when Alvarez said they were pinning a murder on him. He just knew when he looked at that picture that he'd see Percy's pretty ass staring back at him, but it wasn't. It was someone else.

"*Real* shit, my friend. You were one of the last people to be seen with Rick Jenkins, and we got the picture, so don't try to run game like you don't know this cat." Detective Alvarez jabbed his finger at the picture.

Ashanti didn't know the victim personally, but he had seen him at a dice game a few nights before. He had a big month and seemed shifty but hadn't done anything to Ashanti personally, so there was no need to even talk to him, let alone kill him. The only reason Ashanti even remembered him was because Zo kept asking about him.

"Man, just because you got a picture of me with him doesn't mean I killed him," Ashanti said.

"Oh, I know you didn't kill him, it isn't your MO. You like big automatics; this guy was killed by a revolver . . . a .357, to be exact," Alvarez informed him.

INTERROGATION ROOM B.

When the uniformed officers rushed into the room, they found Cain on top of Detective Brown, choking the life out of him. The first officer who tried to pull Cain off was rewarded with an elbow to the nose, sending blood flying. Within seconds, the officers dog-piled on Cain.

"Hold that muthafucka up," Brown ordered. The uniformed officers held Cain up with his arms pinned behind his back. "You got a nice right hook, kid, but mine is better." He punched Cain in the face. He followed up with two blows to the ribs.

"No more, man! I'll talk. Just don't hit me anymore," Cain said. His lip was bloody, and he looked woozy.

"That's what the fuck I thought. Now, tell me something good," Brown said, standing nose-to-nose with Cain.

"A'ight, it went down like this . . ." Cain began, then spit his blood into Brown's face.

"You piece of shit!" Brown roared, and started raining punches down on Cain. Brown and the uniformed officers gave Cain an ass-whipping that he'd remember for a long time. He thought they were going to kill him, until someone came into the room, and the beating abruptly stopped.

"What the fuck is going on in here?" the police captain asked. His white shirt was crisp, the gold badge on his chest freshly polished.

"The suspect attacked me," Brown informed the captain.

"Bullshit, and you know it. This toy cop and his partner jacked me and my homie up for no reason. Then, when I wouldn't sign a confession for something I didn't do, he pulled his gun and threatened to kill me."

"Is this true?" the captain asked Brown.

"Cap, you gonna take his word over all of ours?" Brown motioned to the uniformed officers. They would surely back up his lie.

"You ain't gotta take my word for it, just ask the eye in the sky." Cain nodded to the security camera in the corner above the door.

Brown had completely forgotten that they'd installed the new cameras in some of the interrogation rooms. "Look, Cap, I can explain—"

"Save it." The captain raised his hand to silence him. He

pulled the detective to the side and whispered to him. "What do you have him in for?"

"Right now, him and his buddy are in for weed, but—"

"All this for some fucking weed? Have you lost your mind, Detective?" The captain looked like he wanted to smack the detective.

"Sir, he is also a person of interest in a murder," Brown explained.

"And this was the best way for you to start your investigation? I've told you and your partner about this Nazi shit before, Brown. The last thing we need is more bad press on the NYPD." He turned to Cain. "Sir, do you require medical attention?"

"Nah, I'm straight." Cain wiped the blood from his mouth with the back of his hand.

"It's my duty to ask if you would like to press charges against this detective for striking you."

"Cap, you can't be serious!" Brown was in disbelief.

"Shut up, Brown. Sir," he said to Cain, "do you want to press charges?"

Cain thought about it. "Nah, where I'm from, blacks don't send blacks to jail."

"Fine." The captain nodded. "Brown, get this kid cleaned up, and turn him and his friend loose. Then I want to see you and your partner in my office."

"Yes, sir," Brown grudgingly agreed. When the captain left, he turned his attention back to Cain. "You're lucky, but luck only goes so far. I'm gonna see you again, nigga. Count on that."

"I hope so, because next time, the playing field will be even." Cain made his fingers into the shape of a gun and pointed it at the detective.

"Get this piece of shit out of here before I kill him," Brown ordered the uniformed officers.

INTERROGATION ROOM A.

"By that dumb-ass look on your face, I can tell you know something, so you might as well spill the beans," Detective Alvarez said with a smug grin.

"I ain't seen shit, and I don't know shit." Ashanti folded his arms.

"Ashanti, you and I both know this is bullshit. You might not have pulled the trigger, but it doesn't take a rocket scientist to know who did. All I need you to do is say his name so I can lock his ass up and turn you loose."

Ashanti gave the detective a disbelieving look. "Man, you really got me fucked up. Since when you ever known me to be anything other than a stand-up nigga? I'm afraid I won't be of any help to you on this one, *Detective*."

Alvarez knew threatening Ashanti wouldn't do any good, so he tried another tactic. "What are you, eighteen now?"

"Nineteen," Ashanti corrected him.

"You're just a baby, but by the time you come out of prison for this, you'll be an old man. You really wanna take that kind of weight for something you didn't do? Now, you and I both know you didn't pull that trigger, but this picture of you and the victim don't look good. I think I can build a pretty solid case with it. What do you think?"

"I think you need to stop trying to bullshit a bullshitter. If that were true, you'd have me in here for murder instead of weed. Now, stop insulting me, fam. You keep saying you want me to talk, so I'm gonna talk. Get me a fucking lawyer!" Ashanti demanded. He knew once he invoked his right to counsel, it would bring their little interrogation to an end and buy him some time. He needed to get word to Zo about what was going on.

"OK, tough guy, we'll do this your way," Alvarez said.

There was a knock on the interrogation-room door, and a few seconds later, it came open, and Detective Brown poked his head in. "I need to holla at you, Jay."

Alvarez spared Ashanti one more glance before getting up and stepping outside with his partner. Through the door, Ashanti could hear raised voices. Something was going on, and he wasn't sure what, which made him nervous. Five minutes later, Alvarez came back into the room, and he didn't look pleased.

"Raise up," Alvarez ordered.

"What's going on?" Ashanti asked suspiciously.

"I'm cutting you loose," the detective said through clenched teeth. He undid the handcuffs and yanked Ashanti to his feet.

"I guess it's true what they say," Ashanti said.

"And what's that?" Alvarez asked.

"The sun even shines on a dog's ass at least once." Ashanti smirked.

"Get the fuck out of here before you turn up missing." Alvarez shoved Ashanti toward the door.

"OK, I'm going." Ashanti headed for the door. "You have a good one, Detective," he said over his shoulder.

"Fuck you, Ashanti! You think you're getting away, but nigga, you're on borrowed time. This isn't over, not by a fucking long shot! And you tell your boy Zo-Pound that

I'm coming for him. You hear me? Tell that muthafucka I'm coming!"

When Ashanti got outside, he was surprised to find Cain sitting on a police car talking to Fatima. Her hair was pulled back into a tight bun, so you could see her features: high cheeks, full lips, and perfectly sculpted chin. She was a fly little chick who lived in the neighborhood Ashanti and his crew did dirt in. She was only five-five, but the wedge boots she wore gave her two inches. She paced back and forth, shaking her head from side to side, causing her big door-knocker earrings to rattle. Her hands moved fluidly as she spoke heatedly to Cain. It seemed like the more she talked, the redder her face got. She was in her feelings.

The first to spot Ashanti coming out of the precinct was Cain. He abruptly stopped talking to Fatima and moved to meet Ashanti at the bottom of the stairs. "Glad to see you out." He extended his hand. Ashanti ignored it, eyes locked on Fatima.

"Did you call her?" Ashanti asked.

"Nah, when I walked out, she was on her way in. I thought you called her," Cain said honestly.

"How did you know?" Ashanti asked Fatima.

"You know how the ghetto grapevine works." Fatima hugged him. "When I heard they had my man hemmed up, you know I had to come down and see what was good."

"No doubt." Ashanti grinned. Fatima was a rider. She was young, wild, and loyal, just like him. Their union was almost perfect.

"What did they want with you?" Fatima asked.

Ashanti shrugged. "Just some bullshit. I had weed on me when they rolled."

Fatima's expression said she didn't believe him. "Ashanti, Cain already told me half the story, so you can fill me in, or I'll get it from the streets. Talk to me, baby."

Ashanti gave Cain a disapproving look for opening his mouth. "I told you, it was nothing," he said to Fatima. "They wanted to ask me about a murder, but when do they not want to ask me about murders? These niggaz act like every time somebody dies, it's my fault."

"Ashanti, I hope you ain't tied up in no crazy shit. We've barely made it through one storm, so let's not dive into another one if we don't have to. You know I don't get in your business, but you hot on these streets, so you need to take a step back. You don't see Zo out here like that, so maybe you should chill, too."

"Speaking of Zo, I need to holla at my dude. You seen him today?" Ashanti asked.

"Ashanti, Zo and that bullshit on the block can wait. You hot, baby," Fatima told him. "Dig, me and you are about to dip off to Yonkers and get a room for a few days. You need to be off the block, and I need to be fucked, so let's make this happen. And don't worry about the costs. I got it."

Ashanti pulled Fatima to him and kissed her on the forehead, then the lips. Moments like these made Ashanti wonder if he loved Fatima. He had never loved a woman, so he wasn't sure what it felt like, but he imagined it'd feel like what they had. "That sounds like a plan, but I still need to holla at Zo before I do anything, and it's not a conversation we can have on a telephone. Where was the last place you saw him?"

NINE

ALONZO, A.K.A. ZO-POUND, SAT ON THE BENCH in front of Building 3150 of the General Grant Houses, sipping a cup of coffee and reading a newspaper that was spread across his lap. The temperature had dipped, so he was huddled in a camouflage army jacket with the matching cap, which he wore pulled low over his eyes. Zo was a handsome young man, with cocoa skin and a near-perfect smile. He could've easily been a male model, but instead, he walked the path of a dope boy. He was a lieutenant in King James's army.

A few yards away, a young cat served the occasional fiend who wanted to get a morning blast. Normally, there would've been a constant flow of addicts creeping back and forth to buy drugs, but in light of recent events, it was slow motion. As the saying went, the block was hot.

Two years before, if you'd told Zo that he'd be back on the streets, in the thick of the bullshit, he'd have called you a liar. After his first prison bid, he came back into society a changed man. He hustled his way up to an assistant manager position at the supermarket he was working at and successfully put his old life behind him. He was done with the streets, but the streets weren't done with him. What was supposed to be a fun night at the strip club with his older brother, Lakim, ended in tragedy and placed Zo in the passenger seat of a long and dangerous ride. And with every dirty deed, he was pulled a little farther away from his goal of being a better man and back into old habits. He toed the line of good and evil but remained hopeful that one day, he'd be able to turn it around, but everything changed the night he agreed to help a friend who was in a jam.

Ashanti was his friend and surrogate little brother. The two were thick as thieves. Zo was a few years older than him, but Ashanti was very mature for his age. He had been through a lot. Growing up, he ran with a notorious crew of bandits led by a kid they called Animal, who was a legend in the hood. Years ago, Animal had vanished during what some speculated was an assassination attempt, so Zo was beyond shocked when he resurfaced and enlisted him and Ashanti in his cause. In the end, Animal was taken out, for the final time, and Zo and Ashanti found themselves at the top of Shai Clark's shit list, which dashed any hopes Zo had of going back to the life of a square. He was in it now, and there was no getting out.

"Break yo self!" Zo heard someone shout to his left. Zo looked up and saw his brother Lakim ambling toward him, wearing an oversized green Champion hoodie pulled over his head. While Zo was tall and handsome, Lakim was short and had a hard face. His whole swag screamed *goon*, which is the word that best described Lakim. He walked with a diddy-bop that said he was the hardest dude in the world, and in his mind, he was. Lakim had a quick temper, and it didn't take much to get him to pop off. He was a throwback street cat, with the mentality of the hustlers who had come before him in the eighties and nineties. In addition to being a beast on the streets, he was King James's second in command.

"You play too much, La," Zo told him, and went back to thumbing through the newspaper.

"I ain't playing, I'm trying to keep you on point, baby bro. *There's a war going on outside no man is safe from,*" Lakim said, quoting Mobb Deep's lyrics.

"I'm straight out here," Zo said.

"How you straight and you out here reading shit instead of being on point? What you woulda done if I had been one of Shai's goonies?" Lakim asked.

"I would've shot you." Zo raised the newspaper and showed Lakim the .357 hiding on his lap—.357s and .45s were his calling cards. He preferred to only use guns with the number five in them, which is where the word *pound* came in with his nickname.

"That's what the fuck I'm talking about," Lakim said proudly, and gave his little brother dap. "Word is bond, kid. Niggaz gotta be on point out here. Cats getting stunk left and right, know what I mean?"

"Yeah, I know what you mean. What's good with you, though?" Zo asked.

"Ain't nothing, B. Just coming through to make sure everything good. I should be asking you the same thing. I told you it ain't smart to be just sitting around on the block like a sitting duck. You like prime meat to the enemy or for po-po if they decide to run up in the Ps again."

"I'm good, La. I ain't on shit. I just came out to get some air, and I'm waiting on somebody," Zo said, checking his watch.

"What, you got some pussy coming through or something? Damn, ain't you too old to be still fucking bitches in fiends' cribs? Get a hotel or something," Lakim teased him.

"Man, the only ones still knocking bitches off in rock houses are you and that damn fool Ashanti," Zo shot back.

"Speaking of Ashanti, where the fuck is that lil' nigga at?" Lakim asked.

"Last time I seen him, he was with Cain and Abel. They said they were going to the movies," Zo said.

Lakim gave him a disbelieving look. "Fuck outta here. You know them niggaz don't spend no dough on flicks. They'd rather get the bootleg joints. Them lil' niggaz probably up to no good."

"Nah, I don't think so. Ashanti's calmed down some since that thing that happened with Animal," Zo said.

Lakim shook his head sadly. "Yo, that was some tragic shit, God. Animal was a good nigga, a solid solider. He fucked around and let his heart be his undoing. I keep telling y'all, getting caught up with these broads ain't no good when you out here playing for the stakes we playing for. A bitch will have your head screwed on backward."

"I'd expect somebody who ain't got a girl to say that. Go ahead with that antirelationship shit," Zo told him.

"Nah, I ain't on no antirelationship shit, bro. I'm dead-ass. Think about it, if Animal hadn't been out here chasing behind Gucci, he might still be alive now. Word life, that nigga had it made. He beat the system, and instead of staying low, he comes back and gets his wig split. What the fuck would make him put it all on the line like that?"

"Love," Zo said simply.

Lakim gave him a disapproving look. "Man, ain't no pussy good enough to get my head blown off over."

"See, this is why I can't talk to you, La. Love ain't about pussy, it's about finding someone you want to spend the rest of your life with and doing anything and everything you can to keep them safe."

"Whatever, God. It all sounds like some sucka shit to me," Lakim said. "He did all that and still got pushed and took his bitch along for the ride."

"Damn, ain't you got no respect for the dead?" Zo asked.

"I got plenty of respect for the dead, B. How many of our niggaz have returned to the essence? I don't mean it like that. All I'm saying is that Animal shoulda came and fucked with us, and we coulda rode on that nigga Shai as a team. Every nigga needs a team."

"Nah, La. Not every nigga needs a team," Zo told him. He could tell by the expression on his brother's face that he was going to ask him to elaborate, but a booger-green Audi pulling to the curb on the other side of the short gate drew his attention.

Lakim squinted to try to see through the heavy tints. "Yo, son, that's the same whip you just bought."

"It sure is," Zo said, getting up off the bench. He shoved the .357 down the front of his pants and started walking toward the car.

The Audi drew more than a few stares when it pulled into the bus stop in front of the projects. The curious stares turned into full-out ogling when the driver stepped out. She was a short chick, with flawless dark skin and wearing a pair of expensive-looking sunglasses. When she stepped from around the car onto the curb, it gave the onlookers a better view of her outfit. She was rocking a short cropped leather jacket, with skin-tight blue jeans and black thigh-high boots.

Zo-Pound came strutting up the block, hands shoved into the pockets of his army jacket and eyes locked on the female who had hopped out of the car. He gave her his Billy Dee Williams smirk, and she responded by twisting her lips and rolling her eyes behind the sunglasses. Zo, being Zo, wouldn't be denied, so he approached her. A few of the homies on the block who were watching the exchange made smart remarks and laughed. They just knew Zo-Pound was going to get shot down by the pretty girl. All the laughter stopped when Zo slipped his arm around the girl's waist and kissed her on the lips.

"Did you miss me?" Porsha asked, using her thumb to wipe a smudge of lipstick off Zo's upper lip.

"You know I did," Zo replied. "I see you brought my baby back in one piece." He nodded at the car.

"Stop playing, you know I know how to drive," Porsha told him. "Thanks for letting me use your car to run my errands." She handed him the key.

"All good, baby. I hope you put some gas in it, and not that cheap shit, either," Zo said.

"Yeah, I put gas in it. That reminds me, you owe me fifty dollars."

Zo was confused. "How the hell do I owe you fifty dollars?"

"Because I only had thirty in my gas budget, and it was eighty to fill this muthafucka up. Since when did gas become so high?"

"When the American government started the oil wars in

the Middle East," Zo joked. "Don't worry about the money you spent. I'll kick it back to you, ma."

"I know you will."

"Where's Frankie? I thought y'all were rolling together," Zo asked.

"We were together earlier. I dropped her off at my place after we finished shopping," Porsha told him. "By the way, she said to tell you thanks. She wouldn't say what for, but she said you'd understand."

"No doubt," Zo said, with a smirk that made Porsha uncomfortable.

"You got something you wanna tell me?" Porsha asked with an attitude.

"Cut it out, ma. You know I ain't even that kinda nigga." Zo threw his arms around Porsha and pulled her close. "My heart only beats for you."

"So what's the big secret you and Frankie are keeping?"

"It ain't my story to tell, Porsha. When Frankie is ready, she'll tell you," Zo said. "I was kinda hoping she came, though, so we could've all hung out, like we used to. I was gonna spring for a bottle and some trees."

"You know Frankie, Zo. Ever since she got out of the hospital, she ain't been playing the block like that. Physically, she's healing, but mentally, I think she's still kinda fucked up over what happened," Porsha said.

Frankie Angels was one of Porsha's closest friends and a former roommate. While coming out of her building one day, she got jumped by some hating-ass chicks from her block and the dudes they hung out with. It wasn't enough that they beat Frankie up, but for good measure, they slit her throat. Frankie lived, but the incident had changed her. She was no longer the outgoing, fun chick. These days, she was more withdrawn.

Zo shook his head sadly. "They ever find the ones who done it?"

"Not yet. Frankie wouldn't cooperate, so by the time the police got a lead, them bum bitches were long gone."

"That's crazy. Even when she's wronged, Frankie Angels stays true to the code." Zo said.

"Well, it's a dumb-ass code, if you ask me." Porsha snaked her neck. "If it had been me that got carved up like that and I knew who did it, I'm telling the police. You can call me a snitch all you want, but you'll be calling me a snitch from behind somebody's prison bars."

"A nigga touch you, getting locked up is the last thing they'd have to worry about," Zo said seriously. "Well, if them broads know like I know, they better hope the police catch them before the streets do. A lot of *real* niggaz have love for Frankie out here."

"Yeah, then that crazy shit with Dena didn't help the situation," Porsha said.

"Damn, I almost forgot about her. Didn't she turn out to be some weird stalker chick?" Zo asked.

Dena had been a confused young girl who had fallen in love with Frankie. They had started out as friends, as Dena lived in the same building, but the friendship eventually grew into a romance. The only problem was, for Frankie, it had been a fling, but to Dena, they were soul mates. When Dena got clingy, Frankie cut her off. Still, Dena stalked Frankie in hopes that they would reconcile. Ironically, it had been Dena's stalking that saved Frankie's life. She was the one who found Frankie on the stoop with her throat cut. Had Dena not thought quickly and kept the bleeding in check until the ambulance arrived, Frankie would've died.

"Yeah, she was definitely on some different shit. Hanging with her, you would've never known she had those kinds of tendencies. She seemed cool as hell," Porsha said.

"They always do until they show you that they're fucking nuts," Zo said.

"That is such a mean thing to say, especially after what happened to her," Porsha scolded him. "Has anybody heard anything on Cutty?"

Cutty was an old-school gangster, whom Frankie had owed a debt. To get the debt repaid, he sucked her into his high-risk lifestyle and strong-armed robbery and refused to free her until the debt was settled. Dena blamed Cutty and his influence for what happened to Frankie. In her mind, it was the bad karma that rubbed off from him that got her assaulted. She hated him for this and vowed to take his life as revenge. It was too bad that when she tried to make good on the vow, Dena ended up in the morgue and Cutty ended up back in prison.

"I spoke to Fatima. She said it's looking like her old man is finished. She didn't take it too good when she got the news," Zo told Porsha.

"I guess not. I'd be taking it pretty hard, too, if my father was looking at life for a murder I committed," Porsha said.

Word on the street was that Cutty had been the one who shot Dena that day outside the hospital, but the truth was that it was Fatima who had committed the murder. She saw a woman holding her father at gunpoint and did what any little girl would have done: tried to protect her dad. When the police showed up, Cutty claimed the gun and confessed to Dena's murder. Growing up, Cutty had never been there for Fatima, but in the end, he had made the ultimate sacrifice to give her a shot at life.

Zo looked around nervously to see if anyone had heard her, before moving in and grabbing Porsha by the arm. "Dig, don't you ever let me hear you speculating on some shit like murder. Whoever the streets say killed that girl is who killed her. Do you understand?"

"Zo, I didn't mean anything by it. Regardless of what happened, I like Fatima. I think she's a good kid who was just put in a fucked-up situation."

"It ain't on you to *think* anything about it, it's on you to forget that you even know about it," Zo told her.

"What's this, a lovers' spat?" Lakim walked up.

"Nah, just talking to my shorty," Zo told him.

"What up, sis?" Lakim greeted Porsha with a nod.

"Hey, La," she replied dryly. Porsha and Lakim never really saw eye-to-eye. They both felt like the other was a bad influence on Zo but kept the peace out of love for him.

"Yo, I'm about to go across the street to the liquor store. You gonna be here for a minute, Zo?" Lakim asked.

"No, we about to leave in a little while. Zo is taking me on a date," Porsha answered for him.

"Damn, Zo, I didn't know you were a ventriloquist," Lakim capped, and walked across the street.

"Why y'all two always at it?" Zo asked Porsha.

"Because your brother is an asshole. All he does is play the block and wants you to play the block with him, and the shit be cutting into my quality time. He needs to get a fucking girl, so he can stop being the third wheel with us," Porsha said with an attitude.

"I love it when you get all jealous." Zo pinched her cheek.

"Boy, cut it out before you ruin my makeup." She swatted his hand playfully. Porsha pulled out her phone and glanced at the time. "We should probably get going. I know you wanna change your clothes before we head out, or do you plan on taking me to eat dressed like an extra in *Paid in Full*?"

Zo looked at his outfit. "This is classic Harlem, you better recognize. But yeah, I do wanna throw something else on right quick. Let's bust a move."

Zo and Porsha were making their way to the car at the same time Lakim was coming back from the liquor store, talking on his phone. Zo could tell from his body language it was a heated discussion. When he saw Lakim pause, crack the bottle, and take a deep swig, he knew shit had just gotten real.

"Word is bond, son. It's about to be kufi-snatching season out here. I'll see you in a few, peace." Lakim disconnected the call.

"Everything good?" Zo asked.

"Nah, everything ain't good. Some shit just went down. I need you to help me round up the troops so we can handle business," Lakim told him.

"Oh, hell, no, not today, Alonzo," Porsha said, calling Zo by his government name. "You've been promising to take me out all week, and you ain't gonna pull this on me again."

"Porsha, cool the fuck out. Take the car, and I'll come meet you at your crib once I find out what's going on." Zo tried to hand her the car keys, but she just glared at him with her arms folded.

"Zo, I'll be in the lobby waiting for you. Hurry up, B." Lakim stormed off.

"Porsha—" Zo began, but she cut him off.

"Why are you always doing this, Alonzo? Every time we're supposed to do something, I gotta take a backseat to Lakim, Ashanti, or whoever else needs your attention. Are you fucking them or me?" Porsha asked.

Zo sucked his teeth. "Go ahead with that dumb shit, Porsha."

"It ain't no dumb shit, Zo. You know what dumb shit is? Neglecting your girl so you can go play with your friends. I'm too old for this shit, Zo, and so are you."

"Porsha, he's my brother," Zo said.

"Yeah, I know. He's your brother, and I'm just the chick you claim to love. I guess there's no contest. I'm so off this bullshit." She snatched the car keys and headed back toward the Audi.

"I'll be by to scoop you in an hour, I promise," Zo called after her, but Porsha was already pulling out into traffic. He stood there and watched her peel out down Broadway, feeling like a complete dick because he'd broken yet another promise. He hated hurting Porsha, but Lakim was his older brother, and they were all they had. She was mad now, but eventually she'd get over it . . . or so he hoped. Adjusting the .357 in his pants, Zo turned and walked toward the building to meet Lakim. Whatever was going on had better be life-or-death, or Zo and his older brother were going to have an issue.

TEN

IT WAS A SMALL NOISE THAT BROUGHT Frankie Angels out of her sleep. It was so faint that the average person wouldn't have heard it, but circumstances in life had left her anything but average. One of the benefits of being extremely paranoid was that it gave you super hearing. She cocked her head to one side, brain still heavy with sleep, and listened.

When Frankie heard the noise the second time, she knew she wasn't bugging. Someone was fucking with the locks on the apartment door. With one hand, she pushed her long hair back from her face, while the other disappeared under the sofa she had been sleeping on. When it reappeared, it was holding a .380. Frankie slid from under the comforter and tip-toed across the floor, commando-style. She was wearing nothing but a tank top and a pair of purple panties that were almost swallowed by her supple brown ass. Around her neck she wore a black bandanna. It covered the scar from the slashing.

She peered around the corner to the foyer in time to see the doorknob wiggle. Her heart pounded in her chest. Frankie's mind went back to the last home invasion, when Scar and his people rushed her apartment in the projects. She remembered the feeling of being violated, the touch of death as she lay on the floor, barely conscious. At that time, that was the closest she had ever come to death, but a few years later, getting her throat slashed on a stoop in Brooklyn trumped it. With those situations, and many others, it had been Frankie's will to survive that carried her through. That was the story of her life; she was a survivor.

Frankie placed her hand over the doorknob. Her palm was sweating and left a print. She'd have to wipe it down later or take it with her when she left. She took a deep breath and held the .380 at eye level. Exhaling, Frankie snatched the door open and fingered the trigger. She was able to stop herself before she accidentally blew Porsha's head off.

"What the fuck, Frankie!" Porsha jumped back, startled.

"Jesus, I thought you were a burglar." Frankie lowered her gun.

"Who breaks into their own house?" Porsha snapped. "My key got stuck in that cheap-ass lock, and I was trying to wiggle it loose."

"My God, I'm sorry, Porsha. I heard somebody messing with the locks, and I thought—"

"It's fine, Frankie. Don't worry about it." Porsha walked into the living room. She was trying to act calm, but she was really scared shitless. This was the second time she had been greeted by a gun when she came home. Frankie had been staying with her for the past few weeks, and it had been quite an experience. When Frankie got out of the hospital, there was no way she was going back to the apartment in Brooklyn, so she found another spot. She had given the realtor every dime she had saved to cover the deposit and three months' rent in advance, only to find out later that she had been scammed. She was flat broke and out on her ass, so Porsha took her in.

Porsha and Frankie had been roommates before, but this time, it was different. Frankie had been through some terrible things, and she wasn't the same. She was paranoid and skittish. She barely left the house, and even when she did, it wasn't without a pistol. She was suffering from posttraumatic stress disorder but refused to admit it. Porsha wanted her to get help but didn't force her. All she could do was be there as best she could for her friend during her trying times.

Porsha tossed her purse onto the couch and went into the kitchen, where she proceeded to raid the refrigerator. When she came out, she was carrying a cold bottle of tequila. She plopped down on the La-Z-Boy and screwed the top off the bottle. Forgoing a glass, Porsha took a deep swig.

"Well, damn, what's going on with you?" Frankie asked. She'd never known Porsha to be much of a drinker, especially not that early in the evening.

"I'm just stressed out," Porsha said in a huff.

"Porsha, I said I'm sorry about the whole gun thing," Frankie said.

"It's not you, Frankie. Zo just got me in my feelings," Porsha told her.

"Trouble in paradise?" Frankie asked. She sat on the couch and tucked her legs beneath her.

"Paradise, my ass. I'm about sick of Zo and his bullshit. Every time we're supposed to spend time, something comes up, and I have to take a backseat to his brother or one of his dumbass friends," Porsha fumed.

"The life of a dope boy," Frankie said. "Zo is out there chasing a dollar, so shit like this is to be expected."

"I think I liked him better when he was working in the supermarket," Porsha said.

Frankie gave her a disbelieving look. "Yeah, right, you wouldn't give Zo the time of day when he was stacking boxes, but now that he's stacking paper, that's ya boo," she joked.

Porsha looked offended. "Frankie, don't come at me like that. I'd love Zo if he was up or down, so don't act like I'm just in this for the paper."

"I was just kidding, Porsha. Why don't you relax?" Frankie suggested.

"I wish I could, but I'm wound up tighter than a clock. My job got me stressed, my parents are on my nerves, and I ain't been fucked properly in a week. I'm about to go postal out this bitch!"

"Well, baby girl, when life gets me down, I look for guidance from the most high," Frankie said.

"God?" Porsha asked.

"No." Frankie plucked a rolled blunt from the ashtray. "The weed man, since he's always the *most high*!"

Porsha laughed. "Frankie, your ass is shot out."

"Indeed I am." Frankie lit the blunt. "Now, why don't you get shot out with me?" She extended the blunt to Porsha.

Porsha happily accepted the weed. The two girls smoked and caught the last half of a funny movie that was on cable. When the munchies kicked in, Frankie went into the kitchen and fried up some chicken wings. Frankie was as hard as any dude on the streets, but she was all woman when it came to the kitchen. Porsha smashed her wings while Frankie picked over hers. She was laughing at the jokes in the movie they were watching, but Porsha could see something was troubling her. Frankie had a great poker face, but Porsha had known her so long that it was transparent to her.

"What's on your mind, Frankie Angels?" Porsha asked.

Frankie gave a weak smile. "Is it that obvious?"

"Only to someone who knows you," Porsha said. "Now, what's good?"

"Same shit, just stressing over this shitty hand life has dealt me. I'm damn near broke and homeless."

Porsha waved her off. "Frankie, you know as long as I got a place to lay my head, you do, too. We family, boo."

"I know, and I love you for that. At the same time, though, this is your space. Your apartment is small enough as it is without my grown ass crowding you. I'm looking online and in the newspaper trying to find something but haven't come up on anything in my price range yet that isn't a slum or a room for rent," Frankie told her.

"You know rent is high as hell in the city, Frankie. It ain't like when we was living in the projects. That whole situation was a pain in the ass, but I can't even lie, we had mad fun in that apartment," Porsha said.

"Yo, do you remember that house party we threw that summer?"

"Do I? Poor Sahara threw up so much I thought we were gonna have to take her to the hospital." Porsha laughed.

Frankie sucked her teeth. "That was her damn fault. Who told her to drink all those cans of Four Loko?"

Porsha shook her head, thinking back to how they had to carry Sahara to the bedroom. "She was always going overboard, but that was my bitch. Have you spoken to her lately? I tried to call her last week, but the number I had on her isn't working."

"Nah, I haven't spoken to her in a good minute. You know her, she's probably somewhere chasing a dollar." Frankie thought back on her friend and all her get-rich-quick schemes. "Oh, and speaking of a dollar . . ." Frankie picked her handbag up off the table. She pulled out an envelope and handed it to Porsha.

"What's that?" Porsha asked suspiciously.

"Open it and find out," Frankie urged.

Porsha tore the envelope open and found cash inside. "What's this for?"

Frankie shrugged. "For whatever you wanna spend it on. I been laying on your couch and eating your food for weeks. The least I can do is try to kick you a little something for your troubles. It isn't but a stack, but as soon as I get some regular cash flow coming in, I'll try to do more."

"Frankie, where the hell did you get a thousand dollars?" Porsha asked.

"Don't worry about it. I didn't break any laws for it. A friend of mine owed me a favor and came through recently," Frankie said a little too slyly.

"And speaking of favors, what's up with all this secret shit between you and Zo-Pound?" Porsha asked.

"What do you mean, Porsha?"

"I mean whatever y'all got going on that neither of you seem to want me to know about. Now, if you were one of my other friends, I'd probably be beating your ass for going behind my back with my man on some sneaky shit, but I know that ain't your MO. You wouldn't dare fuck Zo behind my back, and if it ain't sex, I gotta assume it's dirt. What are the two of you up to?"

Frankie didn't answer at first. She was going to lie, but she saw it was really bothering Porsha. She couldn't tell her the whole truth, so she told her enough of it to put her mind at ease. "A'ight, Porsha. Just hear me out before you say anything. You know when I got beat out that money, I was flat on my ass. Anybody I could've gone to for money is either dead or in prison. So when all else failed, I turned to Zo."

"You borrowed money from my boyfriend?" Porsha asked with an attitude. Frankie was her home girl, but she wasn't comfortable with another woman asking her man for money.

"No, I didn't ask Zo for no money. You know better than that, Porsha. I broke my situation down to him, and he offered to help me out. At first, he flipped and wanted to go find the dude who took my money, but you know I ain't about to let Zo get in no trouble. He did offer to give me the money, but I couldn't accept that in good conscience. What I did was I pawned what little jewelry I had and gave Zo a few hundred dollars to flip for me. That's how I got the money I gave you."

Porsha couldn't believe all that had been going on right under her nose. She was slipping. Frankie would never do her dirty, but that didn't mean another female wouldn't have taken advantage of being able to get close to Zo without her knowing. She trusted Zo, but the fact that he refused to tell her what was going on between him and Frankie even when she called him on it meant that he could keep a secret. In her experience, she'd learned that men with secrets were a problem that just hadn't occurred yet. It made her wonder what else he had been keeping from her.

"Frankie, Zo is a good dude, and I'm glad he was able to help you out, but in the future, if you need something from *my* man or he offers you something, I'd appreciate it if I didn't have to hear about it after the fact," Porsha said.

"You got that, and I apologize," Frankie said sincerely.

Now that the air had been cleared, the tension left the room, and everything was back to normal. Frankie rolled another blunt, while Porsha surfed through the channels. She settled on the twenty-four-hour news station to see what she'd missed during the day. A story came on about a murder that had taken place in Harlem, so Porsha turned it up to see if it might've been anyone she knew.

Frankie paused from her blunt rolling to take a sip of her soda. She had the cotton mouth from the weed. When she looked up to see what had Porsha so entranced, she spit her soda all over the table and the living-room floor. On the screen was a picture of the murder victim, along with his name, Rick Jenkins.

"Are you OK, Frankie?" Porsha asked as her friend continued to choke on the soda.

"Yeah, I'm cool. It just went down the wrong pipe," Frankie lied. Her eyes and ears remained focused on the television screen and the news anchor describing how they'd found a con man named Ricky Jenkins dead in a motel room from a .357 slug to the chest.

ELEVEN

IN THE HOOD, NEWS TRAVELED FAST, ESPECIALLY when it came to death. It didn't take long for the streets to start buzzing about the murder of the pretty young pimp in the barbershop. Percy wasn't a big enough player in the game for his loss to cause much of a ripple effect, but there was one man in particular who didn't take his death well.

Swann sat on the park bench, as he had been doing for the past hour or two, drinking and thinking. He always sat on the same bench when he was in that park. It had sentimental value to him. It had been on that very bench where he had murdered a man he had once called his homie, Tech. Of all the lives he had taken, Tech's was the only one he regretted. His friendship conflicted with his loyalty, and in the end, he had to put young Tech's lights out. It was for the greater good; at least, that's what he told himself so that he could sleep at night.

Swann looked nothing like his normally immaculate self. His clothes were wrinkled, his face was ashy, and his hair needed to be braided. Mussed black hair hung down around his face and gave him an insane look. His appearance matched his mood. A few hours before, he had gotten word about the execution of Percy. Percy had been like family to him; Swann and Percy were very close. He was a pompous homosexual who sometimes let his mouth write checks his ass couldn't cash, but that didn't mean he had deserved to die, especially the way he'd been murdered. Swann had to go to the city morgue and identify the body because Percy's mother wasn't up to it. The woman was a wreck over the loss of her only son. When he got there, he was glad that he'd come instead of her. No mother should have to see her child like that.

The killers had tortured Percy with sharp instruments before cutting the skin from his face. The police had searched for hours but were unable to find the missing flap of skin. The police chalked it up as a drug-related hit, but everyone knew Percy didn't sell drugs. The murder had been a message for Swann, and he heard it loud and clear. It was war!

Swann wasn't alone in the park. He was surrounded by several of his goons, thirsty young cats who would do anything to eat from the Clark table. In the midst of the goons were two of Swann's most trusted comrades, Holiday and Angelo. After being shot in both legs, Holiday was confined to a motorized wheelchair until the wounds healed. Although his legs were ruined, his trigger finger still worked just fine, and he was itching to put it to use.

Angelo stood at attention, dressed in a blazer and jeans. His once smooth dark face was now marred by a nasty scar down the side of it. It had been a gift from a woman named

Kastro, who was affiliated with Animal. Kastro and Animal had both paid for the disrespect with their lives, but killing them had made them martyrs. Instead of their deaths deterring the upstarts, it only riled them up more. Where Animal had fallen, another vicious young killer had risen to take his place. His name was Ashanti, and he was currently the focal point of Swann's hatred. Word on the streets was that it was he who had killed Percy. Ashanti and his band of misfits had been violating and pulling capers for weeks to try to get the attention of the Clarks, and now they had it.

"Are we just gonna stand around and watch him drink that bottle, or is he going to say something?" a young goon called Ty asked. Ty was a chubby Haitian kid from out of Brooklyn who served as one of Swann's street soldiers. Ty made good money working the streets for the Clarks, but he knew his profits would be doubled if he could get promoted to the rank of lieutenant. In order to do that, he had to put in the work, which was why Ty was always the first to volunteer when someone needed to be made to bleed. When Swann had called the meeting, Ty couldn't get to Harlem fast enough to see what it was about.

"Why don't you relax?" Holiday said. He, too, was getting annoyed just standing around, but he was smart enough to keep his annoyance to himself.

"I don't mean no disrespect, fam, I'm just anxious, same as everybody else here," Ty explained. "The OG calls an emergency meeting, I know it's something big, and I'm just trying to see what's popping."

"Cool out, and keep your mouth closed. Swann will speak when he's ready and not a minute before. If you don't feel like waiting around, take a fucking walk," Angelo snapped. He had seen Swann in dark moods before, and someone almost always died immediately after he snapped out of it.

"Fifty thousand," Swann said just above a whisper. Everyone was shocked, because he hadn't said a word since they'd gotten there.

"What'd you say?" Angelo asked.

"I said fifty thousand," Swann repeated. "That's the price for that little nigga Ashanti's life."

"Swann, Ashanti is just a foot soldier, so maybe—" Angelo began, but Swann cut him off.

"You heard what I said." Swann turned to address the goons. "Spread the word, my niggaz. I got fifty stacks for the man who puts that juvenile delinquent Ashanti in a fucking bag and an extra ten stacks for each additional person who goes along for the ride."

"What if his pretty little girlfriend is with him? Should we stall her out because she's a civilian?" Ty asked.

"Fuck him and his bitch. If she's there, she dies, too."

Swann had barely finished his sentence before the goons took off in all directions. Fifty thousand dollars was more money than most of them had ever seen, and they were beyond eager to accept.

Angelo waited until the goons had gone and it was just him, Holiday, and Swann left in the park, before speaking. "Swann, that's a lot of money to put on a foot soldier. King James is the real problem. Cut the head off, and the body dies."

"Fuck that. When Ashanti touched my people, he moved into the number one slot on my shit list." Swann stood up.

"So what about the nigga King, we supposed to put him on

the back burner while everyone else is off chasing Ashanti?" Holiday asked.

"Nah, I didn't forget about him. I'm baking a special cake for King James." Swann looked down at his watch. "And it should be just about done cooking."

TWELVE

"WELCOME TO NEWARK," THE SIGN READ AS King James exited 21 North onto Broad Street. He rarely ventured out of the hood unless he absolutely had to, but the way things had been going lately, he needed a change of scenery to get his thoughts together.

When he'd been released from state prison a few years before, he felt displaced in time. He had been born and raised in Harlem, but the Harlem he had come home to after his bid wasn't the one he remembered. Gone was his beautiful slum, replaced by a trendy tourist attraction with overpriced housing, leaving very few corners for a crook to make an honest dollar on. Still, for as much as the landscape had changed, the game remained the same, and that was his main concern. King James was a man with a plan, and that plan was to be the next king of New York.

The plan was simple: fly under the radar and gobble up as much territory as he could before any of the heavy hitters realized what was going on. By the time they woke up to the usurper in their midst, it'd be too late to do much about it except roll with the movement or get wiped out. King James had the right people backing his play, shooters who would kill or die for him, and a bomb-ass product. It was the perfect plan, but even the best-laid plans were subject to unforeseen complications. In King James's case, the complication was named Shai Clark.

Shai was the boss of bosses in New York City, and nothing moved unless he told it to or got a piece. The hood respected Shai, but King James did not. To him, Shai was a spoon-fed rich kid who had inherited the title instead of earning it. From the moment King James had met Shai in Brick City, he knew he didn't like him. Shai was arrogant, and his people were disrespectful. When King had tried to reach out to show Shai the proper respect, he was dismissed like he was little more than a common thug. The slight at the strip club had been the incident that planted the seeds of contempt, and they had been growing in King James for months. All he needed was a reason to strike, and it had been two of his young shooters, Ashanti and Zo-Pound, who had given him that reason.

When Ashanti and Zo-Pound had joined in Animal's personal war against the Clarks, that pulled King James into it by association. King was aware of neither Animal's resurrection nor Ashanti's and Zo's roles in his mission, and by the time he found out, it was already out of his hands. Ashanti and Zo were soldiers in his army, so they were his responsibility. At least, that was the excuse he used when he was called to answer for deviating from the plan. King's partners frowned on the heat he was bringing to the organization from his street wars, but King didn't care. He was the one taking all the risks, so he would run the show however he saw fit. King James had never been big on diplomacy; he was a gladiator.

For a change of scenery, he shot out to Newark to see this young broad he fucked with named Drea, who lived off South Orange Avenue. Her crib was smack in the middle of the hood, but it was the last place anyone would think to look for King. He pulled up in front of the three-family house where her apartment was and parked at the curb. He never pulled into the driveway. Before getting out of the car, King checked himself in the rearview mirror. His waves were spinning like high tide, and his thick beard was freshly trimmed. He moved to brush a speck of imaginary debris from his pecan-colored, butter-soft leather jacket he was wearing. Last, he adjusted the huge rope chain that hung around his neck. The medallion on the end of it was about the size of a bread plate. Carved into the gold was the number seven resting in a crescent moon, with a star hanging from its tip. It was the Universal Flag of the Five-Percent Nation, his calling card. From between the seats, King pulled out his .32, checking to make sure it was loaded before stuffing it into his jacket pocket and hopping out.

The first thing he noticed was how quiet it was. Drea lived two doors down from a liquor store, so her block was always busy. That day, it seemed calm. Standing in his yard, where he usually was, was Drea's next-door neighbor. He was a slightly older cat, with long dreads that could stand a good washing. He was sitting on a lawn chair, drinking a forty-ounce and smoking something that smelled like he had plucked it out of a random backyard. King had seen him a few times when he'd come through but never communicated with him beyond the cordial nod.

King could feel the neighbor's eyes on him as he passed, so he turned and met his gaze. The neighbor turned away. King jogged up the stairs to the apartment and knocked on Drea's door. A few seconds later, he was greeted by a pretty brown-skinned girl draped in only a bathrobe and house shoes. She was dressed like she had just been lying around, but her hair was flawless, and you could still smell the spray in her weave.

"About time you made it," Drea said with a fake attitude.

"You know I keep a hectic schedule." King invited himself in. Drea was a hood chick, but her apartment was nicely furnished and always spotless. King took his jacket off and laid it on the arm of the sofa before plopping down and grabbing the remote to the big-screen television. The .32 was sticking him in the hip, so he took it out of his pants pocket and slipped it into his coat.

"Arrogant-ass Harlem nigga." Drea shook her head. She climbed onto King's lap, straddling him. "And how you gonna come into my house and not show me no love?" She tried to kiss him on the lips, but he gave her his cheek. "What's the matter, baby?"

"Nothing, but you know I'm not really into all that," King said. "So what's good with you, though?" King slipped his hand inside her bathrobe to throw her off the subject. His fingers traced over her soft skin.

"Waiting on you to come give me what I need." Drea slipped her hand between her legs and squeezed King's dick through his jeans. She leaned in so close that her breath brushed his neck when she whispered in his ear. "You got something to get me in the mood, baby?"

King knew what time it was. "You know I do." He reached

over to his coat and pulled a rolled-up brown paper bag from the inside pocket. "Get right, and get me right." He tossed the bag to Drea.

Drea squealed like a schoolgirl when she emptied the contents of the bag onto the coffee table. The bag contained the three Bs: beans, blunts, and blow. Drea was a party girl, and King knew what turned her on. He sat back like a proud father and watched as she began her dance with the dark side.

Drea did a few lines, washing them down with a blunt filled with high-grade weed, and was feeling no pain. She got up from the couch and started dancing to the song playing on the television's music station. With a blunt pinched between her lips, she started doing a striptease. Her weed-slanted eyes looked down at King hungrily as she pushed her robe off one shoulder, then the other. She was naked except for a pair of purple lace panties. Drea licked her fingertips and began playing with her nipples, daring King James to conquer her.

He rose to the challenge.

King got up from the couch. He felt a bit light-headed, but he wasn't sure if it was from the weed he'd smoked or the beating of his heart. So much blood was flowing to his dick that he thought it would explode in his pants. She scooped her hands under her armpits. She knew what it was, so she wrapped her legs around his waist. The pill had Drea's skin on fire, and the blow had her swerving. King held her up with one hand and undid his pants with the other. When his dick was finally free of the restrictive jeans, he guided it to her love cave.

Drea gasped when King entered her. His thickness threatened to tear her open, but it hurt too good for her to tell him to stop. She wanted him to go deeper. He did. King stroked Drea slow and deep, making her a little wetter every time he speared her. She tried to bite his neck, but he pushed her face away. Out of spite, she slammed herself harder on his cock. Drea locked eyes with King, and no words were necessary. He knew what she wanted and was happy to give it to her.

King pulled out of Drea and turned her around. He entered her from the back and found her box to be just as inviting as it had been from the front. He wrapped his massive hands around her waist and pulled her to him while stabbing deep inside her. He felt Drea release herself down his legs and smiled before he plunged deeper into her. It was like magic.

The next forty minutes were a blur. All King could remember were flashes of pleasure and pain as he and Drea ravaged each other. When he was about to blow his load, Drea jumped off him and took his dick in both hands. She jerked it fast and furiously, spitting on it and talking to it. King grunted, letting her know that he was about to cum, and she opened her mouth as wide as she could. A spray of white jizz coated Drea's face and lips. For good measure, she took him in her mouth and squeezed his dick until it was empty. King collapsed on the couch, breathing heavy and waiting for his leg to stop shaking. He looked over at Drea, who was propped on one elbow, playing with the excess cum on her lips.

"Damn, you are one freaky muthafucka," King said breathlessly.

"And you love this freak bitch." She tugged his dick and gave it a little lick.

King heard his phone go off in his pocket. He pulled it out and read the text message that flashed across the screen. His face immediately soured. It was Fatima hitting him to let him know Ashanti got popped. Ashanti was one of King's best, and losing him would hurt. "Damn," he said, replying to the text. He dropped his phone back into his pants pocket and got off the couch. "Yo, I gotta dip back to the city right quick," he told Drea.

She looked at him as if he had lost it. "Oh, hell nah, nigga, how you just gonna come through, blow in my mouth, and keep it moving like I'm some bird?" She was upset.

"Drea, it ain't even like that. Some shit popped off on the block with my lil' mans, and I gotta go see about them," he told her before disappearing into the bathroom. He took a quick shower, then came back into the living room to jump into his clothes. Drea sat at the dining-room table, with her arms folded, staring daggers at King the whole time he dressed. He thought about just breaking down to her everything that was going on, but he figured why bother? Family business wasn't Drea's business. She would either understand or she wouldn't. He didn't have time to care.

After slipping his Timberlands on, King looked to the arm of the chair where he had laid his jacket and didn't see it.

"Here." Drea handed him his jacket off the back of one of the dining-room chairs. At some point, she must've moved it.

"Thanks, ma. I'm gonna call you later, OK?" King told her.

"Whatever." Drea got up and walked into her bedroom, slamming the door.

King decided to leave it be, so he just slipped his jacket on and headed out. When he was coming out of Drea's apartment, he spotted the guy from next door. Instead of sitting in his driveway, he had moved his lawn chair to the front of Drea's spot. Two of his friends had joined him, and they were shooting dice at the bottom of the stairs, directly in King's path.

"Pardon self," King said, coming down the stairs. The three moved to the side and let King pass. One of them was staring at his chain like it was the *Last Supper*.

"What you claiming?" one of the dudes asked King. King's face said that he was puzzled, so the kid explained. "You got a seven and a star on your chain. What gang is that?"

King looked from his chain to the dude. "It ain't a gang, brother. It's a way of life."

The other dude spoke up. "You know we ride that five over here, so some might take you flagging as a sign of disrespect."

King could smell bullshit a mile away. "I hear you talking, shorty." He turned to leave, but two guys blocked his exit.

"Yo, my dude, you been coming around here for a minute, and I been racking my brain trying to think where I know you from, and it didn't hit me until today," the dread from next door said.

"Fam, whoever you think I am, I'm not that nigga," King told him, and kept walking. His hand was already jammed into his pocket and clutching the .32.

"Yeah, I think you that nigga," the dread continued. He had fallen into step behind King, with his friends in tow. "Word is one of the homies put a red light on you. You know OG Swann, don't you?"

King's jaw tightened at the mention of Swann's name. He disliked him more than he disliked Shai. "Listen, shorty, what's between me and Swann is between me and Swann. Don't make the next man's problems your problems. Shit like that never ends well."

“This is all business, big brah.” The largest of the goons stepped forward. He had a hard black face and yellow teeth that were on the verge of falling out. “Swann got some paper on your face, and we aim to collect. But I’m a sporting man, so I’ll tell you what, give up that chain, and I’ll give you a five-minute head start before me and my homies eat your food.”

King James laughed. “Check this out, son. I spent years in prison and ain’t never been robbed, so it sure as hell ain’t gonna happen on the streets.” He pulled his .32 and, without hesitation, pointed it at the kid and pulled the trigger, but nothing happened.

Drea listened for King to go out the door before she retrieved her cell phone from the dresser and dialed the dread from next door. He and Drea were more than neighbors; they were occasional fuck buddies. The dread was hardly her speed as far as the men she seriously dated, but he had a decent dick game. More important, he was pussy-whipped off Drea’s goodies and would do anything she asked, including kill.

“Yeah, he on his way down,” Drea said once he’d answered the phone.

“He strapped?” the dread asked.

“Yeah, but I don’t think it’ll do him much good,” she said sinisterly, juggling the bullets in her hand that she’d removed from King’s gun while he showered. What she was doing was filthy, but she figured the bounty on King James’s head could buy her enough soap to wash away the sin.

“Shit,” King said, looking at his gun in disbelief.

Using his moment of confusion to their advantage, the

Jersey cats moved on him. The big dude, who had asked for his chain, struck first, catching King on the chin with a solid punch. King retaliated by slamming the empty gun into the side of his head. That hurt him, but it was the left King followed with that knocked him out.

King took a boxer's stance and addressed the last two. "You niggaz wanna dance? Let's get it!"

They had planned on stomping him out and snatching his chain before turning him over to Swann's people, but seeing their friend sleeping on the curb gave them pause. Any ideas they had about seeing King James in combat went out the window, so the weapons came out. One produced a bat and the other a gun.

King was by no means a punk, but he knew that a good run beat a bad stand any day, so he threw the empty gun at them and bolted for the truck. A shot whistled past his ear and shattered the rear window. He got low and dipped around to the driver's-side door, hitting the automatic locks. He had just made it inside the truck when the driver's-side window shattered. Glass sprayed him in the face, cutting his cheek and forehead. Before he could fully recover, the guy with the bat proceeded to bust out his windows. Frantically, he threw the truck into gear and tried to make his escape.

King crashed back and forth into the car in front of him and the one behind him, trying to get out of the parking spot. Just as he burst free, the dread who had pulled the gun jammed it through the broken window and tried to blow King's face off. King avoided the bullet by mere inches; it whizzed past him and struck the glove compartment. King grabbed the dread by his arm, locking it in position, and stepped on the gas.

"You tried to assassinate me, pussy?" King snarled. "I'm King James, nigga. I'm invincible!"

The gunman felt the car pick up speed and fired another shot in panic. This one struck the passenger seat. King jerked the dude's arm and snapped it, causing the gun to fall into his lap. "Let me go, muthafucka!" the gunman shrieked. His feet were skidding along the ground as he tried to keep up with the truck.

"Gladly." King released his arm. The dread hit the ground and rolled end-over-end until he slammed face-first into the fire hydrant. He was dead on impact.

King James did one hundred miles per hour until he was back on the highway and safely out of Newark. He couldn't believe what had just gone down. He pounded the steering wheel in frustration as he replayed the tail of the tape in his head. Of all the speeches he had given his soldiers about pussy being the downfall of many great hustlers, he couldn't believe he had almost joined that number. Drea was food when he next saw her. That went without saying. The bad part about it was that he was starting to like Drea, but she had proven to be as scandalous as the rest. The heart had no place in the game.

The most surprising revelation was that Swann had set it up. King had gone out of his way to keep Drea a secret. Not even his closest comrades knew exactly who she was or where she lived, but Swann had been able to get to her. He had underestimated his enemy's reach, and it had almost cost him his life. He wouldn't make the mistake again.

King pulled out his cell and punched in a number.

"Peace." Lakim answered on the second ring.

"Ain't shit peace right now, sun. Shorty in Newark tried to lay me down for a nap," he said, speaking in code.

"Yo, God, I told you about fucking with them snake bitches out there. They don't play by anybody's rules but their own in Newark. Essex County is the Wild West."

"True indeed, but dig the punch line. Pretty boy put the battery in her," King said, referring to Swann.

"On everything, I'm at that nigga like a tweet as soon as I hang up the jack," Lakim vowed.

"Easy, my nigga. This is chess, not checkers. I'm on my way back to Mecca right now, so hold ya head until I get there. In the meantime, round up the crew, and tell them this is not a drill."

"You already know!" Lakim said.

"Nigga tried to send a bitch at me, but that's cool. This shit just taught me a lesson," King James said.

"And what's that, God?"

"Ain't no rules in war."

AIN'T NO RULES IN WAR

"I keep thinking that if I blink, the image will fade, and you'll be gone again."

—Gucci

THIRTEEN

IT DIDN'T TAKE PRIEST VERY LONG TO find the Little Guy. Shai's spies had been keeping steady tabs on him since Gee-Gee had called in the contract. They kept a nice little file on him that included just about everything there was to know about the Little Guy, except the fact that there was nothing little about him.

Priest was taken aback when he first saw the mountain of a man in person. He had been staking out the motel room he was staying in. When the Little Guy came out, Priest had to do a double take. The Little Guy stood at least six-foot-six and was well over two hundred pounds. He was a typical grease ball, with overgelled hair and a jogging suit that fit him a little too snugly at the wrists. All his jewelry was slum, with the exception of the chain around his neck, fitted with a diamond square.

As the Little Guy crossed the parking lot, he was joined by two more men. They were both wearing cheap suits and sunglasses at night. They were either the feds or the last few soldiers loyal to the rat. They climbed into a black SUV with heavily tinted windows and pulled out into traffic. Priest had hoped to hit him at the motel, but there were too many people around for him to risk it. He'd have to follow them and hope another opportunity presented itself.

He followed them out to Queens, where the SUV pulled into the parking lot of a seedy-looking strip club, and they jumped out and made happy steps toward the entrance and were greeted by the bouncer. He hugged the Little Guy like a long-lost family member. When Priest caught a glimpse of the badge hanging around the bouncer's neck, he understood. They were playing for the same team. The bouncer directed the Little Guy and his men around the metal detector and ushered them inside. It was all VIP treatment for the Little Guy. Here was a man who was about to turn state's evidence on his friends, the same friends he had broken the law with, and he was parading the streets like a rock star. The sight of it disgusted Priest. The fact that the snitch could walk around without apparent fear for his life was just further proof that the game had changed. The rules went out the window.

Priest waited a few seconds before following the Little Guy. He knew when he saw the off-duty officer and the metal detector at the entrance that bringing his gun inside was out of the question, so he left it in the car. It complicated things but changed nothing. The Little Guy wouldn't live to see another sunrise, but Priest would have to be creative about the way he killed him.

The inside of the place was more crowded than the parking lot reflected. There were mostly more grease balls, dressed just as badly as or worse than the Little Guy, and a few anorexic strippers with balloon breasts dancing on the stage. Most of the guys in the bar seemed to know one another, which confused Priest at first. When he looked up at the banner hanging on the wall that read "Fond Farewell," everything started to make sense. Obviously, the rest of the organizations hadn't gotten the memo about the Little Guy's extracurricular activities yet, and they were throwing him a going-away party before his phony prison sentence was to begin. Little did they know their going-away parties were right around the corner. It took everything Priest had to keep from laughing and bringing attention to himself.

He found a table in the back, in the darkest corner of the joint, and tried his best to remain inconspicuous. It wasn't an easy task, considering he was the only minority in the whole establishment who wasn't wearing some type of server's uniform or shaking ass on the stage. He watched patiently as the Little Guy and his goombas toasted and told war stories. After about an hour, the Little Guy's bladder finally started talking to him, so he got up to use the bathroom. That was when Priest made his move.

When Priest entered the bathroom, the Little Guy had his back to him, relieving himself in the urinal. Seeing him up close, Priest now knew that what he had mistaken as fat was all muscle. The Little Guy must've felt he was being watched, because he looked up from his leak and at Priest through the mirror. Priest lowered his eyes and went to the urinal on the other side, where he pretended to be taking a leak, too. When he moved to the sink to wash his hands, the Little Guy was still pissing. Priest let the water run while he slipped his hands up the sleeves of the suit jacket he was wearing. He was about to make his move when the Little Guy spoke.

"I've been coming to this spot for a long time, and I've never seen you. Did you just start working here?" the Little Guy asked, still facing the urinal.

"I don't work here," Priest said.

"Figured as much. The only time I ever seen one of your kind in here, they were either washing dishes or dancing. You're dressed too sharp to be a dishwasher, and you ain't got enough curves to be a dancer. So I gotta ask, what brings you to these parts?"

"I guess lying would be pointless at this stage." Priest turned around, holding two small knives. They were made of hard plastic and no good for cutting, but their pointed edges made them ideal for stabbing. "If you must know, I've come to kill you."

The Little Guy shook himself. "I figured that, too. Well, I guess we might as well get to it." He spun, holding a .22.

Before the Little Guy could get off a shot, Priest was on him. He lashed out with a roundhouse kick that sent the gun flying under one of the stalls. Priest swung one of the plastic blades overhand, only to have the Little Guy block the strike with one of his thick arms. The Little Guy's fist shot forward like a rocket and landed in Priest's gut, knocking the wind out of him. Before Priest could catch his breath, the Little Guy slugged him in the chin and sent him skidding across the bathroom floor.

"I'm going to break your neck, you fucking monkey!" The Little Guy charged.

Priest was able to roll into a kneeling position just as the Little Guy reached him. He buried one of the plastic knives into the Little Guy's side, causing him to wince but not stopping him. He tried to stab him with the other one, but the Little Guy caught him about the wrist in mid-swing. The Little Guy pulled Priest up by the arm and smiled at him menacingly before head-butting him in the mouth, busting his nose.

"What's the matter? You don't wanna play anymore?" the Little Guy asked the dazed assassin.

In response, Priest kicked him in the balls. When the Little Guy released his grip, Priest stuck him with the second blade in the shoulder and then drove the first blade into his back. The Little Guy grabbed Priest around the waist and lifted him into the air. Hurling himself forward, he slammed Priest into the wall. Priest stabbed him over and over, but the Little Guy wouldn't release him. Twirling the plastic knives downward, he drove them into both the Little Guy's shoulder blades.

The Little Guy threw Priest across the room, but the blades stayed lodged in his flesh. In an instant, Priest was on his feet and back at him. The Little Guy swung, but Priest ducked the blow and launched two of his own into the Little Guy's stomach. When the Little Guy tried to grab him, Priest slipped under his arms and came up behind him. He pulled out his rosary and tried to wrap it around the Little Guy's neck, but a powerful swing from one of his opponent's arms sent him stumbling. In an attempt to keep his balance, Priest tried to grab the Little Guy's jacket, but his fingers fell short of the jacket and popped his chain. The diamond square that had been hanging on the end flew off and slid across the floor.

The Little Guy seemed to totally forget about Priest and dived for his diamond. Priest leaped onto his back, grabbing hold of the plastic blades and driving them deeper into the Little Guy's skin. A stiff elbow knocked Priest off the Little Guy's back, and he continued crawling toward the diamond.

Priest was back on him within seconds, this time looping the rosary around the Little Guy's beefy neck. He pulled with everything he had, forcing the Little Guy into a kneeling position. "Die already, you big son of a bitch!" He choked him. The Little Guy tried futilely to reach for Priest, but it was over. When Priest released his grip, the Little Guy's lifeless body collapsed to the floor.

Priest dropped to his hands and knees, breathing heavily. His lungs felt like they were going to explode in his chest. "I'm getting too old for this shit," he said to himself. When he had caught his breath, he crawled over and retrieved his plastic knives from the Little Guy's back. "Shai was very specific in his instructions." He rolled the corpse over onto its back. He stuck his hand into the Little Guy's mouth and pulled his tongue out. "And who am I to deny his requests?" He stabbed the Little Guy through the tongue. It took him three attempts to carve it loose with the plastic knife.

"May your rat-fuck mouth never speak the name of a stand-up nigga in a court of law, you piece of shit!" Priest spit on the corpse. After securing the tongue in a piece of cloth, he walked over to the bathroom door, where he plucked the diamond from the floor. "You must be worth a fortune if even on the threshold of death, that fat muthafucka was more concerned about you than his own life." He held it up to the light and examined the diamond. Behind the stones, he could see that something looked off. Priest placed the diamond on the sink and retrieved the Little Guy's .22. Using the butt of the gun like a hammer, Priest smashed the jewel. "What have we here?" He held up the SD card that had been hidden within the diamond. It didn't take a rocket scientist to know what he would find on the card. "I guess not all your dirty little secrets made it to the grave with you, huh?" He kicked the Little Guy's corpse.

"He's been gone for a while. Let's go check on him to make sure he didn't fall in," Priest heard someone say from the other side of the bathroom door.

A few seconds later, two goombas came into the bathroom to check on the Little Guy. All they found was a bloody bathroom and the corpse of the would-be snitch.

FOURTEEN

THERE WAS AN UNCOMFORTABLE SILENCE IN THE room. Kahllah had gone out to run errands, so it was just the two lovers.

Animal hadn't said much since he'd come back from his expedition with Priest. Gucci had tried to bring it up in conversation, but Animal didn't seem to want to talk about it. He sat at the computer desk, taking deep pulls from a Newport cigarette. He'd been telling himself that he was going to quit but just hadn't gotten around to it yet. Through the cloud of smoke, he watched Gucci, sitting on the couch with her hands folded. Her face held a million questions, but her lips were still. So many things had come to pass, and so many more were still unfolding. This was the first time the two of them had been alone together in years. What once felt natural had regressed to first-date butterflies. They were both waiting for each other to say something to break the awkward quiet. It was Animal who spoke first.

"How're you feelin'?" he asked.

Gucci ran her fingers through her rough edges and thought about how badly she needed a perm. "Better than I look."

Another long pause.

"Is your shoulder OK?" Gucci asked.

Animal rotated his arm. "A little sore but still functional."

"Good. For a minute, I thought Priest had really hurt you."

"It'll take more than a separated joint to hurt me. I've been through quite a bit these last few years."

"I can imagine," Gucci said, before going back to looking at her hands.

"What's wrong?" Animal asked.

"What makes you say something is wrong?"

"Because you've spent more time looking at your hands than at me." Animal got up from the chair and walked to stand in front of Gucci. She glanced up at him briefly before averting her eyes again. He knelt and gently turned her chin so that she was facing him. "Why can't you look at me?"

"It's hard for me, Animal . . ." Gucci began. "I spent so much time looking for glimpses of your ghost that now that I have the genuine article, it almost doesn't seem real. I keep thinking that if I blink, the image will fade, and you'll be gone again."

"I'm not going anywhere, Gucci. Now that I'm back in your life, we'll never be separated again. I promise," Animal assured her.

"That's what you said the last time, Animal, but it didn't stop you from being ripped from me. My heart bled for so long that I thought it'd never stop, and as soon as I start to heal a little, you pop back into my life and reopen the wound. I'm still trying to process it."

"Baby, you know if I'd had it my way, we'd have never been apart, not even for a second, let alone years. When I was away, there wasn't a minute of a day that went by when I didn't think about you and the life I was forced to leave behind," Animal said.

"Do you mean it?" Gucci asked.

"I put my soul on it," Animal replied. "The thought that I'd be able to get back to you one day was the only thing that kept me going out there in them jungles."

"What was it like?" she asked. It was an unexpected question.

"Honestly, it was hell." Animal sat on the couch beside her. "I was in a strange place around strange people, nothing familiar to hold on to. I mean, my brother Justice was out there, too, but it wasn't the same between us. After how we parted company, I doubt if it'll ever be the same again."

"Did you get close to anybody else while you were there?" Gucci asked. The question had been weighing on her since his return.

Animal considered lying to her, but he and Gucci were better than that. "I'd be lying if I said in all the years I was gone, my body didn't crave attention, and there was a period when I gave in to the urge."

The admission hit Gucci like a slap, but she didn't show it. "I see," was all she said.

Animal had known her long enough to be able to read her body language. "It wasn't like that, Gucci."

Gucci held up her hand to silence him. "No need to explain, Tayshawn. You're a man, and you have needs, so you went out and scratched that itch. I'd expect nothing less from a nigga."

"So now I fall into the category of being just a *nigga*, huh?"

Gucci looked at him. "What do you expect me to say, Animal, when you've just admitted to having random flings with only God knows how many bitches while you were away?"

"Gucci, you act like I was on spring break with my boys. I was a fugitive!" Animal stressed. "Fucking with my brother and K-Dawg, I did a lot of shit I'm not proud of, ma. It was real out in that jungle, and all we had was one another, so we were all close."

"Some closer than others." Gucci rolled her eyes.

"Gucci," Animal began, "we were worlds apart and had no way of knowing if we'd ever see each other again. Yeah, I slipped, but I'm sure you haven't spent the past few years sitting at home knitting blankets. I know you was out there dating and doing ya thing, but I don't hold that against you."

Gucci cut her eyes at him. "Yeah, I might have gone out a few times since you've been MIA, but that was just for drinks and almost always with my girls. Can't no nigga breathing say they even know what my pussy smells like since you. And while you're trying to flip the script, our situations ain't the same. I thought you were *dead*. Do you know what that was like for me? I thought the only man I'd ever truly given my heart to was gone! You, on the other hand, knew that I was alive. Alive and out here going to pieces over what happened to you, while you were vacationing and swimming in ho soup!"

"It wasn't a vacation, I was a captive. Do you know how many times I thought about trying to bust out of there to get back to you?" Animal asked.

"I'm sure you did, and it only took you two years to act on it," Gucci shot back.

Animal felt his anger rising but held it in check. He knew she was speaking from a place of hurt. "Gucci . . ." He reached for her, but she jerked away, so he let his hand fall to the space between them. "I wish there was a way for me to paint you a picture of what I've been through, but there aren't enough colors in the rainbow for me to do it justice. Things were different . . . I was different, but I'm back now. I came back for you."

"Did you really come back for me, Animal? Or did you come back to settle your score with Shai and Swann over what happened to Tech?" Tech had been Animal's best friend and mentor, the one who taught him the game. Years ago, he had been executed over a slight to Shai Clark. His death rocked Animal, and he had never fully recovered from the loss.

"Gucci, this was never about Tech. I can't ever forgive Shai or Swann for what they done to my homie, but at the end of the day, Tech was a soldier and understood the rules of this shit, same as the rest of us in the Dog Pound who took the oath. We live by violence, so we are cursed to die by violence. When they called Tech's number, he went out like a G. It was an honorable death for a soldier," Animal said.

"And what about Tionna's death? Where was the honor in an innocent girl being tossed out of a window all because she got involved in this madness with us?" Gucci asked with tears in her eyes. This was the first time she had really gotten a chance to process the fact that her best friend was gone, and it hurt.

Animal lowered his head. Part of him hated Tionna for betraying him, and part of him felt guilty for putting her in that position. "I'm sorry for your loss, Gucci. I truly am."

"Jesus, her mother had to hear it on the news instead of from me! This is all so fucked up. " Gucci put her face in her hands.

Animal draped his arm around her. "Everything is gonna be OK."

"No, it isn't, Animal. For as long as this feud between you and the Clarks continues, it's never gonna be OK."

"I know, ma. I'm ready to put this shit to bed, but I'm afraid Shai is going to do something to Ashanti, and it'll be on me, because this was my beef and he was just trying to help," Animal said. He saw a look of sadness cross Gucci's face. "Gucci, if you want me to walk away—"

"No." She cut him off. "I know how you feel about Ashanti, and I'd never ask you to turn your back on him in his time of need. You'd never forgive me or yourself for that."

"Thank you for understanding," Animal said.

"Just because I understand doesn't mean I like it. Animal, you've got a big heart, no doubt about that, but I wonder if there's enough room in your heart for me and your mistress."

"Gucci, I was fucking that girl, but she wasn't my mistress. It wasn't that serious," Animal explained.

"I don't mean that whore you laid up with in Puerto Rico, I mean your *real* mistress, the same woman who has been coming between us since I've known you: the streets. She's got a firmer hold on you than I ever have. Is she ever gonna let you go?"

Animal thought on it. "I imagine she will when she's done with me. Let's not dwell on that right now, ma. It's been so long since we've been together, and I don't wanna ruin the moment with talk of death or revenge. Let's just enjoy each other." He embraced her.

Gucci was tense at first, but as the warmth from his body spread over her, she loosened up. She looked up into Animal's sad brown eyes and found herself falling hopelessly in love with him all over again. When he kissed her, it woke up parts of

Gucci that had long been sleeping. She ran her hands over his back, refamiliarizing herself with a body she had once known as well as her own. He had put on some weight, but it was mostly muscle.

Animal pried his lips from Gucci's and slowly undressed her. His hands trembled as he helped her out of her sweatpants. Seeing her naked stole his breath. He had been with other women since he'd fled New York, but none compared to Gucci. She was his soul mate, the air he breathed, and his body craved her.

Gucci was self-conscious about her surgical scar from the shooting, so she covered herself with her hands. Gently, Animal moved her hands and looked at the scar. It ran from just below her breasts to her belly button. Seeing her once-perfect skin now blemished hurt him. Not because she was any less beautiful to him but because he knew he had been the cause. He knelt and kissed her from the top of her scar to its end.

Feeling Animal's lips on her skin made Gucci giddy. The warmth of his breath on her panty line made her so moist that she was almost embarrassed. With the greatest of care, Animal slid down her panties and continued his kissing. When Gucci felt his tongue brush across her clit, her body stiffened. She relaxed as best she could while his mouth explored her privates.

Animal laid her on the couch and pushed her legs apart so that he could get a better angle. He kissed the interior of both thighs, working his way to her love cave. His tongue was like a hot spear when it entered her. He did tricks with his tongue that he had never done to her before, and she couldn't help but wonder if he had practiced on the other women he'd been with during his time away from her. With this thought in mind, she grabbed two fistfuls of his hair and forced his face deeper into her. No matter whom he had been with before, Animal belonged to Gucci, and she intended to remind him of this.

When Animal finally came up for air, his lips were wet with her juices. She pulled him down to kiss her. She wanted to taste herself. They kissed deeply and passionately, both of them becoming more aroused. Animal slipped his hand between them and guided his dick toward her opening. She was wet but tight, so he had some trouble entering her. This brought a sly smile to his face, and added truth to her statement about having not been touched since he left.

Animal was finally able to slide all the way inside her womb. It was warm and inviting, more inviting than he remembered. She let out a gasp, which made him stop. "Are you OK? I can stop if I'm hurting you." He tried to pull out, but she wrapped her legs around his waist and held him in place.

"No, I don't want you to stop. I want you to fuck me. I want you to be the Animal, not Tayshawn," she ordered.

Animal was surprised by the demand but more than happy to oblige her. He grabbed Gucci by the hips and forced himself as deep into her as her walls would allow. When he looked down and saw that the shaft of his dick was covered in white froth, he knew he was hitting her spot. Animal pushed inside her, slowly and rhythmically, until she had loosened up, and then he picked up the pace.

When Animal flipped Gucci onto her stomach and entered her from behind, she felt like she had died and gone to heaven. Every time his balls slapped her ass, it sent waves of pleasure through her body. She had to bite the pillow to keep from howling like a wolf. When she felt his grip tighten around her waist, she knew he was getting close to climaxing, so she started throwing it back. She wanted to remove any doubts he may have had in his mind about who his dick belonged to. Animal growled, and she felt his seed flood her. He came so hard that after it had filled her, his cum ran down her legs. When it was done, he lay on top of her, dick still in her, breathing like he had just run a marathon.

Gucci and Animal lay there for a long while, quiet and listening to each other's breathing. When Animal leaned in to kiss her, she turned her face.

"What's the matter?" he asked.

"Nothing, just thinking," she said.

"About what?"

Gucci rolled over and positioned herself so that they were side-by-side and facing each other. "Did you make love to her, like you do to me?"

Animal sighed. "Gucci, why do you keep going there?"

"Because it's fucking with me. Now, please answer my question."

"A'ight, Gucci. No, I didn't make love to her like I do to you. When we're together, it's special. It symbolizes our love and our union. With me and Sonja, it was just fucking, no emotional attachments, just sex."

"So that's her name?" Gucci asked, doing a poor job of masking her attitude.

"Yes, Red Sonja. She was the daughter of the man who employed us." Animal reflected on the steel-eyed beauty who had shared his bed in Puerto Rico.

Gucci felt the tears coming back, but this time she wouldn't allow them to fall. "This is too much. I feel like I don't even know you anymore."

"Gucci, I'm the same Tayshawn you fell in love with that night at the club in Harlem."

"The Tayshawn I fell in love with wouldn't have given what was promised to me to another woman," Gucci shot back.

"Gucci, I am deeply sorry for hurting you. I mean that," Animal said sincerely.

"I know, Tayshawn. I'm trying to be understanding about it, but right now, the wound is still fresh, so it's hard."

"Baby, just tell me what I can do or say to make it right."

"Promise me you'll never hurt me again. Promise me that you belong to me and only me, like I only belong to you," Gucci said.

Animal looked her directly in the eyes when he spoke. "On everything I hold dear, I will never hurt you again."

Gucci studied his face. "I believe you, Tayshawn. I'm going to try to get past this, but before we start on the road to reconciliation, let me be clear on something." She grabbed him by his nuts and squeezed them as hard as she could. Animal was in so much pain that all he could do was stare at her dumbly. "If you ever in your life give away what belongs to me again, I'm gonna cut these hairy muthafuckas off! Do you understand me?"

"Yes, baby, now please let my nuts go." Animal gasped. When she finally released him, he rolled over onto his back and felt his nuts to make sure she hadn't crushed them. "Your ass is crazy."

"You ain't seen crazy, but I'm gonna show you if any of your whores come busting out the woodwork," Gucci assured him.

"Well, can't say I expected to come back and see this," a voice said from the doorway.

Gucci covered herself, but Animal was on his feet, naked and ready for battle. Kahllah lingered in the doorway. In her hand, she held a pink and black motorcycle helmet, which matched the pink and black custom bike she rode. Over her shoulder hung a large pocketbook. Judging by the strain on the straps, it was too heavy to be carrying only feminine products.

"Don't you know how to knock?" Animal snapped.

"I would've, had the door actually been closed," Kahllah said. Her eyes wandered to Animal's swinging dick, and she raised an eyebrow.

"Animal, cover yourself," Gucci called from the bed, and threw a pillow at him.

"My fault." Animal picked the pillow up and placed it over his privates.

Kahllah let her eyes linger a little longer before she focused on his face. "Get dressed. I need to talk to you, and it's important."

"Can't it wait?" Gucci asked with an attitude.

"I'm afraid it can't. It's about Ashanti," Kahllah said. She set the motorcycle helmet and the key to the bike on the writing desk next to the laptop.

At the mention of his friend's name, Animal hurriedly grabbed his clothes from the floor and darted into the bathroom. A few seconds later, he came back out, fully dressed and with a worried expression on his face. "What's good with my nigga? Is he OK?"

"For now, but I don't know how long that'll hold true," Kahllah said. There was sadness in her normally confident tone.

"Talk to me, Kahllah," Animal urged.

Kahllah was hesitant. "I wasn't supposed to say anything, but my conscience won't let me keep it, even if it goes against Father's wishes. Your little friend's name is floating around on a piece of paper. I trust you know what that means."

Animal did. It was a term used when a hit was placed on someone. "That ain't nothing new. Since all this has popped off, a lot of people want Ashanti dead because of his affiliation with me or King James."

"This has nothing to do with either of you. Word is, Ashanti and his crew murdered someone very close to Swann, and he isn't taking it too well."

"Fuck Swann and whoever got bodied. We all soldier and understand the risks," Animal said.

"This wasn't a soldier. It was a low-level pimp who didn't have any parts in this war, outside of his affiliation with Swann. Swann is going crazy over this," Kahllah explained.

Animal shrugged. "Niggaz die every day. Why is Swann taking this so personal?"

"Probably because this time it hit a little closer to home. Swann and the boy were close, very close. Some say it was Swann's nephew, but I have other suspicions, which I won't speak on. Swann has put a bounty of fifty thousand dollars on Ashanti's head, and I don't need to tell you that every scum bag looking for a come-up is going to come crawling out of their holes for that fifty stacks. As we speak, there are killers en route to try and collect."

"I gotta go to him." Animal stepped toward the door, but Kahllah blocked his path.

"Now, you know I can't let you go running the streets and

compromise what we have going on," Kahllah told him. "Father says that I am to make sure that you two stay put, which is what I intend on doing." She set her purse on the floor near the door. You could hear the distinct clang of metal inside. "Ashanti is in the hood right now, among all his troops, so he'll be fine . . . at least, I hope. Either way, I can't let you leave. All we can do is pray for him.

"Kahllah, I don't know what planet you grew up on, but where I'm from, bullets are more reliable than prayer. Now, let me go!" Animal barked.

"You can talk as loud as you want, Animal, but ain't nothing popping." Kahllah folded her arms.

"Kahllah, I don't want to hurt you," Animal warned.

"Nor do I want to hurt you, Animal. So let's not dance this dance if we don't have to. Now, I've got a phone call to make, and the reception is horrible up here, so I'm going *way* over to the other side of the church to use the phone in the office. While I'm gone, I strongly suggest that you mind your manners and *do not* snoop around in things that don't concern you." She tapped her purse with her foot. "Do we understand each other?"

Animal was stumped. He wondered if this was some sort of trick. He searched Kahllah's face, but she was impossible to read. "Yeah, we understand each other."

"Good." Kahllah turned and left, leaving behind her purse and key.

"What the hell was that all about?" Gucci asked.

"A wise man once said, 'Never look a gift horse in the mouth,'" Animal told her, and scooped the motorcycle key off the writing desk. He started to grab the helmet too, so as to conceal his identitiy, but figured it might do him more harm than good. A grown man riding around on a pink bike was bad enough, but a helmet to go with it would draw more attention than he needed. Next, he went to the bag she'd left and began to rummage through it. At the bottom, he found a welcome surprise—two, actually. Wrapped in a customized leather harness were a pair of twin rose-tinted chrome Glocks with red rubber grips. "My bitches!" Animal said excitedly. "Pretty Bitches" was the pet name he'd given the guns when he received them as a birthday gift many years before. He thought he'd never see them again after Shai's men had disarmed him in the scrap yard. "It's on," Animal said, slipping into the harness and sliding the guns into their holsters.

"Animal, I know you want to help Ashanti, but think on it for a minute. Are you sure we can trust Kahllah? This may be a trap," Gucci pointed out.

"Baby girl, right now, I'm sure of two things: the fact that I love you and the fact that Ashanti ain't gonna die on my watch. I gotta go." Animal kissed Gucci on the lips and slipped out before she could protest further.

Gucci sat there alone, wrapped in the sheets and staring at the empty doorway. She wanted to be mad at Animal for rushing off and leaving her again, but she couldn't. Gucci knew his heart better than anyone, and his heart wouldn't allow him to leave a friend in time of need, even if it was at the risk of his own life. His loyalty was one of the reasons she loved him so much.

From the tiny window, she heard the loud roar of a motorcycle engine being revved. A chill swept across her shoulders, and she was suddenly overcome with an eerie feeling. She was afraid, afraid that history was repeating itself and that she had been reunited with her lover only to lose him again, far too soon. Animal had already cheated the Reaper twice, and she hoped that the third time wouldn't be the charm.

"Please bring him back to me," Gucci said, offering up a quiet prayer.

Priest arrived back at the church just in time to see Animal go whipping by him on Kahllah's motorcycle. He wished that he could say he was surprised that his son had made a break for it. He'd expected as much, only not quite so soon.

"Because the law worketh wrath: for where no law is, there is no transgression," Priest said, quoting Romans 4:15. "Let your hand be stayed no longer, my fallen angel. Loose your wrath, and make your enemies tremble in your wake."

FIFTEEN

BY THE TIME ASHANTI MADE IT TO the hood, he had missed the meeting King James had called, but he didn't need to be in attendance to get the gist of what it was about. On the whole ride back to the block from the precinct, the ghetto grapevine worked overtime delivering varying accounts of what had happened. The one thing all the stories had in common was that somebody had tried to off King James, and that was all Ashanti cared about. King had taken him in and treated him like family when he didn't have shit, so Ashanti was taking the attempt on his life personally.

"You cool, baby?" Fatima asked when the cab pulled to a stop on the corner.

"Yeah, I'm straight," Ashanti answered, but he didn't turn to look at her. His eyes were locked on the playground in front of the building and all the people in it. It seemed like everybody in the hood was outside.

Abel met them at the curb. He was wearing a black army jacket and black fitted cap, pulled low over his eyes. A scowl crossed his normally jovial face.

Ashanti jumped out of the cab first. He extended his hand and helped Fatima out before giving Abel dap. Abel was about to say something, but Ashanti gave him the signal to hold on while he tended to his lady. "Baby, I'm about to hit the turf and see what's going on out here."

"I already know," Fatima said. "Listen, don't bullshit around out here all night. I still wanna dip off."

"Let me just see what the situation is, then we'll figure it out," Ashanti told her.

"Baby, whatever the situation is tonight, it'll still be the same situation tomorrow. I wanna get out of the city, even if it's just for the night."

"OK," Ashanti said, agreeing in a less-than-sincere tone.

Fatima grabbed the front of his shirt and pulled him to her. She kissed his lips passionately, sucking on his tongue. "Come take care of this pussy tonight, and you can play with your friends tomorrow," she whispered, grabbing his dick through his jeans.

"You playing dirty." Ashanti smiled.

"You ain't seen dirty until you see the outfit I'm going upstairs to get. Act like you know." Fatima sauntered off. She waved to the few people she knew in the playground and disappeared into the building.

Once Fatima was gone, Ashanti's mind was back on business. "What's popping?" he asked Abel.

"Man, shit crazy out here. Some Jersey niggaz tried to push King. They saying Swann set it up."

"Then Swann is a dead man," Ashanti said, heading toward the playground where everyone was congregating.

Ashanti picked his way through the crowd, dapping those

he knew personally and nodding to those he was only familiar with by face. It seemed like everybody was out, from the soldiers to the nosy-ass locals who were just trying to figure out what was going on. King James was a like a celebrity in the hood, so whenever something went on with him, it was big news.

"Yo," Ashanti heard someone call. He turned and saw Zo-Pound huddled in the shadows of the playground. Zo was almost invisible in a big black hoodie. All you could see was the cherry from the blunt he was smoking, burning within the dark folds of his hood.

"What it do, Zo?" Ashanti went over and embraced him.

"Quiet, but 'bout to turn up." Zo exhaled the smoke. His red eyes passed over Cain and Abel. "Why don't y'all give us a minute?"

The twins looked at Ashanti. Only when he gave them the signal did they leave.

"You got them two trained, huh?" Zo asked.

Ashanti watched the twins as they walked off whispering to each other, before they disappeared into the flow of people. "Nah, they ain't trained, they loyal."

"Never give a man that much credit until he proves it," Zo told him. "But fuck that, what's good with you? I heard one-time grabbed you up."

"Yeah, Brown and Alvarez ran down on us earlier. You know they stay on some ho shit," Ashanti said, as if it wasn't a big deal.

"What did they want?" Zo asked.

"Pressing me for a body," Ashanti said.

"Damn, them boys staying reaching. Who got dropped?"

"Some lame-ass nigga named Rick Jenkins," Ashanti said, watching Zo's face for a reaction.

"Who is that?" Zo faked asking as if he were clueless.

"You remember the dude from the dice game. The one you kept asking about," Ashanti reminded him.

Zo cocked his head to one side as if he was trying to remember. "Oh, yeah, the dark-skinned nigga with the trick dice? That wasn't about nothing. I thought he was somebody else, but as it turns out, he wasn't. Them bitch-ass niggaz Brown and Alvarez must be really hard up if they're trying to pin a random murder on you."

"It ain't me they looking at for clipping old boy. It's *you*," Ashanti informed him.

There was the telltale facial twitch. "I ain't killed nobody," Zo said, but he didn't sound very convincing.

"Zo, you've been in my corner through thick and thin. You're more than just a homie, you're family. Family rides for family, right or wrong, so you know I got your back, but I need you to keep it one hundred with me about this, so I can know what we're up against."

Zo was silent for a few long moments. When he looked at Ashanti, there was a coldness to his eyes that Ashanti had only seen once before, and that was when he and Zo-Pound had murdered the boy Sean near the park.

"Talk to me, Zo," Ashanti urged him.

"Ashanti, let me tell you a story . . ." Zo began. "I was watching a movie once. I think it was a biopic about Harriet Tubman. There was this scene when she was about to lead the slaves north, and all their loved ones came to see them off. There was an old woman among them wearing a blindfold.

When they asked her why she was wearing the blindfold, she replied it was so that if she was ever implicated in it, even under the threat of torture or death, she could say in all honesty that she hadn't laid eyes on them and didn't have to die with a lie on her tongue."

Ashanti was about to press the issue when King James walked up. He was with Lakim, Dee, and a neighborhood kid they all called Shorty. Shorty was from the neighborhood but wasn't a part of their crew. He was barely into his teens, so King didn't allow him to touch drugs. Instead, they helped him keep money in his pocket through odd jobs, like going to the store or delivering messages that couldn't be spoken on telephones. Ashanti had always like Shorty because he reminded him of himself when he was that age: young, dumb, and far too willing.

"What up, my nigga? I heard you got bagged. Glad to see you back on the streets." King James embraced Ashanti.

"Yeah, that shit wasn't about nothing. Those dicks, Alvarez and Brown, were just busting my balls," Ashanti told him.

"I think being questioned about a murder is a little more than busting your balls," King said.

Ashanti seemed surprised that King knew what had gone on and he hadn't told him yet, but his face revealed nothing. "That shit didn't have nothing to do with me."

"What did you tell them?" Lakim asked.

"What the fuck do you mean, what did I tell them? I didn't tell them shit," Ashanti said with an attitude.

"Don't get your panties in a bunch, lil' nigga. I was just asking. Can't be too careful with snitching being at an all-time high," Lakim said, half-jokingly.

Ashanti's face became serious. "Dig this, my nigga, you ever mention me and snitching in the same breath, and I'm gonna need that fade from you."

"I'm just fucking with you." Lakim slapped Ashanti on the back. He was laughing, but Ashanti wasn't.

"You know my nigga is built Ford tough," Zo said, speaking up in his partner's defense.

"Word, life. Ashanti is the last of a dying breed." King James gave him dap. "But in the future, if the pigs ever run down on you, call that lawyer I plugged you with. You ain't gotta say shit, just let him handle it, ya heard?"

"No doubt," Ashanti agreed.

"So I hear y'all went and handled that lil' business with Percy," King said.

Ashanti shot Abel a look, because he knew he'd been the one who spilled the beans. Cain was locked up with him, and they were the only three who knew about it. "Yeah, Percy is no longer with us."

"He tell you anything good?" King asked. He watched Ashanti closely to see how he would respond.

Ashanti thought about lying, but he felt like King's eyes were staring directly into his soul. "Yeah, but—"

"Yeah, that bitch nigga fed us a bunch of bullshit," Cain said, cutting him off. "We're gonna follow up to see what's true and what's false. You know a nigga will say anything when he's been tortured, but who's to say how much stock you can put into it?"

"You're right, Cain. I need y'all lil' niggaz to get on that for me ASAP, though, feel me?"

"You got it, King," Ashanti assured him.

"Yo, you need to promote me so I can help out." Shorty

stepped up. The black hoodie he wore nearly swallowed his small frame.

"Shorty, go sit down somewhere. This is grown folks' business," Zo-Pound told him.

"Zo, stop treating me like a kid. If I'm old enough to hold guns for y'all, I'm old enough to pop guns for y'all," Shorty reasoned.

"He's got a point," Lakim said.

"Don't fucking encourage him, La," Zo said.

"Man, why y'all acting like that? Ashanti was about my age when he started putting in work," Shorty pointed out.

"And look at me now," Ashanti said. "Shorty, you my lil' nigga, but you ain't ready for this life. If your heart is really in it, the streets will swallow you up in due time, but for right now, focus on being a kid."

"This is some bullshit." Shorty kicked an empty beer can. He looked up to King James and his crew, and since he had started hanging around, it had been his dream to be a part of their inner circle.

"Shorty, you'll get your chance to prove yourself, but wait a while," King told him. Shorty was still sulking, so he threw him a bone. "Dig, why don't you go across the street and pull my truck around to the front of the projects?" He tossed Shorty his keys.

"You gonna let me drive your truck?" Shorty beamed like he had just been handed the best Christmas gift ever.

"Yeah, but be careful. You scratch my whip, and I'm gonna fuck you up," King warned.

"Don't worry, I won't," Shorty said excitedly, and took off running across the street to where King had parked his truck.

"I have never seen a kid so eager to fuck his life up," Ashanti said, watching Shorty, who had stopped to talk to some little girls from the neighborhood.

"Have you looked in the mirror lately?" Zo asked jokingly. "Let me holla at you for a sec." He led Ashanti off to the side. "Look, I know I ain't gotta tell you that we about to turn up out here."

"Yeah, I know, Zo. You know when it pops, my gun is gonna be the first to bang." Ashanti reached for his gun, then remembered he'd left it in the crib.

"See? You slipping already," Zo teased.

"It won't happen again. I'm about to get a room for the night with Fatima, but before I come back to the block tomorrow, I'll stop by my crib to arm up," Ashanti told him.

"You might wanna handle that before you leave," Zo suggested.

"Nah, I don't feel like going all the way back home to get my strap. Fatima is already tripping about me not spending no time with her," Ashanti told him.

Zo thought back to how he had promised Porsha he'd pick her up in an hour, three hours ago. "I know the feeling. Looks like we both need to take care of business tonight and resume the war effort tomorrow."

As if on cue, Fatima came out of the building. She was carrying an overnight bag over her shoulder and some shopping bags in her hand. "I hope you're ready to go, because I sure as hell am."

"Damn, that's an awful lot of bags for just one night." Ashanti took some of the bags from her.

"It isn't all mine. I was out shopping earlier, and I picked you up a few things," Fatima told him.

"A thoughtful woman is a rare find. If I were you, I'd hold on to her," Zo told Ashanti.

"I intend to," Ashanti said with a smile. "I'm out, my nigga." He gave Zo dap.

"I'm about to get out of here, too," Zo said. "Oh, before you go, hold this down." He reached under his hoodie and handed Ashanti a big .357.

"I told you, I'm getting out of the city for the night. The only gun I'm gonna need is between my legs," Ashanti said slyly.

"Better to have it and not need it than to need it and not have it," Zo said.

"You right." Ashanti accepted the .357. "But if you give me your strap, won't you be out here naked?"

"Nah." Zo lifted his hoodie and showed Ashanti the butt of an identical .357, only that one was scuffed and worn. "I always got a spare." The gun Zo kept with him was the same gun he had used for the motel hit. Normally, he didn't keep guns after he'd killed someone, but he hadn't had a spare moment to get rid of it. He figured it couldn't hurt to hold it for one more day until Ashanti returned the other one.

"Say that." Ashanti dapped him one last time, then left with Fatima and got into the waiting cab.

Zo walked over and rejoined Lakim, King, and Dee. "Yo, I'm getting outta here, unless y'all still need me tonight?"

"Nah, you good. Go take care of that fine-ass woman you got waiting on you," King said with a smile. He was like an oracle and seemed to know everything.

"Pussy-whipped-ass nigga," Lakim teased him.

"Dry-dick-ass nigga," Zo shot back.

"Let's get outta here. I'm starving and wanna get something to eat before we hit the Bronx. What we waiting for?" Dee asked.

"Waiting for that slow-ass nigga Shorty," Lakim said. He

spotted Shorty still talking to the girls across the street. "Yo, Shorty, hurry the fuck up!" he called to him.

Shorty gave him the thumbs-up and hopped behind the wheel of the truck. The first sign that something was wrong was when the truck wouldn't immediately start. The next sign was when it began to smoke.

"Something isn't right," Zo said, and took off running toward the truck. "Shorty, get out of the truck! Get the fuck out!" he was shouting as he ran. He could see Shorty trying to open the doors, but they wouldn't open.

"Somebody help me!" Shorty pleaded while futilely trying to free himself. Those would be his last words before the truck exploded, raining both car parts and body parts all over 124th Street.

"Fire Bug make the trap go BOOM!" the youngest of the Savage boys sang while dancing in the passenger seat of the Yukon he was in. He watched with childlike amusement as the truck went up in flames. On his lap was the remote detonator for the explosives he had planted in King James's truck an hour ago. It was wired to alert him the moment the engine was started, so he could trigger it from a safe distance.

"That's a mighty fine piece of work you done there, Bug," Big Money Savage said from behind the wheel. They called him Big Money, but he never seemed to have much of it. He was Bug's first cousin, but he wasn't a killer like the rest of them. Still, he was a Savage, and they wouldn't leave him out in the cold. He was the odd-jobs man of the family.

"Fucking right it was. I'm a damn perfectionist," Bug told him.

"Well, this one didn't go so perfect, seeing how you killed the wrong person," Big Money told him, and pointed a few feet to the left of the burning truck. He saw Lakim and Zo holding a distraught King James back to keep him from charging into the wreckage.

"That lucky muthafucka!" Bug raged. He pulled his gun out from between the seats. "Big Money, pull up on this nigga so I can blow his brains out. The Savages ain't never fucked up a hit, and we ain't gonna start now."

"Save it for another day, Bug. After an explosion like that, the police and everybody else are gonna be crawling over the block in a few ticks," Big Money said.

"I can take him," Bug insisted.

"Bug, if you wanna go to prison, you can do it on your own time. Ain't no way I'm gonna be the one to tell Ma that you got knocked over some dumb shit." He started the engine. They slowly pulled out into traffic.

The Yukon slow-rolled past the burning truck. King James dropped to his knees and began sobbing. Seeing the self-proclaimed king of Harlem on his knees gave Bug a cheap thrill. It took the combined efforts of two of the other men to get King James back on his feet. Whoever had died in that truck must've been close to him, so Bug felt a little better about the situation. As the Yukon passed the grieving soldiers, Bug and King James made eye contact. Not being able to resist the temptation of kicking a dog when he was down, Bug blew King a kiss before the Yukon peeled through the light and disappeared.

SIXTEEN

"DAMN, WHAT WAS THAT?" FATIMA WAS STARTLED by the loud noise.

"Probably kids playing with guns. Welcome to the jungle, young lady," the cab driver said, as if it was nothing.

"We from the jungle, and that don't sound like no gun I've ever heard. And if it was a gun, I pray I'm never on the wrong end of that big muthafucka," Ashanti said. His hand drifted to the .357 in his pants.

"Baby, try to relax. When we get to Yonkers, I'm going to drain all that tension up out of you. Bet that." Fatima played with his ear. Ashanti loved when she did that.

"Don't start nothing you can't finish," he told her.

"Let me show you how good of a finisher I am," Fatima whispered in his ear. She ran her hand down Ashanti's stomach, en route to his dick, but was stopped by the big gun. Fatima plucked it from his pants.

"Be careful with that," Ashanti warned.

"I got this." Fatima placed the gun on the floor of the cab.

She undid his belt and pulled out his dick. Ashanti was hard as a rock. "That's what I'm talking about." She gave his dick a tug and caused Ashanti to moan. Fatima spared a glance at the cab driver, who was trying to act like he wasn't watching through the rearview mirror.

"Keep your eyes on the fucking road," Ashanti snapped at the driver.

"No trouble, buddy, no trouble," the driver said, and wisely turned his attention back to the street.

"Now, where was I?" Fatima dipped her head down in his lap.

When Fatima took Ashanti into her mouth, he felt his toes curl in his boots. He wanted to tell her to stop for fear that someone would see what she was doing, but he couldn't find the words. For as experienced as Ashanti was at war, he was a novice at love. She played with the head of his dick with her tongue for a few seconds before closing her lips around it. Ashanti closed his eyes and put his head back while Fatima handled her business.

Ashanti was in his own little world while Fatima serviced him. The biggest grin was plastered across his face as he thought about what he was going to do to her. In the middle of his pleasure trip, Ashanti was suddenly overcome with an eerie feeling. His eyes snapped open, and he took stock of his surroundings. They were in the Hunt's Point section of the Bronx.

"Dude, what the fuck are you doing? Why didn't you just take the highway?" Ashanti asked the cab driver, who was chatting away on his cell phone in a language that Ashanti couldn't understand. It sounded like French.

"The highway coming up through Manhattan is too crowded

at about this time. I'm taking a shortcut through the Bronx, and I'll jump on Eighty-Seven a little further up so we can beat some of the congestion. No worries, my friend," the driver assured him, and he closed the plastic partition between the front of the cab and the back. He then went back to talking on his phone.

Ashanti tried to relax and go back to enjoying his oral pleasure, but he couldn't. Something didn't feel right in his gut. One thing Animal had always taught him was to trust his gut. The cab stopped at a red light in a desolated area. A van pulled up alongside them. On the side of the van was painted "First Church of Jesus Christ," but the cat in the passenger's seat of the van didn't look like he'd ever seen the inside of a church. He glanced over at Ashanti but didn't let his eyes linger. Something about the kid seemed familiar, but Ashanti couldn't place him. Before he could twirl the mystery any further in his mind, the side door of the van slid open, and all hell broke loose.

Ty sat behind the wheel of the long van, drumming his gloved fingers on the steering wheel. The van was so beat to hell he was surprised he was able to get it to start. It was a clunker that he'd stolen from the parking lot of a church. It wasn't much to look at, but it was big enough to carry his cargo: five shooters armed to the teeth with automatic weapons. He wasn't hunting some street punk; Ashanti was a certified killer, and he wasn't taking any unnecessary chances.

"There that nigga go right there," No-Good said. He was an older cat who used to get money with King James, until the night Ashanti whipped him out over Fatima and banished him from the hood. Since then, he had been working for Ty and his crew in Brooklyn.

"You sure?" Ty asked, watching the young man milling around with King James's soldiers. A pretty light-skinned girl came out of the building and handed him some of the bags she was carrying. He had never actually seen Ashanti, but from his reputation, he'd expected him to be bigger.

"Hell, yeah, I'm sure. I'll never forget that face," No-Good said, thinking back on his ass-whipping. The fact that he was going to be able to pay Ashanti and Fatima back at the same time made him so excited he could hardly contain himself.

"Well, if you remember his face, then nine times outta ten, he remembers yours, too. Get your ass in the back, and let one of the other niggaz ride shotgun," Ty ordered.

"A'ight, but don't forget to let me get mine off when it's time to kill him," No-Good said, and he climbed into the back of the van, letting one of the shooters take the passenger's seat. Ty watched Ashanti and Fatima get into the taxi and pull off, before setting out behind them.

The whole time they trailed the cab, Ty was on his phone talking to someone. He had switched to a French dialect, so No-Good had no idea what he was saying, and he was uncomfortable with it.

"What's up with all that foreigner shit? Speak English in here, dawg," No-Good said.

"Shut up so I can hear," Ty said over his shoulder, and went back to his conversation. What no one but him knew was that Ashanti's cab driver was Ty's cousin. Ty had promised him some money if he helped set the couple up. What his cousin didn't know was that he would be dead, too, before Ty made good on that promise. No unnecessary chances. "We gonna take him at the light," he told the shooters.

The sounds of guns being cocked and loaded resonated through the hull of the van.

"Yeah, I'm ready to put a hole in this lil' nigga," No-Good said anxiously. He had one hand on the van door and the other on an MP5. His fingers twitched nervously, and he was ready to spring. As soon as he felt the van come to a stop, he snatched the door open and let it rock.

Ashanti moved less than a second before the first slugs ripped through the cab. He threw himself on top of Fatima to shield her from the spray of glass and bullets. When the second wave came and tore through the front of the cab, the driver had finally gotten the memo that he'd been double-crossed and peeled off.

The cabbie sped through the streets, trying to escape his larcenous cousin and his pals, weaving in and out of traffic. There weren't many cars on the street, so it ended up a race between the cab and the van. The van gained on the cab, bumping it and trying to run it off the road. No-Good let go with the MP5 again, this time tearing through the front of the cab and the cabbie. The car swerved, slammed into a parked truck, and flipped over twice before it finally came to rest, right-side up, a few yards down. The van pulled up next to it, and the men filed out.

Ashanti lay on the floor of the backseat, dazed and in tremendous pain. Fatima was crushed beneath him, her face cut and starting to bruise. They were both covered in blood, and Ashanti was so pumped full of adrenaline that he couldn't tell if she was shot or he was. As he was pushing himself up, the door to the cab came open. When Ashanti looked up, he was confronted by a face that he had thought he'd never see again, especially on the winning side of a gun.

"Remember me, lil' nigga?" No-Good spat. He leveled the MP5 with Ashanti's face. "I'm gonna enjoy capping the both of y'all."

"Not on my watch, muthafucka," Fatima said, startling both of them. She was lying on her back, under Ashanti, with the .357 pointed up at No-Good. His mouth dropped open in wide-eyed shock, and Fatima promptly put a bullet in it. The top of No-Good's head shot off like a Roman candle.

Seeing No-Good fall sent the shooters into action. They began spraying the cab, riddling it with bullets. Glass and sparks flew everywhere, and the car caught on fire. Ashanti pushed Fatima out the open door and crawled out behind her, just as the car went up in flames. Fatima fired through the flames at their attackers, laying cover fire for her and Ashanti's escape.

"We gotta move." Ashanti grabbed her by the hand, and the two of them made a mad dash toward an abandoned warehouse. The couple ducked and dodged down the walkway that led to the warehouse entrance, trying their best not to get shot. Ashanti pulled at the door and found it secured by a heavy chain and a padlock. "Shit, we can't get in."

Fatima shot the lock off. "Now we can." She pulled him inside the darkened warehouse.

Ty and his men approached the warehouse entrance with caution. The fact that Ashanti was hurt and cornered made him that much more dangerous. Before they entered, he had some last-minute instructions for his crew. "I'll go around back while Dave, Chess, and Will go in the front to flush him out." He pointed to each man respectively. "Paulie, you cover the door," he told the last man, who was also the youngest.

"Ty, why I gotta stay out here while them niggaz see all the action?" Paulie asked. It was clear that he wasn't happy about being left behind.

"Because I said so, muthafucka!" Ty snapped. "There's too much paper riding on this lil' nigga's death for me to risk letting him get away. You guard this damn door and put a hole in any muthafucka who tries to come in or out unless it's me! That goes for the rest of y'all niggaz, too." Ty turned to the trio. "I want this nigga dead at all costs! Tonight Ashanti draws his last breath!"

SEVENTEEN

"I'M SURE GLAD I DIDN'T HOLD MY breath waiting for you to keep your word," Porsha said when she opened the door to her apartment. She was wearing an oversized New York Knicks nightgown.

"My fault," Zo said in a hoarse voice. He knew he'd be in for an argument when he showed up at Porsha's place hours after he was supposed to pick her up, but he didn't have it in him, not after the night he'd had.

"Fucking right it is." Porsha stepped back so he could enter. When Zo was inside, she closed the door and started right in. "Zo, you know this shit with you putting me on hold for your friends is getting old, right?"

"I said my fault," Zo repeated over his shoulder, walking into the living room. Frankie was sitting on the couch, dressed in sweats and a T-shirt, watching television. She flashed him a dirty look, but her face softened when she got a good look at him.

"Oh, my God, what happened to you?" Frankie asked, noticing the dirt and soot on his clothes. Normally, Zo was always fresh and clean, even when he was dressed in his hood gear, but at that moment, he looked like he'd just crawled out of the gutter.

"It's a long story," Zo said, flopping onto the La-Z-Boy chair. He fished a half-smoked blunt out of his pocket and lit it. "Y'all got any liquor up in here? I need a drink bad as a muthafucka right now."

"I think there's some Henny in the kitchen. Let me go check." Frankie got up and went into the kitchen.

"Zo, baby, are you OK?" Porsha asked, checking him over. She felt bad about going in on him, not noticing something was clearly wrong.

"Not really," Zo said, exhaling a cloud of smoke. "Shorty died tonight."

"What Shorty, the little guy who's always hanging around King James?" Frankie was coming out of the kitchen with a half-empty bottle of Hennessy, a can of Red Bull, and three empty plastic cups.

"Yeah," Zo replied.

"Wow, wasn't he only like thirteen?" Frankie asked, pouring Hennessy into each of their glasses and popping the tab on the can of Red Bull.

"He would've been fourteen in a few months." Zo threw the whole glass of Hennessy back without waiting for Frankie to add the Red Bull. He'd barely swallowed the liquor before he grabbed the bottle and poured himself some more. He downed that cup, too, before giving Frankie and Porsha the short version of what had happened.

"That is so fucked up," Porsha said with tears in her eyes. In her mind, she could hear the trump-mouthed little boy pressing her to be his girlfriend like he always did whenever he saw her around the hood.

"The whole hood is twisted behind this shit," Zo said in a solemn voice. "I think this was the first time I ever saw King cry. He feels horrible about it."

"He should, since it was his fault that Shorty died," Porsha said.

"Porsha, you can't put that on King. All he ever did was try to look out for Shorty. He never put him in harm's way," Zo said, defending his friend.

"He put him in harm's way when he started letting him hang around y'all instead of forcing him to go to school," Porsha shot back. "It's a dangerous game y'all are playing out there."

"And you telling me this like I don't know? I'm in the thick of it, remember?" Zo said, a little sharper than he'd intended. The look on Porsha's face said she felt it, too. Zo-Pound was lurking beneath the surface. "Porsha," he said, calming himself. "What happened to Shorty was random. It could've happened to any one of us who tried to start that truck. It's just fucked up it had to be him. I know it's easy to blame King, but it was just as much any of our faults as it was his, because we kept the lil' nigga around so much." He was emotional.

Porsha sat on his lap and stroked his cheek. She could feel the tension drain from him. "Alonzo, I'm sorry if I sounded judgmental, I'm just upset. I keep seeing these kids killed in the streets over bullshit, and it breaks me down every time. I just wish kids had more positive role models in the hood."

"Happy hunting, because those are scarce these days," Zo told her. "When kids like Shorty get of age and start looking around for that love they missed out on because their daddies left, who do you think they're gonna look to? Niggaz like us. Ain't no doctors or lawyers in the jungle, ma, only savages and survivors."

"Call me old-fashioned, but I'm one of those people who don't believe what you come from is what will define you. People can change . . . you changed."

"And look at me now." Zo motioned to his filthy clothes.

"Yeah, I almost forgot you were a mess." Porsha got off his lap and brushed off her nightgown. "I'm gonna go and run you a bath. I want you out of those clothes and in the tub in five minutes, in that order!" Porsha sashayed to the bathroom.

"Yes, ma'am," Zo called after her.

Frankie waited until she heard the water running before she spoke. "I know this ain't necessarily the best time, after what happened, but I need to holla at you, Zo-Pound."

"Talk to me, Frankie Angels."

"First, I wanted to tell you face-to-face, thanks for doing me that solid with the bread. That shit literally saved my life."

"No doubt, ma. I told you I was gonna get that flipped and right back to you before you even missed it," Zo said.

"Yeah, about that . . ."

"What about it? I know you probably expected a little more, but I told you shit got slow with the beef cooking."

"Zo, where did this money really come from?" Frankie asked him flat out.

Zo seemed to be shocked by the question, but he recovered quickly. "I told you, it came from—"

"Alonzo," Frankie said, addressing him by his government name, "I've known you since when you first started working in that supermarket. We got too much history not to keep it one hundred with each other.

"Frankie, I been through too much tonight to try and figure out your riddles. If you've got something to say, spit it out.

"Did you kill the man who took my money?"

The weed and alcohol magically vanished from Zo's system, and he was now quite sober. "Why would you ask me something like that?"

"Don't answer a question with a question, Zo. You heard me. I tell you that someone stole from me, and a few weeks later, the thief turns up dead and you hand me a bag of money. Alonzo, I ain't flew here, I grew here. I'm just trying to see if I should be worried about being picked up on an accessory-to-murder charge."

Zo leaned in close enough to her that she could see clearly into his eyes. Until that moment, she had never realized how dark they were. With a friendly smile, he patted her on the cheek. "You worry too much, Frankie Angels."

"What's all this?" Porsha came back into the living room. She was carrying fresh towels and washcloths.

"Certainly not what it looks like." Zo got up from the La-Z-Boy and headed toward the bathroom. As he passed, he kissed Porsha on the nose and patted her ass.

Porsha stood there for a while, looking at Frankie suspiciously. "Let me find out," she said half-jokingly, and turned to follow Zo into the bathroom. Frankie was her girl, but she wouldn't hesitate to jump on her ass if she came sniffing too close to what Porsha had laid claim to.

EIGHTEEN

ZO STRIPPED HIS CLOTHES OFF AND SLID into the hot water. At first, it burned, but after a few moments, his body adjusted to the temperature. Porsha came in behind him and closed the door. She was carrying the ashtray with the last bit of the blunt in it. She set the ashtray on the table and passed Zo the weed clip. Grabbing the lighter off the edge of the sink, she lit the weed for her man.

"This is just what I needed." Zo exhaled the smoke, while fanning his hands through the bubbles in the tub. He held one of the bubbles in the palm of his hand and blew it gently into the air.

"Don't I always know what you need?" Porsha popped the bubble.

"Indeed you do, love."

"So what's up with what I need?" Porsha slipped her hand into the water and tugged at Zo's dick. He stiffened at her touch.

"You know I like it when you do that," Zo told her, taking

another toke of the blunt. He tried to pass it to Porsha, but she declined.

"I'll get with the weed in a minute. Right now, I'm looking for a different kind of high." Porsha stood and pulled the Knicks nightgown over her head, exposing her nude body. Just above her pelvic area was a tattoo Zo hadn't seen before, so she had to have just gotten it. It was two .357s curved to look like a heart. "You like?" she asked, noticing Zo checking out the tattoo.

"It's beautiful, just like the rest of you." Zo sat up and ran his hand over the tattoo and down her leg. He left a trail of watery fingerprints in his wake.

"I can't be that beautiful if you keep putting me on the back burner, now, can I?" Porsha covered herself with her hands.

"Baby, don't act like that." Zo reached for her, but she moved back.

"You control shit on the streets, but in this castle, I am the queen," she told him. Porsha stepped into the tub one foot at a time. She hovered in front of Zo in all her glory. "How beautiful is your queen, Alonzo?"

"You're the most beautiful woman I've ever seen," Zo said, looking up at her as if he was in a trance.

"Then prove it to me." Porsha slipped her hand gently behind his head. Slowly, she began pushing Zo's face toward her pussy, and he didn't resist. She let out a low hiss when Zo's tongue made contact with her box. "How does it taste, baby?"

"Like candy," Zo muttered, before going back to his vaginal exploration.

Porsha placed one leg on the side of the tub so that Zo could get a better angle and drove her pelvis into his face. When she came, her legs shook, and she feared that she might fall, but Zo's powerful grip on her waist steadied her while he continued to lap at her. Porsha found herself in the throes of pleasure and felt like she could hover there forever, but Zo had other ideas.

"My turn." Zo pulled her down into the water and onto his lap. When his dick entered her, he felt like he would nut prematurely, but his ego wouldn't let him. He hooked his arms under hers and gripped both shoulders, pulling her down on his dick. From the way her eyes were closed, he knew he was hitting her spot. "Look at me, Porsha," he demanded.

Porsha's eyes opened to slits as she gazed at her lover. As usual, Zo's face betrayed nothing, but the twinkling in his eyes said he loved her pussy. She pushed herself down on Zo's dick as far as she could go and started swirling her hips like she was working a hula hoop. When she saw Zo's lip curl, it made her smile. It was their game. Zo always tried to play the role of the stone-faced gangsta when they had sex, and Porsha made it her business to try to break the persona and bring the bitch up out of him.

Every time Porsha bounced on Zo's dick, he felt like it swelled a bit more, threatening to burst at any moment. Zo had slept with his fair share of women, but none was like Porsha. Her pussy was sweet, and not just in a metaphorical sense. It was almost as if he could taste the sugar on the back of his tongue every time they made love. Zo would never admit it, but inside Porsha's pussy was the only place he ever felt safe. Within the tenderness of her walls, none of the burdens he carried in every day life could touch him.

When Porsha felt Zo's nails bite into her shoulder, she knew he was getting close. Leaning in, she wrapped her arms around his neck and began bouncing her ass on him harder. "Let me get that . . . let me get that," she repeated over and over while licking his earlobe.

Zo could feel his face twist into an ugly mask, but there wasn't much he could do about it. He tried to grab Porsha to slow her bouncing, but her body was slick with warm water and bubbles. He tried to hold out, but his dick was fighting against him, so he was left with no choice but to go with the flow. Zo grabbed a fistful of Porsha's hair and yanked her head back. Hungrily, he licked and sucked her neck, while feeling the geyser between his legs about to go off.

"FUCK!" They yelled in unison as they came at the same time.

Zo could feel his heart beating thunderously in his ears as he released himself inside Porsha. Her bucking had ceased, but she was still grinding her ass back and forth, pulling every last bit of semen from his cock. When both of them were completely spent, Porsha laid her head against Zo's chest, with him still inside her.

She breathed heavily in his ear. "Alonzo, word to everything I love, if you ever give this dick to any bitch but me, I'll kill you."

Zo laughed. "Ma, my dick only rises for you."

"Don't say it unless you mean it." Porsha dragged her nails over his ribs, before dismounting him.

After their fuck session, Zo and Porsha took a quick shower together and retired to the bedroom. Porsha was out like a light within minutes of her head hitting the pillow. Zo looked at his sleeping beauty and smiled, knowing that he had fucked her into exhaustion. Their fuck sessions were always epic. Porsha could be the Whore of Babylon in the bedroom and the Queen of Sheba in the streets, and that's why Zo fucked with her the way he did. She was a rider . . . *his* rider.

He watched her sleeping form and marveled at how, even unconscious, with her mouth hanging open and snoring, Porsha was still the most beautiful woman he had ever seen. There was no doubt in his mind about it, and his certainty about this fact is what scared him.

From the first time he'd ever seen Porsha come into that supermarket all those years ago, he knew that he wanted her. At first, it was just a physical thing, but as he got to know her and her story, he found himself becoming emotionally attached. Of course, he'd heard the rumors about her loose ways, but Zo was never one to put much stock in hearsay. He believed in judging people for who they were versus who the hood said they were. The courtship was a long and hard one, because they had been living in the same world but going in two different directions. Both of them fought against it, but eventually, the heart won out and they became a couple. Even if Zo wanted to lie about how much he loved Porsha, he couldn't. He wore it on his sleeve like a button for all to see. Zo had never given his heart to a woman outside of Porsha, which is why he often worried about her breaking it and breaking him in the process.

Unlike what it did to Porsha, sex didn't make Zo sleepy, it only made him more wired. He figured he'd roll another blunt and smoke until he got sleepy, but when he went through his pockets, he realized he didn't have any more cigars. Zo slipped on a sweat suit he'd left at Porsha's apartment so he could run to the store. He grabbed his gun and his jacket and was about to slip out of the bedroom when Porsha's groggy voice stopped him.

"Damn, you just gonna hit it and slip out while I'm sleeping like I'm a jump-off?" Porsha asked.

"Stop playing, Porsha. You know I'd never do that. I'm just jetting to the store right quick," Zo told her.

"The store is just on the corner, what you need your gun for?"

"You know how it is out here, Porsha," Zo told her, looking at the gun in his hand.

"It'd be just your luck if you get stopped on some bullshit and the police find that gun on you. I know how shit is on the block, but nobody in this neighborhood even knows you like that. You don't need to be strapped. Don't invite trouble. Leave the gun here, baby."

"A'ight." Zo reluctantly agreed and placed the gun on the nightstand. He didn't feel comfortable rolling without a strap, but he knew Porsha would worry. He was only running to the corner and coming right back.

When he passed the living room on the way to the front door, he saw Frankie lying on the couch and flipping through the channels. He could tell by the look on her face that she was still feeling some type of way about their discussion, but she'd get over it. She had no choice, because death was the one thing you couldn't take back. What's done was done.

"You leaving?" Frankie asked him.

"Nah, just running to the store. You need anything?" Zo asked.

"I'm good," Frankie said.

"Cool." Zo continued toward the door, but she stopped him.

"Be careful out there, Zo-Pound."

Zo smiled. "Ain't I always, Frankie Angels?" He winked and left.

The walk from Porsha's building to the corner store was a short one. The doors were locked for the night, so he had to place his order through the Plexiglas window. While waiting for the man behind the window to come back with his purchases, Zo scanned the block. There were a few people coming and going, but for the most part, Porsha lived on a quiet street.

Suddenly, the hairs on the back of Zo's neck stood up. He cast his eyes to the right and saw a man coming in his direction. He was wearing a hoodie and looking at the ground, so Zo couldn't see his face. The only people looking to conceal their faces at night were the ones up to no good. Keeping one eye on the man, Zo grabbed his purchases from the window and spun off.

Zo could hear footsteps behind him. He glanced casually over his shoulder to find the man in the hoodie still following him. This time, he had his hand jammed into the pocket of the hoodie. Zo cursed himself for not bringing his gun. He added speed to his steps, and so did the man in the hoodie. *I ain't going out like this.* Zo took off running.

He dashed for Porsha's building, hoping to lose the man there. He had almost reached the building when someone jumped out in his path, and Zo slammed into him. Reflexively, Zo swung, landing a right cross on the roadblock's chin and dropping him. Zo didn't even look to see who it was, he just kept moving.

Before he could reach the door of the building, the man in the hoodie caught up with him and tackled him. Zo and the man tussled around on the floor, with Zo ending up on his back. Zo wrapped the hoodie around the man's neck and pulled, choking him. The man struggled frantically, but Zo kept all his weight on him so he couldn't move. Before Zo could put his lights out, he felt the cold press of steel at the back of his skull.

"Police, muthafucka! Move and I'm gonna blow your head off," the man standing behind Zo informed him. Zo stopped his choking of the man in the hoodie. "Now, get up, and do it real slow."

Zo wisely complied. He turned around and was confronted by a tall Hispanic man, dressed in a leather jacket and blue jeans. His lip was bloody and his chin bruised, courtesy of Zo's right cross.

"Nice to see you again, Detective Alvarez," Zo greeted him.

"You little fucking punk." Detective Brown picked himself up off the ground. His hoodie was stretched out from Zo choking him with it. "You like to swing on police, huh?" He punched Zo in the stomach, doubling him over.

"Hold him up, and let me get some for what he did to my lip," Alvarez said. Brown grabbed Zo in a full nelson and held him defenseless for his partner. Alvarez hit Zo with a two-piece to the face.

"You know this is police brutality, right?" Zo spit blood on the ground.

"Nah, this is excessive force to subdue a murder suspect who resisted arrest." Alvarez hit him again. After he felt vindicated, he threw Zo roughly to the ground and handcuffed him. The detectives searched Zo but didn't find anything on him except some broken cigars.

"Y'all got the wrong dude," Zo said, as they yanked him to his feet.

"Bullshit. We found your calling card, Zo-Pound." Detective Brown held up one of the .357 shell casings from the crime scene at the motel.

"I ain't never seen that before in my life." Zo laughed.

"Let's see what forensics says when we match your prints to them slugs, buddy." Brown ushered him toward the police car.

"Ain't y'all gonna at least read me my rights?" Zo asked.

Brown slammed his head into the car door. "Fuck yo rights, nigga. The only right you got is the right to pray you make it out of this car alive." He shoved Zo inside.

NINETEEN

ASHANTI AND FATIMA MOVED AS QUIETLY AS they could through the abandoned aisles of the warehouse. Some of the shelves still held old drums containing only God knew what, but the drums provided excellent cover. He had retrieved the gun from Fatima. She had proved she would let it fly if she had to, but Ashanti was a much better shot, and they were low on bullets.

"Fatima, this three-fifty-seven ain't gonna keep us for very long, so we gotta escape. I want you to creep to the back of the warehouse and see if there's another exit. I'm gonna distract them to give you time to dip," Ashanti whispered.

"I'm not leaving you, Ashanti," Fatima said.

"Fatima, I'm combat trained, and these dudes are just thugs. I'm better than them, and I can make it out, but I won't be at my best if I'm worried about you, too."

"But Ashanti—"

"Don't argue with me, just go." Ashanti shoved her. Reluctantly, Fatima slunk off into the darkness to try to find an exit. Once she was out of harm's way, he was ready to go to war. "Let's do this." He gripped on the .357 and got low.

Animal trolled the streets, trying to get a line on Ashanti. He drew more than a few stares, riding on Kahllah's pink and black motorcycle, but he was in no position to be choosy about his methods of transportation. He just wished he hadn't been so hasty when he'd left the helmet. Around every corner he turned, he was afraid that he would bump into someone who recognized him. He needed to find Ashanti and get off the streets.

Thanks to Kahllah, locating Ashanti wasn't as hard as Animal thought it would be. Her motorcycle was fitted with a portable police scanner. He knew that when the killers came for Ashanti, he wasn't going down without a fight, and someone was going to report it. Sure enough, the radio call came through over the scanner.

"Reports of possible machine-gun fire in the Hunt's Point area . . ."

"Ashanti!" Animal said. It had to be. Who else would be involved in a machine-gun fight in the middle of the Bronx?

Animal pushed the bike to the limit, trying to make it to the scene of the crime before the police did. When he spotted the remains of the bullet-riddled cab and the abandoned church van along the side of the road, he knew he was going in the right direction. He scanned the night, watching and listening. He drowned out the passing cars and sirens and focused on the sounds that didn't belong. That's when he heard the gunshots.

"No," Animal said, fearing the worst. The thought of his lil' homie stretched out somewhere made him nauseated. "You won't take any more of my family." He revved the bike and whipped it at top speed in the direction of the shots.

The detectives rode around with Zo in the car for about a half hour without saying a word. Whenever he would ask them what he was being arrested for, they simply ignored him. He knew the tactic. They were trying to make him sweat, but it wouldn't work. The fact that they had run down on him alone instead of in force meant they were acting on a hunch and not with the blessings of the NYPD, so he still had a chance.

"I hear you been real busy, Zo-Pound," Detective Brown said over his shoulder. He was in the passenger seat of their notorious Buick.

"I keep telling y'all, I don't know what you talking about. Stop speaking in riddles and shoot straight with me," Zo said.

"OK, how's this for shooting straight? We know you killed Rick Jenkins, and we're going to make sure you fry for it," Detective Alvarez said from behind the wheel.

"Who?" Zo asked, as if he had no idea who they were talking about.

"You think you're fucking cute, huh?" Brown turned around in his seat and tried to stare Zo down.

Zo blew him a kiss.

"Fucking little punk." Brown leaned over the seat and started hitting Zo in the ribs with a blackjack.

"Cool the fuck out before you make me crash." Alvarez kept one hand on the wheel and tried to pull his partner off Zo with the other one.

"You just keep talking slick, and you ain't gonna have to worry about a trial, because we gonna hold court in the streets." Brown gave Zo another whack with the blackjack before returning to his seat.

"Zo, you don't have to play tough. Big brother Lakim isn't here to see you, so you don't have to keep up the front," Alvarez told him. "Look, we know you, Zo. You're a gangsta, but you ain't no cold-blooded killer. That's Lakim's MO. You're a working dude who's just having a hard time, and it's forced you to make some poor decisions. We get that. The way we figure it, if you put Rick Jenkins to sleep, you had to be in a position where you didn't have a choice. So what really happened in that motel room?"

"I keep telling you that I don't know anybody named Rick Jenkins, and I haven't been to any motels," Zo said.

"Well, we've got a witness that says different," Brown said. "Picked up a chick for boosting, and she traded a bit of info for a get-out-of-jail-free card. Seems she was in the motel room with Rick that night when a guy of about your height and build kicked in the motel-room door, armed with a three-fifty-seven."

Zo's mind went back to the girl he'd spared, and he wished that he'd killed her, too. "No loose ends," he said to himself.

"What was that?" Brown asked.

"I said I don't know what you're talking about. That could've been anybody," Zo said.

"Right, it could've been, but I doubt it," Alvarez said. "Most of these little shitheads do their dirty work with automatics. There are very few who are still running around shooting revolvers like it's the Old West. The jig is up, Zo. If you come clean, I'll talk to the DA and see what I can do. Maybe we can get it reduced to self-defense. You do a dime, and you're back on the streets in no time."

Zo laughed. "Man, you want me to hang myself? Now, that's a new one. I'll tell you like this. Fuck you and the nigga sitting next to you. Y'all wanna hang a murder conviction on me, you gonna have to earn it."

"OK, Buster Bad Ass," Brown said smugly. "We'll do it your way. We're gonna take you to the precinct and put you in a lineup while we're waiting for your prints to come back off those shell casings. If the witness can't convict you, I'm willing to bet modern science can."

"Whatever, nigga," Zo said, and tried to get as comfortable as he could in the backseat with his hands cuffed. Outwardly, he didn't have a care in the world, but inside, his heart was racing. He was almost sure that he'd been wearing gloves the night he loaded up to go out, but he wasn't one-hundred-percent sure. There was no telling what would come back once they ran his prints, and it had him spooked. He just hoped they'd let him get his mandatory phone call so he could contact King James's lawyer. He had to get out of there before the prints came back.

The police radio squawked as a transmission came through from the dispatch. "Reports of possible machine-gun fire in the Hunt's Point area of the Bronx . . ."

"Who the fuck could be shooting machine guns in the Bronx?" Brown thought out loud.

"If I had to guess, I'd say it was one of his homies." Alvarez nodded toward Zo-Pound, who looked nervous. "I say we go and check it out."

"What about this idiot?" Brown asked. He wanted to get Zo back to the precinct and booked so he could question him further.

"Fuck it, let's take him along for the ride," Alvarez said.

"You think that's a good idea?" Brown asked.

"Where the fuck is he gonna go? We'll leave him handcuffed and locked in the car while we investigate. Unless his last name is Houdini, he'll keep until we get back."

"It's your call, partner," Brown said, grabbing the handset off the dashboard. "This is car one-eighty-seven, show us responding."

Once inside, the three shooters fanned out. Dave took the right, Will the left, and Chess down the middle. The plan was to drive Ashanti out into the center and overwhelm him.

Dave moved cautiously down the right wall of the warehouse, clutching a Mac 11. His eyes scanned the dark corners and nooks on the oversized shelves, alert for anything out of place. The warehouse hadn't been used in quite some time, but it was still cluttered with trash and abandoned containers. Some were even big enough to hide a man, so there was no telling where Ashanti might pop up from.

A can clanked to the left. Dave spun and saw someone moving between the aisles. Reflexively, his finger tapped the trigger of the Mac 11. The bullets looked like fireflies, whisking through the dark and ripping through their target. Holding the machine gun at the ready, Dave moved in to finish him off. That's when Dave realized that it wasn't a man he'd assassinated but a mannequin draped in a dry-rotted dress.

"You missed, muthafucka." A voice came from behind

Dave. He turned and found himself staring down the barrel of a .357.

Dave dropped his gun and raised his hands in surrender. "Fam, I'm jus' the help. Can I get a pass?"

Ashanti weighed it. "Fuck yo pass." He pulled the trigger and blew Dave's brains out. Before the body hit the ground, Ashanti was already moving in on his next target.

Chess dropped to a crouch and held his weapon at the ready when he heard the gunshots. Unlike Dave and Will, he was a soldier, and battle was his element. This was the reason Ty had asked Chess to come along. He knew that he wouldn't flinch or hesitate when it came time to spill blood. What he didn't know was that Chess was planning on double-crossing him and keeping the fifty thousand for himself.

"And then there were three." Ashanti taunted him from the darkness. His voice echoed off the warehouse walls, so Chess couldn't figure out exactly where it was coming from.

"Why don't you stop hiding like a lil' bitch and let's square off?" Chess swept his gun back and forth, looking for movement in the shadows.

"I've got a better idea. Why don't you get the fuck out of here while you still can?" Ashanti countered. "If you leave now, I won't send you home to your mama missing your face."

"Sorry, but I got fifty thousand reasons to stay." Chess tightened his grip on the gun.

"Fifty stacks? Swann must want me dead pretty bad if that's what he dropped." Ashanti chuckled. "Ever ask yourself why he's so eager to silence me? What do I know that's worth fifty thousand to keep it from getting out?"

"Can't say that I know or care, but those fifty stacks will make a hell of a difference in my life right now," Chess told him. From his peripheral vision, he could see faint movement between one of the shelves and an oversized container on his left.

"Not if you don't live long enough to collect it. This is your last warning. Leave or get peeled," Ashanti told him.

"I think I'll take my chances." Chess fired in the direction of Ashanti's voice.

"Fuck!" Chess heard Ashanti yell.

Chess saw Ashanti hobbling in the darkness, trying to escape, but he wouldn't be denied. He fired twice more, hitting him in the back and dropping him.

"Got you, lil' nigga." Chess moved in on the injured Ashanti. He was crawling on his belly, trying to escape. Chess shot him in the back of the thigh. "You ain't talking big shit no more, are you?" He flipped him over, ready to finish him off. Chess was shocked to see that it was Will and not Ashanti whom he had shot.

"Fuck," was all Chess could say when he felt the cold touch of the .357 behind his ear.

"With no Vaseline," Ashanti said sinisterly.

"As soon as you touch that trigger, I'm gonna touch your bitch." Ty stepped from behind a tall shelf. He was holding Fatima in a reverse choke hold, keeping her body between him and Ashanti.

Seeing his girl hemmed up made Ashanti furious. "You bitch-ass coward." He turned his gun on Ty. "I'll rock yo faggot ass if you touch my lady!"

Ty huddled further behind Fatima and put his gun to her

temple. "All that tough shit sounds good, but you and I both know you don't wanna see this bitch's brains. Now, stop fronting like you don't love this ho and put that hammer down, before I feel it necessary to motivate you." He cocked the hammer back with his thumb.

Ashanti felt like he had just been kicked in the chest, seeing Fatima in the clutches of danger, knowing he had put her there. In his mind, he could hear Animal's voice the day he first taught him how to shoot a gun. *In battle, your weapon is your best friend. Never surrender your gun, even if it means the death of one of your homies. You keep your strap and avenge him another day.* Until that moment, Ashanti had always taken everything Animal said as the gospel without a second thought, but this was different. It wasn't one of the homies, it was his girl.

"A'ight." Ashanti held the gun up. Slowly, he placed it on the ground.

Now that Ashanti was disarmed, Chess rediscovered his courage. He picked the .357 up and held it like a club, barrel first, and approached Ashanti. "So you was gonna fuck me with no Vaseline, huh?" He slapped Ashanti in the head with the butt of the gun and dropped him. "Before I kill your bitch ass, I'm gonna make you hurt," Chess promised, and began stomping the life out of Ashanti.

"That's enough!" Ty shouted. "Bring his lil' ass over here where I can see him."

The shooter dragged the bloodied Ashanti by his shirt across the floor over to where Ty was standing with Fatima and tossed him at Ty's feet. Ty shoved Fatima to the side and hovered over Ashanti.

"So this is the protégé, the one they say was next in line to play the role of the boogey man." Ty shook his head sadly. "Look at you now." He kicked Ashanti in the face.

Ashanti pushed himself up on his knuckles and spit blood onto the floor. "You got me, and that's what it is. Soldiers understand the rules, but my lady is a civilian. Let her go."

Ty twisted his lips. "Yo, what is it with all you niggaz and these broads? First Animal and now you. When are you gonna learn that in war, a chick is only good for two thing: making you lose focus or crippling you with grief when you watch her die over your bullshit." He turned the gun on Fatima.

"No!" Ashanti screamed at the top of his lungs, but his voice was overshadowed by another sound: the loud roar of an engine.

The window overlooking the spot where they were standing was suddenly flooded with light. Against the glare, a silhouette formed. It was a dark angel, wings spread and menacing as it swooped ever closer.

"Sweet Jesus." One of the shooters gasped.

"Not Jesus. The Reaper," Ashanti corrected him, before tackling Fatima to the ground and out of harm's way.

Paulie hated the fact that Ty had left him on guard duty while the others got to join in the hunt for Ashanti. From the amount of money Swann had put on his head, he knew the kid was someone important, and it would've looked good on his résumé if he had been the one to take him down.

"I never get to see any action," Paulie said in disgust, and sat on a milk crate in front of the warehouse.

Paulie spotted something coming in the direction of the

warehouse. Curiously, he got up and squinted to get a better look at whoever was approaching. At first, Paulie thought it might've been the police or reinforcements, but upon closer inspection, he realized it was a lone motorcycle. Whoever it was wasn't the police, and he damn sure wasn't with Ty's crew.

Paulie let off a burst of shots that perforated the dirt around the motorcycle. The rider swerved but kept coming. Paulie squeezed again, this time managing to hit the bike, shredding the front tire. Expertly, the rider popped a wheelie and continued coming at Paulie on one wheel. Paulie tried to fire again, but the gun jammed. It took him three attempts before he was able to dislodge the bullet, and by then, it was too late. Paulie let out a blood-curdling scream as the motorcycle tore up through his chest and his face when the rider used him as a human ramp.

TWENTY

Everything seemed to move in slow motion. The window exploded in a magnificent spray of glass when a ball of smoke and flame crashed through it. Against the backdrop of moonlight, a sneering gold and diamond grille became visible in the smoke. Animal swooped in like a dark horseman mounted on a pink demon steed. His arms were outspread, clutching the Pretty Bitches as he threw himself from the bike.

Ty dove for cover, but Chess wasn't as quick to react. The motorcycle hit him and dragged him screaming across the floor, pinning him in a corner. Animal hit the ground in a roll and came up holding his Pretty Bitches. Chess was in his sights and at his mercy. "Die," he hissed, and pulled the triggers. One by one, the guns flared to life, expelling vengeful hellfire from the barrels.

The bullets tore through Chess's neck and torso, with the last one hitting him between his eyes. Before his light was snuffed out, his last thoughts were of the fifty thousand dollars he'd never get a chance to double-cross Ty for.

"You OK?" Ashanti rushed to Fatima to check her injuries, which he was thankful to see were minor, but she was terribly shaken up.

"Yeah, I'm fine, baby," Fatima said, allowing Ashanti to help her to her feet.

"You've got more lives than a cat," Ashanti said to his mentor.

"I guess that's a blessing for you. Seems like I'm always saving your ass." Animal embraced Ashanti. "Did you miss me?"

"Fuck no, I was just getting used to the title of being the hardest nigga alive," Ashanti joked.

"Wait, is this Animal?" Fatima asked in wide-eyed shock. She had heard many tales of the brokenhearted killer, but seeing him in the flesh was surreal.

Animal greeted her with a nod. "The one and only."

"I heard you were dead," Fatima said.

"I get that a lot." Animal cracked a half smile. "We can exchange pleasantries later. Right now, we need to get gone before the police come." A flicker of movement caught his eye. "Move." He shoved Ashanti and Fatima out of the way, just as several bullets tore through the floor between them.

Ty came from behind the smoky wreckage of the motorcycle, armed with Chess's abandoned machine gun, letting off shots. "You fucked up putting your nose where it don't belong, stranger." He let off another burst, sending Animal scrambling for cover behind a crate. "Before I kill you and this bitch nigga you tried to save, why don't you tell me who you are so I can make sure they spell your name right on your tombstone?"

Animal popped up from behind the crate, holding his Pretty

Bitches. "The name is Animal, cocksucker." He fired twice. The first bullet hit the motorcycle's gas tank, soaking Ty's clothes in gasoline. The second one struck the ground, igniting the flammable liquid.

Ty danced like an extra in Michael Jackson's "Thriller" video as the flames licked his skin. He crashed into a pile of boxes, setting them and the wall on fire. Hungrily, the flames ate at the side of the warehouse and began nipping at the ceiling.

Animal stood over the suffering Ty and shook his head sadly. "Ashes to ashes, muthafucka," he said, before putting two bullets in Ty's head and taking him out of his misery.

"See what you get for fucking with a real nigga!" Ashanti shouted at Ty's corpse.

"Stop playing, and let's get the fuck outta here. I gotta get back to Gucci," Animal told him.

"Where is she?" Ashanti asked.

"Somewhere she shouldn't be, and I don't wanna leave her there alone longer than I have to. Let's make a move." Animal led them to the warehouse door. The three of them left the burning warehouse like they had the devil on their heels. As soon as they made it out into the night air, they were blinded by flashing red and blue lights.

"This is the police. Get your fucking hands up!" someone shouted through a bullhorn. There were so many flashing lights that there was no way to tell how many of them were out there. It was clear that there would be no escape this time.

"Oh, shit, it's the boys!" Ashanti shouted.

"What are we gonna do?" Fatima asked nervously.

"I ain't going back in a cage for nobody. Die, pigs!" Animal raised his Pretty Bitches and started dumping at the police.

As soon as Alvarez and Brown pulled up to the front of the warehouse, they spotted the dead body lying outside the door. "What the fuck?" Brown said.

"Call it in," Alvarez told his partner. While Brown made the call, Alvarez leaned over the backseat. He undid one of Zo's handcuffs and chained him to the door. "In case you get any big ideas," he told him before getting out of the car.

Slowly, the two detectives crept toward the body, guns drawn and alert for danger. Brown kneeled down beside the boy . . . or what was left of him. His face had been ripped apart by what looked like tire treads. From inside, they could hear a machine gun rattling off, which sent them scrambling back to the safety of their car.

"Fuck that, I'm not going in there until backup comes," Brown said.

"Now, that's something we can agree on," Alvarez replied.

As if in answer to their prayers, the first of several blue-and-white units came screeching to a halt near their car. The two detectives straightened themselves and went to meet the uniformed officers.

"There's a possible homicide suspect inside, and I'm not sure how many people he's with or what's going on. What I do know is that they're working with some heavy fire, so proceed with caution. Fan out and surround the building," Brown told them. He was the senior officer on the scene and therefore the one in charge.

The officers did as they were told. Within a few minutes, the building was surrounded by a sea of blue uniforms. The two detectives led a handful of the officers toward the warehouse entrance, ready to go in. Suddenly, the doors burst open, and three people came rushing out.

"This is the police. Get your fucking hands up!" a bullhorn blared. The spotlights illuminated the fugitives.

Just as Brown and Alvarez had suspected, Ashanti was at the center of the disturbance, but when they saw who he was with, both of their jaws dropped.

"Is that Animal?" Alvarez asked, in shock.

"Still think I'm crazy?" Brown raised his gun. He'd been trying to tell his partner for years that he didn't believe the young killer had truly perished in the shootout that had almost claimed all three of their lives, but he was always dismissed as being obsessed.

"I'll never doubt your gut again, partner," Alvarez told him. "I say this time we put him down for good," he whispered.

"That's cold-blooded murder," Brown pointed out.

Just then, Animal opened fire and sent them running for cover. The detectives ducked behind a patrol car as bullets ripped through the hood.

Alvarez looked at his partner. "It doesn't seem like he's going to give us a choice. Let's end this once and for all." He came up from behind the patrol car and opened fire.

Animal stood there, showing no fear, lighting up police cars and officers. His face was hard and determined as he blasted cop after cop. Ashanti was in a state of shock when Animal opened up on the police. Shooting out with cats in the streets was one thing, but this was the law! He was being pulled to the point of no return.

"Fuck it," Ashanti said, and fired the .357. He had wasted most of his bullets trying to fight Ty and his men off, so it wasn't long before the .357 clicked empty. "I'm out!" he shouted, tossing the empty gun.

"Get inside the warehouse," Animal ordered, blowing the leg off a uniformed officer who was trying to creep in on his left.

"The building is on fire," Ashanti pointed out.

"You've got a better chance in there than you do out here," Animal said, ducking a bullet that whizzed past his ear. He returned fire, knocking down the cop who'd shot at him. "Go, Ashanti!"

"What about you?" Ashanti asked.

"Like you said, I've got more lives than a cat. Get inside. I'll be right behind you," Animal told him.

Ashanti didn't want to leave Animal's side, but he knew he'd be more of a distraction than a help, standing there defenseless. He grabbed Fatima by the hand and led her back inside the burning warehouse.

The dozens of police officers on the scene provided Animal with more than enough targets, but he was focused on two in particular. He let off the Pretty Bitches, trying to tear Brown's and Alvarez's heads off, but they managed to make it to the safety of a patrol car. He had spared the detectives' lives when he'd had the opportunity to kill them, and they repaid him by constantly hunting him. The game between them was going to end that night.

Alvarez popped up from behind the car and took a shot at Animal, but his fear kept him from aiming, so the shot went high. Animal returned fire with two shots of his own. There was a thunderous sound, and Animal moved just before a spray of buckshot tore up the ground where he'd been standing. Animal returned fire, backing up toward the warehouse entrance.

Coming to Ashanti's rescue had taken Animal out of the frying pan and put him into the fire. He was outmanned, outgunned, on the losing end of the fight, and he knew it. He could hold the police off for a while, but it would only be a matter of time before they were all overrun and killed. After all the things he'd done, Animal knew that there was no way the police were going to take him alive, and even if they wanted to, he wasn't going out like that. He would rather die than spend the rest of his life in a cage and away from Gucci.

Someone grabbed Animal from behind and pulled him deeper inside the warehouse. He had expected it to be Ashanti and was surprised when he was confronted by his father. He was holding Fatima around the neck, with his hand over her mouth. At his feet lay Ashanti.

"What the fuck are you doing here?" Animal asked.

"It would seem I'm saving the lambs from the slaughter," Priest told him. "You just couldn't resist disobeying me, could you?"

"I couldn't leave my homie," Animal told him. He looked down at Ashanti's body. "Is he dead?"

"No, just unconscious. He was a bit unnerved about my presence, so I had to subdue him," Priest explained. "It's bad enough that you three knuckleheads are trying to get yourselves killed at every turn, but you're involving innocent people in your bullshit."

"Three?" Animal was confused.

"I'll explain later. We haven't got much time." Priest released Fatima. From his robe, he pulled a small black box. He placed the box against one of the shelves and punched in a series of numbers that started a countdown.

"What is that?" Animal asked suspiciously.

"A fuck-you present from us to the police. Always leave your enemies with a fuck-you present. Now, pick Ashanti up so we can go. We haven't much time," Priest told him.

"How the fuck are we going to get out of here? There are police crawling all over this place," Animal said.

Priest simply smiled. "The Black Lotus will provide us with the window we need. Just be ready to move when I say so."

"We've got them trapped," Brown said excitedly. For years, he had dreamed of the moment when they would finally take Animal down.

"Move in!" yelled a beefy police sergeant dressed in a bulletproof vest and a cheap suit. The moment he poked his head up from behind the car, it exploded.

"What the fuck?" Alvarez shouted as pieces of the sergeant's brain splattered on his leather jacket.

The night air was suddenly filled with low whistling, as high-caliber slugs tore through police cars and flesh. The officers who were foolish enough to try to run away were cut to pieces, while the others huddled behind cars and whispered silent prayers that they would live through the firefight.

"Sniper!" someone yelled.

"As if this shit could get any worse," Brown said, creeping around the car and out of the way of the sniper fire.

No sooner had the words left his mouth than the warehouse exploded, knocking him off his feet.

Brown wasn't sure how long he'd been unconscious. He was awakened by a paramedic shining a light in his eyes and asking him if he knew his name and where he was. He saw Alvarez talking to their captain, standing behind the paramedic.

"What the fuck happened?" Brown sat up.

"We got our asses kicked," Alvarez told him. "How you feeling, partner?"

"Like shit."

"That means you're feeling about how you look," Alvarez joked.

"Did we get him?" Brown asked. When he saw the look on his partner's face, he knew the answer. "How the fuck did he get away?"

"When the building blew, he slipped away in the chaos. We thought we might've gotten lucky when we found some bodies in the wreckage, but none of them was Animal or Ashanti."

"That's one slippery little fucker. Well, at least we got Zo-Pound. I want to put the screws to him personally," Brown said.

"We *had* Zo-Pound," Alvarez corrected him.

"What do you mean, *had*?"

Alvarez held up the empty handcuffs. "I guess his last name really *was* Houdini."

LOYALTIES

"Nigga, we gladiators, and there are only two ways out of the arena: on a stretcher as a corpse or on the shoulders of your comrades in victory."

—Lakim

TWENTY-ONE

ANIMAL HAD BARELY CROSSED THE THRESHOLD OF the church when Gucci threw herself into his arms and hugged him as tight as she could. "Thank God," she breathed into his neck. The whole time he was gone, she had feared the worst. When she heard the news broadcast on the radio about the shooting, it didn't help. Although they didn't mention anyone by name, she knew in her heart it had something to do with Animal. "I thought I'd never see you again."

"I told you that I'm back for good. I ain't going nowhere this time," Animal promised her.

Gucci looked past Animal and noticed Ashanti, with a guy and a girl she didn't recognize. The girl looked frightened, but the dude looked confused.

"'Sup, sis." Ashanti hugged Gucci tightly. The last time he saw her, she was in a hospital bed, fresh out of a coma.

"What's up, lil' bro? I see you still can't keep yourself out of trouble." Gucci returned his embrace. "Who are your friends?"

"That's my man Zo—he nodded at Alonzo—"and this is Fatima." He pulled her to his side. "She's my girlfriend."

Gucci was surprised. "Your what? My goodness, how long was I in that coma?" she teased.

Kahllah entered the church, looking worn and tired. In her arms, she cradled a Barrett M82. She gave Animal and Gucci a look but didn't say anything when she passed them. She disappeared somewhere in the back of the church, slamming the door behind her hard enough to rattle the already-broken stained-glass windows.

"The fuck is her problem?" Animal asked. Kahllah had been strangely withdrawn the whole way back. She didn't even say anything about Animal wrecking her bike.

"I'll tell you later," Gucci whispered. She was still unnerved by what she had seen and wouldn't dare speak of it within earshot of Kahllah or Priest. As if reading her mind, the robed assassin entered the church.

"Seeing all of you together like this would make a wonderful family portrait." Priest smiled.

"What the fuck is this freak show, and what am I doing tied up in it?" Zo asked.

"I'll take that as your way of saying thank you for us saving you from what was waiting behind door number two, my murderous friend," Priest said to Zo. "Right now, you'd be in the process of being formally charged with the death of Rick Jenkins, had the Black Lotus not freed you."

Zo had been sitting in the back of the police car handcuffed to the door, racking his brain trying to figure a way out of the mess he had created for himself. When the door swung open, he thought it was one of the detectives, but it was a beautiful woman dressed in all black and holding a gun. She'd freed him from the cuffs, then whisked him away at gunpoint and locked him in a van, leaving him to wonder about his fate. Zo felt like he would shit his pants the whole time he waited but was relieved when she came back, accompanied by some familiar faces.

"Good to see you again, Zo. I just wish the circumstances were different," Animal said.

Zo blinked as if he'd just awakened from a dream. "I guess the saying is true; real niggaz don't die."

"We all must die eventually, just not before our work on earth is done," Priest said.

"I'm sorry, who the fuck is this again?" Zo asked Animal.

"My father," Animal told him.

"Your what?" Ashanti asked, clearly shocked.

"I was just as shocked as you are when I found out. It's too long of a story to tell, but the short version is that the man who was sent to kill me turned out to be the man who brought me into the world," Animal explained. "This is Priest."

"Wait, do you mean *the* Priest, as in the Clark family's executioner?" Zo shook his head in disbelief. "Somebody hand me a shovel so I can dig my own hole."

"I have no claim to your life, boy. At least, not at the moment, but at the rate you're going in the name of your insane king, it won't be long before your number is called," Priest said.

"We didn't start this pissing contest with Shai, but we're gonna finish it," Zo declared.

"Or get finished," Priest countered. "You and your crew are little more than mice being toyed with by an adolescent tiger.

When he's tired of the game, Shai Clark will devour you and everyone you hold dear."

"Then help us instead of stringing us along," Animal interjected. "You said you'd help me end this thing with Shai, but so far, all you've given me are some old-ass stories and riddles. If you're gonna help me kill him, then do that, and if not, let me and mine go about our ways and do what we gotta do!"

Priest gave Animal a sad look. "Animal, you're so blinded by your own rage that you can't see the writing on the wall."

"Then why don't you hand me a pair of fucking glasses!" Animal snapped. He was frustrated; they all were.

Priest turned to Gucci, who had been silently watching the exchange. "Gucci, would you mind taking Fatima up to the apartment while the men speak?"

Gucci looked to Animal, who gave her the nod that it was OK. Without a word, she took Fatima by the hand and led her up the back stairs.

Priest waited until the women were gone before he addressed the men. "Fine, you want me to speak plainly, then I'll do that. None of you have a snowball's chance in hell at winning a war against Shai Clark. He's got more guns and more money."

"Yeah, but we got more heart," Ashanti said.

"Straight like that." Zo gave him dap.

"All of you have more heart than I've seen in a man in a very long time. If more were built like you three, then maybe the game wouldn't be so fucked up. But for as much heart as you have, it won't help you to prevail over an enemy who has the power of a god on earth. When your families are awakened by the rattling guns of Shai's death squads, will your hearts shield them from the bullets?" Priest asked them.

“So then what would you have us do, keep running until Shai eventually picks us off?” Animal asked.

“Heavens, no, my son. Asking you not to fight would be asking you not to be true to your character. No matter how much a man changes, the nature of who he truly is will always be lurking beneath the surface. I’m simply asking you to choose a stronger weapon,” Priest told him.

“Shit, what’s a stronger weapon than a gun?” Ashanti asked.

“Information,” Priest told him. Before he could elaborate, his phone rang. He looked at the caller ID, and a worried expression crossed his face. He excused himself while he took the call.

“So what’s the game plan? Do we roll with whatever Priest is cooking up, or do we take our chances?” Zo asked.

“I say we round up the posse and go at this bitch nigga Shai with everything we got,” Ashanti said.

“A lot of good that’s done us thus far. That strategy has gotten me killed twice and the two of you marked for death,” Animal pointed out. “I ain’t saying Priest is right, but I ain’t saying he’s wrong, either. We need a better plan than bumping our heads against the wall, hoping our skulls don’t crack open. I’m ready to put this shit to bed.”

“As are we all.” Priest rejoined them. “Gentlemen, I think I have a way to get us all what we want, but I need to know how far you’re willing to go.”

“You already know where I stand,” Animal said.

“I’m with the big homie. If he says we roll with your plan, I’m cool with that,” Ashanti said.

“Zo?” Animal turned to him.

He looked at the assembled faces. "I'm down for whatever ain't gonna get me killed."

"You're a wise young man," Priest told Zo.

"So what's this great plan of yours?" Animal asked.

"To bring an end to all this bloodshed between your respective crews without anyone else having to die," Priest told them.

Zo laughed. "Man, you said you had a legit plan, but you're talking about a miracle. Shai hates us, and we ain't too fond of him. Lives have been lost, and there ain't no way to just sweep this all under the rug."

"To an extent, you're correct, but it isn't as complicated as you would make it seem," Priest said. "Although all your reasons for going at Shai are valid, none of them is a wrong that can't be made right. You"—he addressed Animal—"wanted to get at Shai over what happened to your lady, but she's safe and sound now. You"—he looked at Zo—"fight out of loyalty to your brother, but it isn't really what you want. If you had it your way, you'd find yourself a decent-paying job and be content to live happily ever after with your girlfriend. And you"—he turned to Ashanti—"fight because it's all you know how to do. It doesn't matter if it's Shai or some other foe, as long as you get to bust your gun, you're fine with it."

"Sounds like you know us all pretty good, but we don't know you or what your stake in it is," Ashanti said.

"My stake is I don't want to see my son slaughtered in the street like cattle. The only reason I'm entertaining you two is because it's important to Animal. I honestly couldn't care less what happens to you," Priest said bluntly.

"If nothing else, you're honest," Zo said with a measure of respect.

"My game is killing people, not coddling them," Priest told him. "The way I see things is, you can either keep up this war until you're plucked off one by one or take the high road and everything goes back to business as usual."

Zo thought on it. "OK, so let's say that we do try things your way. Who's to say all parties involved will play along?"

"You let me worry about the Clarks. I just need the street crews to stand down," Priest said.

"I'll speak to King and Lakim. It'll be a hard sell, but King isn't a completely unreasonable man," Zo said.

"Dawg, you're as hot as a firecracker right now behind that Rick Jenkins shit. The hood will be the first place they look," Ashanti told him.

"I'm hot?" Zo raised his eyebrow. "Did you forget that you just had a shootout with the cops and blew up a building in the middle of the Bronx?"

"Ashanti has a point," Animal said. "Brown and Alvarez can say for certain Zo and me were at that crime scence and our names are probably on the wire as we speak, but they got no proof Ashanti was there. Let Ashanti go holla at King. We need to stay low."

"A'ight, but I still can't linger around here. I got shit to do in the streets. Porsha is probably worried out of her mind, and I got something else I need to look into before the last dance." Zo thought of the girl he'd let escape. "We can all meet back here in the morning."

"Fine, but I trust I don't have to tell any of you why it's imperative that you stay out of sight," Priest told them.

"I'm good at moving unseen," Zo assured him.

"Handle what you have to handle, and we'll all meet here

in the morning. Is there anything that you'll need in the meantime?" Priest asked.

"Yeah, a pistol," Zo told him.

From the back of a heavily tinted SUV, a pair of eyes watched the old church. The watcher looked on curiously as two young men slipped quietly from the side entrance, with a pretty girl between them. His hand tightened on the grip of the machine gun sitting across his lap, ready to pop off. Upon closer inspection, he realized that neither of the dudes fit the description of the man he'd come looking for. A few seconds later, a third man came out of the church. This man was older and dressed in priest's robes. He said something to the three youths before going back inside. The watcher waited until the trio had gone before picking up his cell phone.

"Yeah, this is the place. You want me to handle that, boss man?" the watcher asked the person on the other line. "A'ight, it's your call, but y'all niggaz hurry up so we can take care of business." He ended the call and went back to his watching. Soon . . . very soon.

TWENTY-TWO

AFTER THE DAMAGED CAUSED IN HARLEM, FIRE Bug and Big Money decided to have a little celebration. Big Money called some hood rats he knew and had them come out to meet them at a hotel in downtown Manhattan. Big Money had promised to get them high and drunk and put a few dollars in their pockets if they came and freaked off with him and his cousin. The thirsty hood rats readily agreed and told him they'd be there within an hour.

Although he kept up his smug persona, Bug was actually quite nervous. When he was around his brothers or other male members of the Savage clan, he would regularly boast about his sexual exploits, but they were mostly lies. Bug played grown men's game, but chronologically, he was still a child and inexperienced. He slept with a few of the girls from his school and a wayward prostitute or two from Maxine's stable when he caught them drunk enough, but Bug was a novice when it came to women. On the cusp of his potential first orgy, he found himself borderline terrified.

"What's taking these chicks so long? You think they backed out?" Bug paced the floor of the spacious hotel room nervously.

"Chill out, Fire Bug." Big Money was putting the finishing touches on the blunt he was rolling. "Shorty texted me a few minutes ago and said the cab was dropping them off in front of the hotel. I left a key for them at the front desk."

"What?" Bug stopped his pacing. "Why you leave them bitches a key? We don't know them hos like that. For all we know, they could be planning a jux." He dashed over to the writing table and retrieved his gun.

Big Money looked at Bug comically. "Boy, why don't you sit your paranoid ass down somewhere? I met these hos at a club downtown, and they jumped on the dick, so we kept in contact. These bitches ain't off shit but get high and a few dollars, so quit working your teenage brain with conspiracy theories. You're worse than Mad Dog with that lunatic shit." The minute Big Money said it, he wished he could take it back.

"What you say about my brother, nigga?" Bug's grip tightened on his pistol. "You putting family business in the street, Big Money?"

The subject of Mad Dog's mental stability was taboo in the Savage household. As a kid, Mad Dog Savage had been hit in the head with a baseball bat while trying to protect their father from some men who had ambushed them. Mad Dog suffered a cracked skull and was in a coma for five days. When he awoke, he said he'd had a conversation with the Grim Reaper, and during their conversation, death had whispered to him the exact moment he was scheduled to die. Mad Dog was never the same again. He lived like a gypsy, moving from place to place, searching for death around every corner and trying to stay one step ahead of the Reaper.

"Bug, you know I didn't mean it like that," Big Money said in a sincere tone. "I got love for my big cousin. I was just trying to get you to lighten up a little, Bug." He lit the blunt and took a deep pull. Still holding the smoke, he passed the weed to Bug.

Bug wasn't a big drinker or smoker, but he'd experimented with both, like most kids his age. Bug frowned as the strong weed tickled his nose. He saw his older cousin watching him from under hooded eyes, daring him to hit the potent weed. Bug put the blunt between his lips and inhaled. At first, he didn't feel anything, but then the aftershock came. The smoke gripped his lungs, forcing him to cough violently. The more Bug coughed, the higher he seemed to become. By the time he composed himself enough to pass the blunt back to Big Money, saliva was dripping down Bug's lip onto his jeans.

"What the fuck was that, some killa?" Bug asked, wiping his mouth with the back of his hand. He had only hit the weed once, but he could already feel the fog trying to settle over his brain.

"That there is some of Harlem's finest, mixed with a little something extra to cap it off. Don't worry, it'll make you feel groovy, little cousin," Big Money said, hitting the blunt like a champ. He passed it to Bug, but he declined. Instead, he went over to the nightstand and grabbed the pint of Hennessy.

"Where these bitches at? I'm ready to get it going," Bug said, swigging from the bottle. He had a nice buzz going on.

No sooner had he said it than they heard someone insert the keycard into the door.

"Showtime." Big Money smiled, sliding onto one of the two queen-size beds and striking his coolest pose.

The door opened, and in slithered two buxom young things, one chocolate, one caramel. The chocolate one was older, maybe in her late twenties, but her body was still very tight. It looked like her blue jeans had been painted on with as much care as her multicolored acrylic nails. The caramel one was prettier in the face but didn't have as much tits and ass as the chocolate one. She came in sucking a cherry lollipop like it was best thing since the television show *Scandal*. It had gotten chilly that night but not enough to persuade her to put on stockings with the short skirt she wore. From the way she struggled to navigate the high heels on her feet, you could tell she was young.

"Glad you could make it." Big Money slid off the bed and stood. He blew smoke into the air confidently and openly ogled both girls. His eyes lingered on the caramel one, but it was the chocolate one who stepped up. Her name was Pam.

"I told you we was coming." Pam hugged him. "This is my girl Tiffany." She nodded to the caramel one. Tiffany just waved.

"I'm glad y'all made it. Whatever y'all had to spend on cabs or whatever to get down here, don't worry about it. I'll shoot it back to you before you leave."

"You'll hit us with more than that." Pam kissed him on the cheek and strode past Big Money. "And what's your name, cutie?" she asked Bug, who was sitting in the armchair with a goofy look on his face.

"Fire Bug," he said in a lazy drawl. It felt like his lips and tongue were going numb.

"Why do they call you that?" Tiffany asked. She had a high voice.

"Because I'm good at blowing shit up," Bug boasted. Tiffany gave him a smile that said she was impressed, and he found himself getting warm and tingly feelings in his gut.

"Well, I hope your little cute ass didn't have nothing to do with the traffic jam in Harlem. That's what took us so long to get here," Pam said.

"What was it, an accident or something?" Big Money asked, passing Pam the high-octane blunt.

"Nah, they said there was an explosion on Broadway, near the projects." Pam took a hit of the blunt, then paused and looked at it funny. She shrugged it off and kept smoking. "They said it was a gas main or some shit."

"Or something else," Bug mumbled, then broke into a fit of giggling.

Pam gave him a look but didn't follow up on his remark. "You know, I don't really be in my hood like that anymore. It's getting too crazy, with all the recent shootings," she told Big Money.

"It's getting like that all over," Big Money said. "But fuck hood politics, what the business really is?" He looked her up and down so there was no mistaking exactly what he meant.

"You ain't said nothing slick to a can of oil." Pam slid out of her jacket and made herself comfortable on the bed. "Let's get to drinking and drugging for a while so we can unwind. Then we can turn this shit into a gangsta party."

Big Money put a few more blunts in the air, minus the special sauce he'd sprinkled on the first one. He and Pam lay on the bed, feeling each other up. Pam stroked his dick through his jeans and whispered into his ear what she planned to do to him. Drinks flowed freely, and everyone began to loosen up, including Fire Bug. He and Tiffany were on the opposite bed, passing a blunt back and forth and both of them pretending not to notice Bug running his hand timidly up Tiffany's skirt. The mood was officially set.

"Well." Big Money got off the bed. "I don't know about y'all, but I'm ready to get into some grown folks' business." He pulled his shirt over his head.

"I can't speak for the kids over there, but I ain't never been shy." Pam wiggled out of her tight jeans.

"Wait, we all gonna do it in the same room?" Bug asked nervously. He was just getting comfortable with the idea of having sex with Tiffany, but he wasn't sure if he was up to doing it in front of an audience.

"It ain't like y'all got nothing we've never seen before. Listen, if it'll make you feel better, we can dead the lights." Pam flipped the switch on the wall and draped the room in darkness.

Bug lay there, not sure what to do next. In the dark, Tiffany leaned and kissed him on the lips. "Don't worry, everything is cool." She helped him get his shirt off.

It didn't take Big Money and Pam long to start getting into some heavy action. She kissed a trail down his stomach and worked her way to his dick. She took the tip of it into her mouth, then hesitated. She sniffed his dick and frowned. "Baby, were you at a BBQ or something? Your whole body smells like charcoal."

Big Money pulled her up from his dick and kissed her. "Nah, just had to take care of something, and I got a little too close."

"You and your fake-ass gangsta stories." Pam bit him on the lip playfully.

Big Money held her at arm's length. "What you mean by that?"

"Nothing, I was just teasing you, because every time I talk to you, you've got a crazy story. Remember the last time you were telling me about the shootout with ten dudes?"

"Those ain't stories, that's my life, ma. What these niggaz rap about, I'm living!" Big Money declared.

"If you say so, boo. I ain't doubting you're gangsta." Pam tried to kiss him, but Big Money turned his face away.

"You think it's a game with me? I'm a Savage. We about that work. If you wanna know the truth, that wasn't no gas main that blew up in Harlem, it was a truck," Big Money told her.

"Nigga, how the hell would you know more than what everybody else is saying?" Pam asked.

"Because it was me that blew it up," Big Money said proudly. It was a lie, but it made him look big in Pam's eyes.

This piqued Pam's interest. She had heard a story about a kid from her neighborhood being killed that night, but she didn't know the details. All she knew was that the whole hood was broken up. She wasn't sure if there was any connection, so she decided to prod Big Money further. "Big Money, that's dumb as hell. Why would you blow up a truck in the middle of Harlem?"

"Because when I body a nigga, I don't do it half-ass. If I have to, I'll take out every muthafucka on the block, too. Dude had to get got, and whoever went along for the ride, that was just their hard luck."

"That's cold-blooded," Pam said.

"Us Savages are cold-blooded creatures, ma. You fuck with us, and you're fucking with the best."

Before Pam could drag any more information out of him, they were interrupted by laughing coming from the next bed. Both Big Money and Pam saw Bug's silhouette rise from the bed, yanking at his pants.

"Fuck is going on over there?" Big Money asked, cutting on the light.

"Your friend had a little accident," Tiffany said, trying to stifle her laughter.

Bug stood in the corner, wiping something off his jeans with a towel. "Shut up," he said sharply.

"I keep telling you it's OK. It's happened to plenty of other guys, though not quite as quick," Tiffany said.

"Bug, I know that ain't what I think it is?" Big Money asked. When he saw the look of embarrassment on Bug's face, he knew what had gone down. Before Tiffany could give him the business, Bug had ejaculated prematurely all over himself.

"Wipe that fucking smirk off your face, Big Money. This shit ain't funny." Bug threw the towel at him.

"Don't worry about it, baby. I'll have your dick back hard in no time." Tiffany reached for Bug, but he slapped her hand away.

"Bitch, don't touch me," he snapped.

"Bitch, who you calling a bitch?" Tiffany asked with an attitude.

"I'm calling you a bitch, funky whore," Bug said.

"Ain't no need for name-calling, shorty. Didn't your mama teach you any manners?" Pam asked. She didn't like the way Bug was coming at Tiffany.

Bug retrieved his gun and pointed it at Pam. "Low-life whore, you wanna see what my mama taught me?"

"Bug, be cool," Big Money urged him.

"Man, fuck that. These bitches gotta go. Get your shit, and get the fuck out," Bug ordered the girls.

"That's how it's going down, Big Money?" Pam looked at him with fire in her eyes. He had been the one who invited her to the hotel, and the fact that he wasn't bothering to try to keep his cousin in check made her angry.

Big Money looked from Bug and his gun back to Pam and shrugged. "Sorry, shorty. I think it's best if y'all just roll out." He was tight that he didn't get any pussy, but Big Money knew Bug and his tantrums. There was no telling what he was liable to do with the gun, and he didn't want to have to be the bearer of bad news when it came time to explain everything to Ma Savage.

"This is some bullshit." Pam snatched up her pants. "Let's go, Tiff."

"Lame-ass nigga," Tiffany mumbled under her breath as she got off the bed.

"What did you say?" Bug asked.

"I said y'all some lame-ass niggaz," Tiffany said defiantly. Without warning, Bug hauled off and slapped her across the bed.

"What the fuck is you doing?" Big Money grabbed Bug.

When the shock of being slapped finally wore off, Tiffany jumped to her feet. "Nigga, is you crazy?" She tried to attack Bug, but Big Money kept his bulk in between them.

"Shorty, please don't make it worse. Just go," Big Money pleaded.

"Fuck it, Tiff. It ain't that serious." Pam pulled her friend away. "Big Money, this is some wack-ass shit, but I ain't gonna hold it against you. The next time you wanna party, bring a grown-up with you."

"Eat a dick, whore." Bug spit at her but missed.

"Ya mama is a whore," Tiffany said from a safe distance.

"Your mouth is gonna get you in trouble one day, shorty," Pam told Bug. "Big Money, can I at least get that paper you promised me so we can bounce?"

Big Money looked at Pam as if she was speaking a foreign language. "Paper, what paper? I didn't bust a nut, so all bets are off."

Pam's eyes narrowed to slits. "Wow, I'd heard around town that you were a greasy nigga, but I didn't know you was that petty. It's OK, though, Big Money Savage. This shit is gonna come back around to you, bet that."

"Whatever, just get the fuck out before my arms get tired of holding this lil' nigga and I'm about to turn him loose," Big Money told her.

"Come on, Tiff." Pam pulled her toward the door.

When the girls were gone, Big Money turned to Bug. "What the fuck was all that shit about, Bug?"

"Bitch was trying to play me," Bug said.

"I hear you, but you can't be pulling no guns on no hos in no hotels. That's just dumb," Big Money told him.

"She lucky you was in the way, or else I would've shot her," Bug promised.

"Dumb-ass kid." Big Money shook his head. "Get your shit, man. We getting out of here. I don't know what might come of this situation you caused."

"Fuck them whores. My last name is Savage. They can't do shit to me," Fire Bug said, tucking the gun into his waistband.

Pam and Tiffany stepped out into the night air, looking a hot mess as they had to dress hurriedly in the elevator and still hadn't had a chance to put their shoes back on. Their disheveled hair and bare feet drew a few glances, but they were too mad to care what people thought.

"This was some bullshit. You said these niggaz you were coming to see were cool," Tiffany fumed.

"When I met Big Money, I thought he was about that life. I didn't know he was gonna turn out to be a clown," Pam explained.

"Him and his bitch-ass cousin better hope I don't tell Lil' Monk about this shit, because you know that nigga would straight clown," she said, speaking of her son's father.

"Tiffany, don't bring that crazy nigga into this. Lord knows they don't want no parts of him, and I don't want my name tied directly to no murder," Pam said. Lil' Monk was a menace in the hood who was known to let his gun fly. "I know how to fix them niggaz, though," Pam said coldly.

"What you gonna do?" Tiffany asked.

"Watch this." Pam pulled out her cell phone and dialed a number. "Hey, this is Pam," she said when the caller answered. "How much is it worth to you to find out the names of the cats responsible for killing your lil' homie?"

TWENTY-THREE

AFTER WHAT HAPPENED TO SHORTY, KING NO longer wanted to go to the Bronx. He needed to be in his hood. It had always been his theory that he drew strength from the concrete streets of Harlem, and he needed the strength of his native soil more than ever.

He stood in the middle of the playground, looking out at the street, eyes fixed on the spot where his truck had exploded and claimed Shorty's life. The city had removed most traces of the crime scene, but he could still see soot resting on cars and the broken grocery-store window that had caved in after the blast. When he closed his eyes, he could hear Shorty screaming for someone to help him out of the truck.

"It should've been me," King said to himself.

"What you say, big homie?" Abel asked. He was sitting on the bench next to his brother, Cain, and Dee.

"Nothing, my nigga," King said, blinking away a tear that was trying to form in his eye.

Lakim came out of the building, face twisted into his usual scowl, with a duffel bag slung over his shoulder.

"What's in the bag, La?" Dee asked.

"Early Fourth of July for anybody who comes through here acting like they wanna get stupid." Lakim patted the bag. "Yo, God," he said, addressing King. "I just got off the jack with the broad I'm fucking who works for the cab company as a dispatcher, and she had some disturbing news."

"Well, don't keep an asshole in suspense. Spit it out," King told him.

"She said that one of their drivers got killed tonight up in Hunt's Point during some wild-ass shootout," Lakim told him.

"I heard about that shit. They were talking about it on the radio a little while ago. They was saying like eight niggaz got killed, including three police officers," Abel said, remembering the news broadcast that had interrupted the hip-hop countdown on his favorite station.

"Good riddance to them fucking pigs." Cain spit on the ground. He was still salty about the beating he'd taken at the hands of Detective Brown and his henchmen at the precinct.

"Why is that relevant to us?" King asked.

"Because she said the last fare he picked up was a guy and a girl leaving this location," Lakim told him.

"Ashanti and Fatima?" King's heart was filled with dread. The last thing he wanted to hear was that he had lost two more people he'd promised to look after.

"Sounds like it might've been," Lakim said sadly. "They found the cab driver murdered in his car and a few more bodies in a warehouse that blew up a few blocks away. I don't know who it was, though."

"Yo, word to everything I love, if somebody did something to my big homie, I'm stretching them and they mamas!" Cain said emotionally. Both twins were close to Ashanti, but he and Cain shared a special connection. Ashanti was like the big brother Cain never had, and he loved him just as much as he did his own twin.

"Be cool, Cain. It could've been anybody. Don't put negative energy into the air," King told him. "Has anybody spoken to Ashanti since him and Fatima left?"

"I tried calling his phone a few times but kept getting the voicemail," Abel said.

"It ain't like Ashanti not to have his phone handy at all times," Dee added.

"Let's get our people on it. If somebody did something to Ashanti, they gonna die for it. No questions asked," King vowed. He had always had love for little Ashanti. Not just because he brought money into the organization but because he was *real* nigga.

"I didn't wanna say nothing, but I been thinking about a few things," Lakim said. "Ashanti was acting strange after the police picked him up for questioning about that murder, and—"

"You better think long and hard before you finish that sentence, Lakim," Cain warned.

"Don't get to puffing up on me, lil' nigga. I'm just laying all the possibilities on the table," Lakim said to Cain. "I'm just saying, yo, Ashanti got a rap sheet a mile long. I'd have expected them to keep him at least overnight for questioning, but he was out within a few hours."

"And when did you get your law degree?" Cain asked. "They popped me and Ashanti at the same time but didn't have nothing on us. While you're bumping your gums about shit you don't understand, you should probably factor in that the police are on camera beating the shit out of me. That's why they sprung us, nigga!"

"Both of y'all cool out," King interjected. "I got the word earlier about what happened at the precinct, so I know neither one of y'all rolled over, Cain. If you had, I'd have put you to sleep personally the minute you hit the block. I know better than most how Ashanti is built, so I would never question his loyalty. Neither would Lakim. He's just making a point."

"Well, he's pointing in the wrong direction," Abel added. "Instead of arguing over Ashanti's loyalties, we need to find out what happened to him."

"You can ask him yourself." Dee pointed to the curb, where a taxi had just pulled up. Ashanti and Fatima got out of the backseat.

When Ashanti walked up, he noticed that all eyes were on him. "What's popping?"

"You," Lakim said, giving him a look.

"Ain't I always?" Ashanti matched his stare.

"'Sup, Fatima? You good?" King asked, noticing that she looked a mess and her clothes were filthy.

"Hey, King. Yeah, I'm straight," Fatima told him. Her voice sounded tired.

"Baby, go upstairs and get some rest. I'll call you when I turn in for the night." Ashanti kissed her.

"OK, but let me talk to you real quick." She led him off out of earshot of King and the rest.

"What's good?" Ashanti asked.

"Ashanti, you know I love you, right?"

Ashanti gave her a look. "Fatima, that's always what the chick says on *Maury* before she reveals some crazy shit."

"Ashanti, stop being silly, because I'm serious. I love you, and I would go to the ends of the earth with you, but this is some deep shit you're tied up in," Fatima said.

"I know, and I'm gonna get it worked out. The homie Animal got a plan."

"Animal? Ashanti, the way I hear it, every time Animal has a plan, somebody dies or goes to prison, and I don't want either of those for you or us."

"Fatima, ain't nobody dying or going to prison," Ashanti assured her.

"But how do you know? Tomorrow isn't promised, and the chances get slimmer when you decide to go to war with somebody who runs the entire city."

"What am I supposed to do, tuck my tail and run?" Ashanti asked.

"No, baby, I'm not telling you to run, I'm telling you to pick your battles. Listen, my father might be locked up, but his name still holds weight out here. I could have him reach out to the Clarks and work something out," Fatima offered.

"I don't need your daddy to speak for me, Fatima. I'm a man, and this is gonna be what it's gonna be. I just need to know if you riding with me or not," Ashanti said.

Fatima looked at him lovingly and ran her hand down the side of his cheek. "Ashanti, I love you more than anyone I've ever been with, but I'm young, and I want a life that doesn't involve living like a hunted animal or marrying my future husband in a prison visiting room. You know I would do anything in this world you asked of me, but please don't ask me to die for you unnecessarily."

She kissed him on the lips as if it would be the last time. "Goodbye, Ashanti," she told him, and disappeared into the building.

Ashanti stood there for a while, breathing in and out slowly. It felt like someone had punched him in the stomach and knocked the wind out of him. Since he'd hooked up with Fatima, his life had revolved around her, and the thought of her leaving him made him weak in the knees. Nobody had ever told him that love was supposed to hurt. On shaky legs, he walked over to rejoin his crew.

"Isn't that touching?" Lakim said sarcastically.

Ashanti cut his eyes at Lakim. "My nigga, it's been a long night, and I've been through a lot. I'm really not in the mood for your bullshit."

"We were just out here discussing what you may or may not have been through today. You care to fill in the blanks?" Lakim asked.

Ashanti knew Lakim was testing him, but he was too drained to play the game with him. "The short version is, I've been through hell and back, and I've come to the table with an offer from the devil."

"Offer?" King asked, not understanding what Ashanti was talking about.

Ashanti nodded his head. "Indeed, King. So much has gone on that I don't know where to begin, but I'll give you the short version. If you down for it, we might be able to negotiate a cease-fire with the Clarks."

"Cease-fire?" Lakim jumped in before King could respond. "Nigga, we gladiators, and there are only two ways out of the arena: on a stretcher as a corpse or on the shoulders of your comrades in victory.'"

"I know all about being a gladiator, La, but I also know math," Ashanti said. "For every one of Shai's men we take down, they take five of ours. When we ain't losing cats to bullets, we're losing 'em to the system because of all the dirty cops and politicians Shai's got on his payroll."

"So what, you saying you scared or something?" Lakim asked.

"I wouldn't know fear if it smacked me in the face, so you talking to the wrong one about that, homie." Ashanti turned to their leader. "King, look at who we lost already. Dump is in the system, Meek is in the ground, and Shorty is in pieces. All for what, because Shai was disrespectful at the club? Not only are Shai's goons on our asses, but so are the police. All these murders got us hot, and we can't even cross the street without getting pinched for something. I can't speak for y'all, but I'm ready to get back to the business of making money."

King couldn't deny that Ashanti had a point. All he wanted to do was talk to Shai and maybe do some business, but alcohol and egos came into play, and everything went to the left. King James never wanted an all-out war with the Clarks, but he had to do something after the slight at the club so as not to look weak. One thing had led to another, and the next thing he knew, he was losing soldiers and money left and right. In his heart, he knew that they had slim to no chance at beating the Clarks without decimating their own whole operation, but he had gone too far to turn back and not run the risk of looking soft. If he had it to do all over again, he would've done things differently.

"I know you ain't actually considering what this nigga is saying?" Lakim asked, noticing the contemplative look on King's face.

"Lakim, just chill. I ain't even said nothing," King said.

"You ain't gotta say nothing, I can see it on your face." Lakim was getting tight. "Who the fuck is you to come around here talking about negotiating shit?" He turned on Ashanti. "We put you on the team, and you getting too big for yourself. Lil' nigga, this is our army!"

Ashanti had finally had enough. "Check this fly shit. I'm getting a little sick of your mouth, dawg. You a stand-up nigga, and I'd never disrespect you by suggesting anything less than that, but I think it's *you* who is getting too big for himself. King James is the head of this, he feeds the pups, and for that I'm grateful, but it's me who holds the leash on these dogs in the streets. Never forget that."

"I don't think I like how you're talking to me." Lakim puffed up.

"Then that makes two of us, because I don't like how you're talking to me, either, *blood*," Ashanti said, matching his tone.

"Bang bang, anywhere gang." Cain stood next to Ashanti. He didn't draw his weapon, but he kept his hand close to it.

Sensing the tension building, King James stepped between them. "Knock it the fuck off. It's bad enough we going at niggaz in the streets, but if we start turning on each other, we don't stand a chance. Y'all dead that."

Ashanti was reluctant, but he extended his fist to give Lakim dap. Lakim just stared at him, seething. Eventually, he pounded his fist and mumbled an apology.

"Ashanti"—King draped his arm around him—"it's been a long and trying night for all of us. Why don't you take it down and come see me in the morning, and we'll talk some more, a'ight?"

"No doubt, King." Ashanti gave him dap. As he was leaving, King had a question.

"Ashanti, what makes you so sure Shai is even willing to let it go?"

Ashanti thought on it. "I'm not, but it's worth a shot. I got an insider working on putting it together."

"You've been keeping quite a few secrets these days, huh?" King asked.

Ashanti just smirked. "Never let the left hand know what the right hand is doing. I'll see you later, my G." He headed toward the Ave.

Abel followed, but Cain lingered, glaring at Lakim.

"Fuck you looking at, ugly?" Lakim asked harshly.

"Nothing, man, just thinking that you have a very unique face." Cain grinned wickedly before going to join his brother.

"Fucking weirdo," Lakim said, watching Cain walk away. He caught up with Ashanti and Abel. The trio huddled together at the curb like they were scheming.

"Why don't you leave them little dudes alone? What is it that you have against Ashanti lately?" King asked. When Ashanti first joined their team, he and Lakim were close, but as Ashanti got older, they seemed to be growing apart.

"Nah, sun, shorty be feeling his self a little too much for my taste, and it irks me," Lakim said. It was half true. His real beef with Ashanti was that he was growing up and growing out. King had started delegating more and more of the street responsibilities to Ashanti, including things that Lakim used to handle. King called him pulling Lakim off the streets a promotion; they were upper management now and didn't need to play the block so heavy, but to Lakim, it felt like he'd had his power stripped. It was to the point where even the soldiers were deferring to Ashanti, and Lakim didn't like it.

"Ashanti has his hang-ups, but he's a good soldier, one of the most solid cats we got with us. That kid is an important piece of this puzzle," King told him.

"He still needs to stay in his fucking lane," Lakim spit.

King's cell phone rang. "Peace," he answered. "Oh, what's good, Pam?"

TWENTY-FOUR

"NIGGAZ ALWAYS FLEXING FOR NOTHING," ASHANTI SAID as they were walking down the block. He was going to go home and sleep, but the confrontation with Lakim now had him wired. So Ashanti suggested they go get hero sandwiches before he dipped.

"I don't like that dude . . ." Cain chimed in.

". . . never did," Abel added.

Ashanti knew the twins were upset when they started finishing each other's sentences, as if they were one person instead of two. "I ain't stunting Lakim. His bark is worse than his bite."

"Well, all I know how to do is bite . . ." Cain said.

". . . Fuck barking," Abel continued.

The three of them walked to the twenty-four-hour deli and placed their sandwich orders and got some junk food. Cain told the man behind the glass to add two forties of Old English to their items.

"Yo, I swear I think y'all are the only two niggaz I know who still drink fucking forties," Ashanti told the twins.

"You bugging, this here is the food of the gods." Abel put the bottle to his lips to take a swig, but Cain stopped him.

"Ain't you got no etiquette?" Cain asked his brother. "This is for the brothers who ain't here." He poured some of the beer out onto the curb before taking a sip.

"Word up." Abel tipped his forty, spilling beer before taking several deep gulps. He then extended the bottle to Ashanti.

"I'm good," Ashanti told him.

"Stop acting like I'm offering you crack. It's just a lil' drink," Abel said.

"For the fallen comrades," Cain added.

"A'ight." Ashanti accepted the bottle. "This is for Shorty." He poured a few splashes out. "Rest in peace, lil' homie." He turned the forty to his lips and drank deeply.

Ashanti, Cain, and Abel slow strolled back toward the projects, passing the beers back and forth. Ashanti, who claimed not to like beer, knocked out half of Abel's forty and was working on Cain's, too. He didn't know if it was the alcohol or exhaustion setting in, but he felt like he was walking on clouds. When he rounded the corner, leading back into the projects, he collided with a kid they called Dub. Dub was a fat black cat, with a face that only a mother could love, but he was working with a few dollars, so chicks overlooked him being facially challenged. Around his neck, he wore a thick chain with diamond letters that spelled out his name. With him was a cute Spanish girl named Sarah who lived in the next building. Dub wasn't from the hood, but he was always over there to see her. Ashanti was about to offer him an apology, but Dub spoke first.

"Damn, watch where you're going, shorty," Dub said with an attitude. When Ashanti bumped into him, he accidentally stepped on Dub's brand-new white Nikes and left a scuff across the toe.

"My fault," Ashanti said.

Dub examined his sneakers and turned his angry face to Ashanti. "I just got these muthafuckas, and now they're ruined."

"I said my fault. What the fuck do you want me to do, clean them with a toothbrush or something?" Ashanti asked sarcastically.

Dub glared at Ashanti murderously. "You trying to be funny?"

"Let it go, baby. It ain't that serious." Sarah tugged at Dub's arm. Unlike her boyfriend, she knew who Ashanti was and how he gave it up.

"Word up, listen to your girl, my G," Ashanti told him. He was buzzing from the beer, but sensing a potential threat, his brain started sobering him up.

"Fuck all that." Dub pulled away from Sarah. He stood toe-to-toe with Ashanti, whom he had by at least an inch or two and easily one hundred pounds. "What you trying to say?" he pressed Ashanti.

"*Check yourself before you wreck yourself*," Cain sang in a half-drunken voice.

"What, y'all gonna jump me for your man? I ain't no sucka, I'll scrap with all three of y'all." Dub started taking his jewelry off and passing it to Sarah to hold.

Cain stood at attention, hand inching toward his gun and ready to end Dub if Ashanti gave the word. Abel had stealthily positioned himself to Dub's left. As if by magic, a retractable baton appeared in his hand. From that angle, he could crack Dub's skull and probably kill him with one swing. It was moments like these that they had trained for. In battle, they moved as one unit, attacking like a pack of synchronized dogs.

Ashanti saw his pups ready to attack. "Stand down," he told them. Like a set of bookends, Cain and Abel took two simultaneous steps back. "I'll bang with any nigga, big or small. I got this." He stared up at Dub defiantly. "You really wanna go there?"

In answer, Dub swung on Ashanti. Ashanti had been expecting it, so he was able to easily duck the blow and rock Dub's flabby stomach with a combination of punches. Dub tried to grab Ashanti and throw his weight on him, but Ashanti slipped the hold and clocked Dub twice in the side of the head. The fat man tripped over his feet and crashed clumsily to the ground, trying to figure out exactly what had just happened. The fight was clearly over, but Ashanti wasn't done.

Ashanti jumped on top of Dub and delivered two punches to his exposed face. "See, you couldn't just leave with your bitch." He punched Dub in the face again. "You wanted to be a fucking tough guy, but look at you now, pussy!" Ashanti continued to rain on Dub until a blue-and-white police car skidded to a stop at the curb.

"Rollers, nigga. Let's dip!" Abel pulled Ashanti off Dub.

"Hey, stop!" one of the cops yelled, swinging the car door open.

"Fuck you, toy-ass cops!" Cain yelled, and hurled his forty at the patrol car. The bottle smashed against the car's windshield and drenched the cop in malt liquor.

"Come the fuck on!" Abel pulled his brother by the shirt.

Cain stumbled forward, ready to make his great escape when he had a thought. "Let me take care of that for you." He snatched Dub's jewelry from Sarah's hands. "Good looking out," Cain called over his shoulder as he disappeared into the night.

Zo stood on the corner, fishing around in his pocket for change and cursing up a storm. When he'd left the church, he had two very important phone calls to make, with the second one to Porsha to let her know he was OK. When Zo tried to use his cell phone, he realized that the battery was dead. Through pure luck, he had managed to find one of the last functional pay phones in New York City, and he placed his calls.

Porsha was relieved to hear that Zo was safe, but that relief quickly turned to anger when she started asking him to go into detail about his whole ordeal. Zo told her about the police picking him up, but he lied and said it was drug-related. He knew she could smell the lie through the phone. Things took a turn for the ugly when she offered to come pick him up and he declined. It was bad enough that he'd left her hanging in the middle of the night when he was only supposed to be going to the store, but now he was telling her that he wasn't coming back, and the best excuse he could give her was "I'll explain it to you when I see you." She had hung up the phone on Zo twice already, and he was trying to call her a third time to explain, but he was all out of change.

"Fuck!" Zo kicked the pay phone. He was going to have to work his ass off to make this up to Porsha, but first he needed to make sure he'd remain free long enough to even make the attempt.

The girl he had spared at the motel was returning the favor by trying to put Zo away for the rest of his days, and he didn't intend to sit by and let that happen. She had to go. Finding her was Zo's biggest problem, but it proved to be far easier than Zo imagined. It was a shot in the dark when he called the precinct, impersonating Detective Brown, telling the half-asleep desk sergeant that he'd misplaced the address for the witness in the Jenkins murder and needed him to have someone pull it from a file on his desk. The sergeant put Zo on hold. The whole time, Zo kept looking up and down the block, thinking they had seen through his ruse and were tracing the call. Every car that passed he thought was an undercover, ready to pounce on him. A minute later, the sergeant came back to the phone and rattled off the girl's information. He was asking the detective how he was feeling after being caught up in the explosion, but Zo had already hung up the phone. The sergeant would likely be fired and, with any luck, brought up on charges when his blunder was discovered, but that wasn't Zo's problem; the girl was.

Her name was Linda Carver, and she lived in an apartment building off 161st Street and the Grand Concourse in the Bronx. The lobby door to her building was locked, but Zo just waited around until someone was coming out and slipped in. Bypassing the elevator, Zo hiked up the eight flights of stairs to her floor. He crept to Linda's door and listened for sounds of movement inside. Zo could hear the television playing softly. He wasn't sure if anyone was awake in the house at that late hour or if they'd just left the TV on, but he had to go in regardless. Time wasn't his friend, and he had to silence the witness before she could bury him.

Getting past the apartment door lock was simple enough for Zo. Breaking and entering had been his thing before he'd started trapping with his brother, and there weren't very many locks that he couldn't pick. Moving as quietly as he could, Zo turned the knob and slipped inside.

The apartment was dark, but Zo could see the light from the television in the living room. With the 9mm he'd borrowed from Priest clutched in his hand, he crept down the hall and peeked around the corner into the living room. There was an older woman sitting up sleeping on the couch. On her lap was the crossword puzzle she'd been working on when she nodded off. Zo left the woman to her slumber and made his way to the bedroom. The door was ajar, and he could see someone sleeping on the queen-sized bed with her back to him. The glow from the street lamp outside the window illuminated enough of her face for Zo to know it was the girl he'd come to murder.

Zo crept into the bedroom, with his gun aimed at the sleeping girl's back. His heartbeat pounded in his ears so loudly that he found it hard to concentrate. He was no stranger to death or murder, but he had never killed a woman before. It went against his code, but Linda hadn't left him a choice. It was her or him.

When the girl stirred, Zo froze like a roach on the wall. She mumbled something in her sleep, followed by loud snoring. Zo figured he had to hurry up before the girl's snoring woke the old woman up. He retrieved a pillow that had fallen off the bed and placed it over his gun. It would muffle the sound of the blast. Zo angled the gun and the pillow at her head and crept forward, finger tightening on the trigger. He was right on top of her and about to ruin her white sheets when he saw what he had missed when he first entered the room: a baby nestled on the bed next to Linda.

She was a beautiful infant girl, with bright and alert eyes

that were staring right up at Zo. She stared at him curiously, while cooing and making little spit bubbles with her mouth. Zo ignored the little girl and lowered the pillow just above Linda's head so he could deliver the kill shot. He tried not to look at the baby and stayed focused on her mother, but his eyes kept drifting back. Even with him holding the big black gun, she seemed to be more curious about the man in her mommy's room than afraid of him. The child was so innocent, so undeserving of the fate he was about to condemn her to by taking her mother away.

"I can't," Zo whispered. He knew that if he didn't kill Linda, then it was likely over for him, but he couldn't bring himself to make that little girl an orphan. Before he accepted that kind of mark on his soul, he'd rather take his chances in the courtroom. As silently as he'd entered, Zo exited the apartment. He could only hope that in the future, Linda would give the child the best possible chance for making something of herself, since it was the child she owed her life to.

Zo made hurried steps down Linda's hallway, shaking his head as he thought back to what he'd almost done and why he was in the position to have to do it. "I'm bugging," Zo said to himself while wiping the gun down with his shirt. When he passed the building's compactor room, he threw the gun down the trash chute. His life was spinning out of control, and he had to restore order to it while he still could. He was going to go to Porsha's and tell her everything. In the morning, he would call the lawyer and see where he stood with the charges the police were trying to slap on him.

Zo walked hurriedly from Linda's building to the corner, where he began trying to hail a taxi.

"What's up, Houdini?" someone called from behind him.

When Zo turned around, something crashed into his face. He fell flat on his ass in the street, dazed and bleeding from the mouth. Stars danced before his eyes, and when he finally got his wits about him, he found himself staring up at Detective Alvarez, holding a nightstick.

"You know, I always pegged you as the smart one of the bunch," Alvarez began. "But apparently, you're just as fucking stupid as the rest of them. Imagine my surprise when the sergeant calls my partner's phone to tell him that he forgot to give him the zip code with the address he requested. I wouldn't have thought much of it, if it weren't for the fact that I've been at the hospital all night with Brown while he was being treated for a concussion."

"I don't know what you're talking about. I was just out taking a late-night walk," Zo told him.

"Horse shit, and you know it." Alvarez kicked him. He reached down and grabbed Zo by the collar, snatching him to his feet. "You just happen to be taking a walk in the same neighborhood where the witness to your bullshit lives?"

"Man, I don't know nothing about—"

"Yeah, yeah, yeah," Alvarez said, cutting him off. "I've been hearing that G-code shit all night, and it's starting to sound like a broken record. I caught you with your hands in the cookie jar this time, Zo-Pound. I'm willing to bet that when we go upstairs to check on the witness, she'll be just as dead as Rick Jenkins, and I can hang two bodies on you instead of one. You're gonna ride the lightning for this one, homie."

TWENTY-FIVE

When Animal entered the upstairs apartment, he found Gucci sitting at the desk, hunched over the laptop. He peered over her shoulder and saw her sifting through news reports of the rash of violence that had broken out in the city. Her teary eyes were fixed on a photo of a charred SUV that marked the final resting place of a twelve-year-old boy.

"Don't be reading that junk, Gucci. It's only going to upset you." Animal closed the laptop.

"I think it's a little late for that," Gucci told him. "Seeing all this stuff, I feel like history is repeating itself. I don't want anyone else to die because of me."

"Gucci, I think this stopped being about you a while ago." Animal pulled her to her feet and hugged her. "We're in a very dark situation, but as long as we hold each other down, there's light at the end of the tunnel. You with me, ma?"

"You know I am," Gucci said confidently.

Animal leaned in and kissed her passionately. "That's what

I'm talking about." He patted her on the ass. "We've decided to give Priest a shot before we exercise plan B."

Gucci frowned. "Animal, I know that's your dad, but you really don't know him enough to place blind trust in him."

"I don't place blind trust in anybody," Animal said.

"Even me?" she asked.

"His plan can't put us in any worse a position than we're already in," Animal said, ignoring her question. "Priest is a wild card, but he's probably the best card in this shitty deck we've been dealt."

"I still don't like him. I wasn't a fan of his after he kidnapped us, but I became less of a fan after what he did to Kahllah," Gucci said.

"What happened?" Animal asked.

Gucci went to the door and peeked up and down the hallway to make sure it was empty. With a soft click, she closed and locked the door. "Baby, I've known some monstrous men in my day, but none quite like your father." She went on to tell him the story.

When Priest had returned and found out that Kahllah had allowed Animal to escape, he was surprisingly calm. Without saying a word, he went behind the pew and opened a small wooden box that he kept on the floor. When he came back, he was holding what looked like two leather whips braided together. Kahllah gave Gucci a weak smile before getting up and removing her shirt. She walked to the altar, dressed only in her bra and leggings, and braced her hands against it. Over her shoulder, she gave Priest a defiant look, just before the first lash fell.

"He beat her like a dog, Animal," Gucci said, trying to keep from crying again. She pitied Kahllah, as Priest tore into her over and over, forcing her to recite verses from the Bible on command. It was the sickest thing Gucci had ever seen.

"That's some dirty shit," Animal said heatedly. He thought back to his childhood and some of the epic beatings he'd gotten from Eddie. "Did she fight back?"

"No, and when I tried to stop him, she wouldn't let me. She said it was her punishment for breaking her vow. She actually believed that she deserved to be beaten."

"Priest has got that girl all fucked up. Makes me grateful that he didn't raise me, but that don't make the shit he's doing to Kahllah OK. I should say something." Animal stood.

Gucci grabbed him by the hand. "Animal, I feel bad for what happened, too, but Kahllah is the classic case of a battered woman. No matter what we do or say, she's gonna always go back to Priest, because she's programmed to think that abuse equates to love. The only person who can cut that chain binding her to Priest is Kahllah."

Gucci had a point, but it still bothered Animal. Kahllah was twisted in the head, but she was still good peoples. She had done what she could to help Animal, including making their escape at the warehouse possible. "I should at least check on her. I owe her that much." He pulled away from Gucci.

Animal knocked on the door he'd seen Kahllah disappear through earlier, but he got no answer. He placed his ear to the door and heard a low mumbling. Curious, he pushed the door open and stuck his head inside.

Kahllah had her back to the door, kneeling in the corner. She was wearing only a tank top and spandex shorts. Her hair was pulled up, so Animal could see the tattoo on the back of her neck. It was a dragon swallowing its tail. Kahllah's body was way more fit than Animal had thought, muscular but still feminine arms, smooth back, and rounded shoulders. Her skin was almost perfect, except for a scar that went from her tank top and over her shoulder. As Animal looked closer, he noticed that the scar wasn't alone. Her body was marked by whelps, some obviously still fresh judging by the faint red stains on her shirt. Animal moved closer and peered over her shoulder. She was hunched over a small altar, deep in prayer. On the altar was a crucifix and a big black gun.

"Are you just going to stand there gawking at me, or do you need something?" Kahllah said, without turning around.

"How did you—"

"In my line of work, maximizing the use of all your senses increases your life expectancy." Kahllah stood and turned around. She tapped her nose. "You stink of smoke."

Animal smelled himself. "I guess I do, don't I? Look, I didn't mean to intrude on you."

"You mean more than you already have with your street war? Don't worry about it, I don't have anything better to do," Kahllah said sarcastically. "So what brings you down here? Someone else need to be rescued from a police firing squad?" Seeing the embarrassed expression on Animal's face, Kahllah gave him a half smile. "I was only joking."

"I didn't realize you had a sense of humor," Animal said.

"In this world, you have to find something to laugh at, or else you'll be crying all the time."

Animal nodded. "That's some deep shit."

"Nah, that's some real shit," Kahllah said, taking her hair

down and letting it spill freely around her shoulders. "So have your friends gotten to their destinations safely?"

"I imagine so. If they don't show up tomorrow morning, I guess I'll know different."

"I wouldn't worry too much about it. If I've learned anything from watching Ashanti and Zo, it's that those two don't lay down easily. Zo's indecisiveness is likely going to get him hurt one day, and Ashanti is an accident waiting to happen, but if you're going to war, then they're as good to have at your side as anyone."

"Yeah, those are my dudes. Kahllah, I never had a chance to thank you for everything you've been doing."

"No thanks necessary. I'm just doing my duty, nothing more," Kahllah said, grabbing a T-shirt from the back of the chair in the corner. When she pulled it over her head, she winced a bit.

"You OK?" Animal asked, meaning the welts.

"These are nothing. I've had far worse injuries," she told him.

"I'll bet, with a name like Black Lotus. Still, I feel kind of fucked up about what happened to you because you helped me," Animal said sincerely.

"I told you, it's fine," Kahllah insisted.

"No, it isn't fine. Priest beats you to keep you loyal to him. Any man who beats on a woman is a sucka, and I can't respect that."

"Priest doesn't beat me, he keeps me disciplined. The pain makes us numb and therefore incorruptible by the evils of the world," Kahllah said, as if she was reading from a script.

"Is that what you believe, or is that what Priest has been

drilling into your head for God knows how long?" Animal asked.

Kahllah didn't answer right away. "Father loves me, he's just trying to keep me from straying from the flock."

Frustrated, Animal grabbed Kahllah by the arm and led her to the mirror mounted on the wall. When he turned her to face the mirror, she didn't resist. "This isn't love." He turned her head so she could see the welt that snaked under her neck from where the whip had landed during her beating. "Love is to protect and nurture, not to abuse."

Kahllah pulled away and turned her eyes from the mirror. "You don't understand. I was broken, and he made me whole . . . he gave me purpose."

"What purpose, to obey him without question or be beaten?" Animal was heated.

"And what would you have me do, Animal? Should I abandon the man who was my salvation and go out into the world to chase love like you have?" Kahllah matched his tone.

"No, but you should at least be given the choice."

"What do you know about choices when you haven't acted of your own free will in years? Everything you do is in the name of someone else," Kahllah spit.

"I don't wanna argue with you, Kahllah. I'm just concerned, that's all," Animal told her.

Kahllah snorted. "Don't let that brother-and-sister shit go to your head, Animal. We share no blood. When this is done, you'll leave here and forget about me, as I'll likely forget about you."

"That's where you wrong, Kahllah. See, we don't have to be blood to be family. To me, actions hold more weight than genetics, or haven't I shown that during my little reunion with Daddy dearest? And contrary to what you think, I won't forget you when I leave here. I never forget kindnesses paid on me, and I always return them," Animal told her, and left the room.

Kahllah stood there for a while, fuming and trying to keep her anger in check. She was frustrated because Animal's words had taken her there, and she prided herself on control. Looking at her trembling reflection in the mirror, Kahllah felt disgusted. With a scream, she grabbed the altar and hurled it against the mirror, shattering the image staring back at her.

"Sounds like a sibling spat," Priest said playfully when Animal came out of Kahllah's room. He was sitting on one of the scuffed wooden benches in the front row of the church. "I wonder what it is that you've done to get a reaction out of the Black Lotus?"

"Why do you wanna know, so you can have a reason to whip her again?" Animal snapped.

"Discipline is a necessary evil, especially with your generation. It's the lack of discipline among you young rebels that has the game in so much chaos."

"So says the man who didn't have the discipline to keep his family together," Animal capped. "Priest, you talk all this shit, but you're a hypocrite and a fucking bully. Tell me, does it give you some kind of thrill when you beat Kahllah with that strap?"

"I do what I must to keep Kahllah focused, so that she can live long enough to look back and appreciate the things I've taught her. You should know better than anyone how cruel the world is. Those who rush off unprepared are swallowed by this madness. What you call abuse I call survival training.

In Kahllah, I have created a perfect specimen. Long after you and I are gone and forgotten, the legacy of the Black Lotus will live on."

Animal looked at Priest as if he had a screw loose. "Do you hear yourself? You're talking about Kahllah as if she's some type of lab experiment. She's a person, you fucking monster!"

Moving faster than Animal's eyes could follow, Priest was on his feet and standing directly in front of him. "You'd do well to watch how you speak to me, boy."

Animal glared at Priest, lips parted, grilles glistening. "That boogey-man shit only works on little girls, homie. I'm a grown-ass man."

"You're talking like you're thinking about doing something. Need I remind you of what happened the last time you tried to raise up against me?"

Animal slipped off his harness and laid it and his two guns on the ground. "Ain't no chain around my ankle this time, Padre."

"I see them nuts getting too heavy for your jeans again." Priest took a few steps back, smiling sinisterly, lips curled up into two perfect pink bows, identical to Animal's lips. He spread his arms. "There ain't nothing but space and opportunity between us. You wanna dance, come on and get your ass kicked."

Animal lunged forward. This time, his attack wasn't wild and mindless; he was focused and calculating with his blows. Priest blocked the first two, but the hook to the stomach caught him full on. He was surprised at how strong his son was when he was at full strength. He lowered his head as if he was winded, and Animal took the bait. When he tried to grab Priest in a headlock, Priest lifted him off his feet and slammed him onto the ground.

"Not bad for an old man, huh?" Priest taunted.

Instead of feeding into it, Animal swept Priest's legs out from under him. He tried to roll on top of Priest, but Priest braced his knees against Animal's chest and pushed, sending him flying across the room and landing in a row of folding chairs.

By the time Animal got back to his feet, Priest was already on him. He caught Animal in the chin with a right, then came back with his left. Animal waited until the last possible second to lift one of the metal folding chairs like a shield and blocked the punch. He followed with an overhand swing of the chair, which Priest blocked with his arms, but the force still knocked him backward.

"So you wanna fight dirty?" Priest asked, pulling his rosary from his sleeve. He began twirling the chain like a helicopter blade, advancing on Animal.

Animal tried to protect himself with the chair, which Priest had expected. He whipped the rosary around the chair leg and pulled, yanking it from Animal's hands. Moving in a fluid motion, Priest faked like he was going right and went left, slamming his fist into Animal's face. He tried to wrap the rosary around Animal's neck, but Animal put his fingers between the chain and his throat. In his ear, he could hear Priest wheezing.

"I know you're not getting tired, old man," Animal taunted him.

"On the contrary, I'm just getting warmed up." Priest kneed Animal in the back, stunning him while he locked the rosary around his neck. "Don't worry, I'm not going to kill you, but

I am gonna put my baby boy down for a nap." He pulled the rosary tighter.

Animal clutched at the chain but couldn't get a grip. As it bit into his neck, he could feel his airway closing off. In the corners of his eyes, Animal began to see spots. He was losing consciousness. In desperation, Animal let all his weight fall, pulling Priest down with him. Priest's chin made contact with the top of Animal's skull and rattled his teeth. Priest released the rosary and fell backward, dazed.

Animal crawled to his feet, pulling the rosary from around his neck. Breathing like he'd just run a marathon, he stalked over to Priest. "Like you said, people need discipline, ain't that right, Daddy?" He brought the rosary down across Priest's back. "You like that? Are you focused?" He whipped the rosary across Priest's back over and over. He tried to tell himself he was beating Priest for what he had done to Kahllah, but in reality, he was letting out all the years of pent-up rage and resentment.

Priest managed to make it off the floor and grabbed Animal in a bear hug.

"Get the fuck off me!" Animal raged, trying his best to break loose, but Priest was far stronger than he looked.

"That's right, let it all out, son." Priest squeezed him tighter. Animal had his face buried in Priest's chest so he couldn't see the tears falling, but Priest could feel his body racked with sobs "Let it all out."

"I fucking hate you for what you did to us," Animal said in a defeated tone.

"I know, Tayshawn . . . I know." Priest continued to hold him. "I hate me for it, too."

"What the hell is going on out here?" Kahllah entered the

room. Gucci came downstairs a few seconds later. Both women stared at the hugging men, confused about what was going on.

"Nothing, just blowing off a little steam." Priest released Animal.

"Are you OK?" Gucci rushed to Animal's side.

"It's like he said, we were just blowing off a little steam," Animal said. He refused to look her in the eye for fear that she would know that he had been crying.

Kahllah looked from Animal to Priest and immediately knew what had taken place. They had let go of their demons. "Must men always show their emotions like Neanderthals?"

"Talking like adults would be too much like the right thing," Gucci said, chiming in.

"Well, if the two of you are done trying to kill each other, I suggest we all get some sleep. The sun will be up in a few hours, and we've got a lot to do."

"Kahllah is right," Priest agreed.

"I believe this belongs to you." Animal handed Priest the rosary.

Priest looked at the length of gold chain. "I've used this for a great many things over the years but never to administer an ass-whipping." He laughed. His laughter died when he saw the small red speck on Animal's shirt. At first, he thought it was blood, but then he realized that blood didn't glow. "Down." He lunged at his son just as the first bullet shattered the window.

TWENTY-SIX

AT SOME POINT, THE MAN WHO WAS watching the church must've nodded off. He was startled awake by a firm knock on the window of his car. He jumped, gun in hand and ready to shoot, but lowered it when he saw who was standing outside the car. He was husky, wearing all black and a permanent scowl on his face.

A broad smile spread across the watcher's face as he rolled the window down. "Damn, you can get shot creeping on niggaz like that."

"And you can die for sleeping when you're supposed to be on point, Steve," the man in all black said.

"I wasn't asleep, I was resting my eyes," Steve lied.

"Whatever." The man in black waved him off. "They still in there?"

"Yeah, but the cat we looking for is still there. He's not alone, though. How many cats you bring down with you?" Steve asked.

"Enough." The man in black nodded behind him.

Steve looked in the rearview and saw the headlights of at

least three cars. "That's what I'm talking about." He rubbed his hands together in anticipation. "So what's the game plan?"

"Go in there and lay everybody who ain't with us." The man dressed in black held up the SPAS-12 combat shotgun he was carrying.

"Damn, you ain't playing, are you?" Steve marveled at the gun.

"Touch one of mine, I touch *all* of yours," the man in black said. He pulled the slide on the SPAS-12 and chambered a round. "Let's go gobble these niggaz the fuck up. This is for my old man."

Animal was dazed from the knock he'd taken on his head when Priest tackled him, but he wasn't so out of it that he didn't recognize the sounds of gunfire. Bullets seemed to be coming from everywhere at once, shredding everything they hit. His thoughts immediately went to Gucci, and he looked around the church frantically. He didn't see her on the first sweep, but then he spotted her cowering in the doorway that led to the upstairs apartment. Her terrified eyes looked to him, and he gave her the signal to stay put. Animal looked around for Kahllah, but there was no sign of her. She had abandoned them. After all the game she talked about loyalty, she left them for dead when the shit hit the fan.

"Fucking mercenary," Animal cursed to himself. A few feet away from him lay Priest. He wasn't moving, and there was blood around his body. "Priest," Animal called out, crawling across the floor toward him. Bullets whizzed over his head, raining glass and wood splinters on him. "God, no." He turned Priest over, expecting the worst. When he saw his father's robes covered in blood, Animal just knew it was over for him, until the one-eyed man looked up and smiled.

"I thought you didn't believe in God."

"I never said I don't believe in him, I just said he doesn't listen to me . . . at least, he hadn't until today." Animal lifted him into a sitting position. "You OK?"

"I'm fine. I think it went straight through." Priest gently touched the wound near his abdomen, just above his hip.

"Damn, I can't believe you took a bullet for me," Animal said in disbelief.

"Don't be so quick to praise me, because had I remembered how much being shot hurts, I would've stayed where I was and let you take it. Don't say your old man has never done anything for you. Who the hell is shooting up the house of the Lord?"

"Beats me. I thought they were your friends," Animal said.

There was the thunderous roar of a very big gun at the front of the church, and less than a second later, the front doors burst off the hinges.

"Lucy, I'm home," the man in all black sang. Out of the shadows of schemes and into the light of action, you could get a better look at him. He was average height, with brown skin and a build that had been gained from multiple stints in various state prisons. A crisscross of scars that had grown into thick keloids marred the left side of his face and neck. Cradled in one of his well-built arms was the smoking SPAS-12.

"Who the in the hell are you, and what do are you doing here?" Priest called to the gunman.

"You stood before God and my family to be named my godfather, and now you don't know me? Shame on you." The man in black let off another slug from the SPAS-12, knocking the back off one of the church benches.

"Chuck?" Priest asked in surprise.

"I see lead showers work wonders at jogging memories." Chuck fired the shotgun again, taking out the podium at the front of the church. "You were my father's friend, and you shot him like a dog in the woods, so I've come to return the favor."

"Chuck, it broke my heart to kill your dad, but I had to. Charlie fucked up big-time. He knew the rules. Put the gun down, and let's talk about this!" Priest shouted.

"Sure, I'll put the gun down . . . down your fucking throat before I blow your spleen out through your asshole!" Chuck fired several more rounds.

Animal and Priest huddled together near the side of the stage. "I gotta get to my guns." Animal looked over at his harness and Pretty Bitches, which were still on the floor where he'd left them. He popped up to try to make a mad dash, but a round from the SPAS-12 sent him scrambling back into his hiding spot, alongside his father. "Shit, all this time you've been worrying about the people I was pissing off, and it's your bullshit that's gonna get us splattered."

"Not on my watch." Priest slammed his elbow into the side of the stage floor, breaking the old wood open. He fished around inside and pulled out an old-looking rifle. "And definitely not in my house."

"Does that prehistoric piece of shit even work?" Animal asked, looking at the rifle. It was dusty and probably hadn't been fired in years.

Priest pulled the lever on the side and chambered a round. "This old girl ain't failed me yet. When I move, you move."

He struggled to his feet. "You've spoken your piece," he told Chuck, "and now I will speak mine." He pulled the trigger, and the rifle kicked to life.

While there was a break in the action, Animal scrambled across the floor and snatched up his guns. He had just cleared them from the harness when a swarm of men dressed in black entered the church. Animal pressed his back to the bench and held his two guns to his chest. After the shootout with the police, he didn't have many rounds left, so he had to make every shot count. The moment the first of Chuck's men came into view, Animal made his move.

"What's popping, slime?" Animal sprang from his hiding place, firing with both guns. The slugs made his target dance, before putting him on his back.

"Kill everything moving!" Chuck roared. His men surged forward, firing their weapons.

Animal darted across the church, banging his hammers, hitting flesh and wood. Priest covered him, licking shots from the rifle. To their credit, Chuck's men had no fear of death, which suited the father and son, because they were skilled at issuing death. The screams of the dying men filled Animal's ears like the sounds of sweet music, and the high-powered slugs from the Pretty Bitches ripped them to pieces. He was giving as good as he got, but there were more of them than he had bullets. He had just laid another of Chuck's men when the unthinkable happened. His guns clicked empty.

"Get back, I got this." Priest limped across the floor toward where Animal was pinned down, firing the rifle. Bullets whipped by, threatening to finish Priest, but he kept shooting as if he didn't even notice. When the old rifle was finally spent,

Chuck's men surged forward and tried to overtake Priest. The older man flipped the rifle around, using it like a baseball bat, and started swinging. He got a few good licks off, but in his injured condition, he was no match physically for the younger men. They tackled Priest to the floor and began kicking and beating him. There was a flash of steel as one of them pulled a knife.

"Don't you dare kill him. That muthafucka belongs to me!" Chuck shouted, pushing his way through the crowd of men. Priest's life belonged to him, and he would not be cheated out of his revenge.

From behind Animal, there was the sound of a door being kicked open. He turned in time to see Kahllah emerge, wearing black body armor over her T-shirt. Clutched in her hands were two Mac-11s. "Demons." She addressed Chuck and his men. "Let the vengeful fire of my Lord wash your evil from this holy place and cast thee back to the foul pits from which you crawled!" She howled and let both guns rip.

Animal watched in wide-eyed shock as Kahllah danced through the aisle, spinning like a ballerina across a stage, firing the machine guns and cutting down her targets. Death was an art form, and she was truly a master at her craft. Two of Chuck's men, who had been hiding in the aisle, got the drop on Kahllah. They overpowered her, knocking one of the machine guns loose and trying to pry the other one from her hands. Animal tried to pick the Mac up off the floor, but another blast from the SPAS-12 knocked it out of reach. He watched helplessly as Kahllah tried to fight off the two men and the rest rushed the front of the church.

Animal watched the scene unfolding like a horror-movie

reel. Priest disappeared beneath a sea of black-clad soldiers, all with plans on ending his life. Kahllah was putting up the good fight, but there was only so long she could keep it up. When Animal looked to Gucci, his heart sank. He had never seen her look more terrified. When their eyes met, something unspoken passed between them. Their journey was reaching its end, and they would not be riding off into the sunset. The sacrifices they'd made to be together had all been for nothing.

"Get busy living or get busy dying," Animal said, quoting one of his favorite movies, *The Shawshank Redemption*, before leaping into the fray, fists flailing. He got off two good punches before he was overrun. Animal covered his face and head as best he could, as Chuck's men kicked and stomped him in every exposed part of his body.

Steve pushed through the crowd of men who were working Animal over. They parted like the Red Sea for Chuck's second in command. "Hold him down," he ordered. The men pinned Animal's arms and legs to the ground. He looked up at Steve defiantly as he hovered over him, holding a gun. "Chuck said Priest's life was his to take, but he didn't say nothing about you, pretty boy." He grabbed a fistful of Animal's hair and pressed the barrel of the gun to his lips. "Any last words?"

"Fuck you," Animal spit at Steve.

"You bitch-ass nigga." Steve shoved the gun roughly into Animal's mouth and down his throat, causing him to gag. "I'm about to give you a real messy tonsillectomy."

Animal looked up at Steve through glassy eyes. He saw his lips moving but couldn't make out the words. He didn't have to hear what he was saying to know what he intended. Steve's finger cocking the hammer back on the gun told that story. Animal let his thoughts drift, trying to escape to a happier place in his head. In his mind, he could hear his mother's voice saying to him, "You ain't gonna be like your daddy. These streets ain't gonna claim you." Once again, she had been wrong.

TWENTY-SEVEN

"GET YOUR HANDS OFF HIM," A VOICE called from somewhere behind the mob. Steve looked up and saw Gucci holding the Mac that Kahllah had lost. Her face was unsure, and her hands trembled.

Steve released Animal and calmly started walking toward Gucci. "Shorty, you too pretty to be a killer. Why don't you put that gun down and knock it off?"

"Only thing that's gonna get knocked off is your head if you don't tell your boys to get off my man," Gucci warned him. She tried to sound tough, but her voice was shaky.

"OK, let's make a deal. You put the gun down, and I won't let these thirsty niggaz gang-rape you when we're done killing your boyfriend," Steve said with a smirk.

"Don't make me do it to you," Gucci pleaded.

"You ain't 'bout to do shit." Steve lunged at the same time as Gucci pulled the trigger. The Mac tore a line up through Steve's chest and knocked half of his face off.

Closing her eyes, Gucci depressed the trigger of the Mac,

sweeping it back and forth. Chuck's men retreated toward the back of the church, trying to find shelter from the rain of bullets. The screams of Chuck's men as they fell to the bullets were terrifying, but what was more terrifying was the prospect of dying, so Gucci kept firing until there was nothing left in the clip.

Cautiously, Animal approached Gucci. She was trembling, still pulling the trigger of the empty gun. "It's OK." Animal plucked the gun from her hands. "It's over now." He embraced her. As Gucci sobbed into his chest, Animal surveyed the carnage she had caused. Looking at the dead bodies on the ground, he knew that Gucci's soul was now stained, too. It would take her a long time, if ever, to recover from it, but he would be there to help her through it. They would heal together.

Kahllah joined them, sweating, bruised, and holding the remaining Mac. Gucci looked up at her over Animal's shoulder, and Kahllah gave her an approving smile. "A woman of her word," she said, recalling Gucci's earlier statement.

Animal looked over his shoulder at Kahllah. "What's that supposed to mean?"

"Nothing, simply that any doubts I had in my mind about her love for you being genuine have been removed," Kahllah said, and went to root out the last of the invaders.

Chuck stood in the middle of the aisle, watching as his remaining men retreated. "Where the fuck are y'all going? This shit ain't over," he barked at them, but his commands went ignored. "Fuck y'all cowards, I'll finish this myself." He hoisted the SPAS-12 and pointed it at Animal and Gucci. When he pulled the trigger, nothing came out.

"One of the most common and fatal mistakes of a rookie is not keeping track of your ammunition," someone said from behind Chuck, just as something cold slipped around his neck, cutting off his air. "You dare to bring war to my doorstep?" Priest tightened his grip on the rosary.

"You killed my daddy—"

"So you've already said." Priest pulled tighter. "Your father was a good friend but also a notorious fuck-up who always felt like he had something to prove. A quality he obviously passed on to you."

"You promised him that you'd take care of him," Chuck said emotionally.

"And so I have, by making sure he died quick and clean. I also promised him that if you came looking for death, I would help you find it." Priest jerked the chain and snapped Chuck's neck, letting his lifeless body fall to the ground. He knelt beside the corpse and traced a cross on his forehead. "In the name of the Father, the Son, and the Holy Spirit, I release your soul from this world."

When Priest stood up, he felt light-headed. He'd taken two steps and pitched forward. If it hadn't been for Kahllah catching him, he'd have hit the ground.

"Father, are you hurt?" Kahllah asked, holding him upright.

"No, just a little winded. Help me sit," Priest said, motioning toward what was left of the bench at the front of the aisle.

Kahllah got Priest to the bench and helped him into a sitting position. When she looked down at the arm that had been hooked around his waist, it was covered in blood. "No," she gasped. Kahllah dropped to her knees in front of him and tore

Priest's robe open. There was a large circle of blood on his side. He had been far more wounded than he'd let on earlier.

"How bad?" Animal asked. Kahllah didn't answer, but her face said it wasn't good. "We've got to get him to a hospital."

"No hospitals. Too many secrets that must remain buried. I just need to rest for a minute," Priest said in a labored tone. "The police will be here soon, and they can't find you or Kahllah here, Tayshawn. You would both be sent to prison for the rest of your lives for your crimes."

"I don't expect they'll overlook you sitting in the middle of all these bodies, either," Animal said.

"I promised myself a long time ago that I would never see the inside of a prison cell ever again, and I don't intend to break that promise now," Priest told him. "Kahllah," he said, addressing his adopted daughter, "get them to safety."

"Father," Kahllah said, still kneeling, hugging him around his waist, ignoring the blood, "I can't leave you."

"But you must, my Black Lotus." Priest ran his hands through her hair lovingly. "I raised you from a child, subservient to my needs and wants, but it is time that I release you from your vow. You have money, and you are beautiful, my flower. Go out and discover the little things like life and love that you've been denied while under my charge. The world is a very big place, and you have it laid at your feet. Explore it."

"What good is the world if I'm alone in it?" Kahllah sobbed into his lap.

"On the contrary, you will not be alone. You have Animal and Gucci now. No matter the circumstances that brought us together, it is what we have endured during our time that makes us family. Is this not so?" He looked to Animal and Gucci.

Animal looked at Gucci, who nodded in approval. "Indeed it is," Animal said, laying his hand on Kahllah's shoulder. "We're all we got left."

Kahllah looked up at Animal, laying her hand over his. Her eyes were red and her face streaked with tears, but she managed to muster a weak smile. "I guess we are," she said.

Priest smiled, and when he did, there was no sign of death in his one good eye, only his love for his children. "Take Gucci outside, Kahllah. I would have words with my son."

"Yes, Father." Kahllah stood. "I love you." She hugged his neck as tightly as she could.

"And I you, Black Lotus." Priest hugged her back. "Now, get going. We haven't much time."

Kahllah and Gucci grabbed what they could carry in the way of weapons and fresh clothes and headed for the back exit. Gucci stopped and looked to Animal with questioning eyes.

"It's fine, love. I'll be right behind you," Animal assured her. He waited until Gucci and Kahllah had gone before he addressed Priest. "This is the last time I'm going to see you, isn't it?"

Priest shrugged. "We cannot predict what the Divine Father has planned for us. If it's my Lord's will that I am to leave this world today, so be it. I have no regrets . . . well, only one. I wish I had been a bigger part of your life. If I had been around, maybe some of this could've been avoided."

"I appreciate you saying that, real talk, but it's like you said, We cannot predict what the Divine Father has planned for us. I guess this was just the road that I had to walk, to become the man I am."

"And I'm proud of the man you've become," Priest said.

"Why, because I grew up to be a killer like you?" Animal asked.

Priest laughed. "No, not because you grew up to be a killer but because you've discovered love, and unlike me, you held on to it. That Gucci's mouth could stand a good soap-washing, but she's a good woman. When times get rough, she will be your backbone. Hold on to her."

"I intend to," Animal told him. His ears picked up the sound of police sirens, and his eyes shot nervously to the door.

"Looks like our guests have arrived. I'll make sure they get a warm reception." Priest pulled himself to his feet.

"I'll stand with you," Animal told him.

"I know you will, and that's why you're a better man that I could've ever hoped to be. Before you go, I would like to present you with two gifts."

"Gifts?" Animal didn't understand.

Priest pulled out his gold rosary and held it to the light. "This has been with me for a great many years. Your mother gave it to me before you were born, but the modifications I made to it came later on in life when I strayed from the path. I've used it for prayer as well as sin, but I have need for neither now. Take it." He extended the rosary to Animal.

"I will cherish it." Animal slipped the rosary around his neck, and a chill went down his back. "What's the second gift?"

Priest reached within the folds of his robes and retrieved a small SD card in a plastic case. "The second gift is your freedom." He handed it to Animal.

"I don't understand," Animal said, looking at the card curiously.

"Show it to Kahllah. She will understand," Priest said. Just outside the church entrance, they could hear the squawk of police radios. "Time for you to go, little one," he told Animal.

Animal tucked the card into his pocket and headed for the door. As an afterthought, he rushed back in and shocked Priest by giving him a hug. "You still ain't shit, but you're my father, and I love you." Before Priest had a chance to respond, Animal broke the embrace and disappeared.

Priest felt like a weight had been lifted off his shoulders. For as much as he wanted to bask in the glow of reconciling with his only son, he had business to attend to. He picked up one of the discarded machine guns, left by Chuck's men, and stood in the middle of the aisle. Several uniformed officers spilled into the church with their guns drawn. All eyes were locked on the priest holding the chopper.

"Come all ye lambs to merciful slaughter," Priest said, before pulling the trigger and cutting down the first wave of cops.

Animal had just made it into the alley behind the church when he heard the first shots. There was a quick burst, followed by at least a dozen or more loud booms. Then all was silent. The life of one of the underworld's most noted assassins had come to an end, but his legacy would live on through his children, biological and adopted. When Animal hopped into the passenger's seat of the idling car, he was wiping his eyes with his shirt.

"Drive," he told Kahllah, expecting at least some type of resistance, but she simply put the car into gear and pulled off.

"You OK?" Gucci asked him from the backseat.

"I'm good," Animal said, trying to keep his voice strong.

"He's gone, isn't he?" Kahllah asked.

"Yes, our father has passed on," Animal said solemnly. He never imagined how strongly the death of someone he barely knew would affect him. It was as if he felt his father's passing in his spirit, and it deeply saddened him.

"Fuck, fuck, fuck!" Kahllah slammed her fist into the steering wheel over and over. Tears danced in the corners of her eyes, but she refused to let them fall.

"I'm sorry, Kahllah," Gucci offered. Priest's death didn't affect her one way or another, because she had no attachments to him, but she could feel the grief coming from Kahllah and Animal.

After a while, Kahllah was able to compose herself enough to speak without screaming. "He's in a better place now, and the demons can't touch him."

"So what do we do now?" Gucci asked.

"I have money and connections. I can get you two out of the country. You can set up someplace where no one knows you and put all this bullshit behind you," Kahllah offered.

"To come this far and not see it through to the end would be to disrespect our father's memory," Animal said.

"Animal, Priest was our best chance, and now that he's gone, it puts us back at square one. Let's just go," Gucci urged.

"As much as I hate to admit it, I agree with Gucci," Kahllah said. "I'm connected, but my reach only goes so far. It was Priest who had the real power. Without him, what leg have you got to stand on?"

"This one." Animal showed her the SD card. "Priest said that this was the key to my freedom and you would know what it meant."

Kahllah's face betrayed her surprise. She was so stunned all she could do was laugh. "Our father, even in death, he keeps tricks up his sleeve."

"What is it?" Animal asked.

"A fuck-you present for Shai Clark," Kahllah told him.

THE TRIPLE CROSS

"Take this bitch in the alley, and put her out of her misery."

—Swann

TWENTY-EIGHT

PORSHA WAS SO TIRED THAT SHE FELT like her ass was literally dragging that morning. She had spent half the night up waiting and worrying about Zo, only for him to finally call from a pay phone with some bullshit secret-agent story with way more holes than Porsha cared to fill in. Her mind was telling her that enough was enough and she was through with Alonzo, but her heart made her reluctant. The downside about love was that it was the one thing you had no control over.

For as much as she wanted to lie around in bed all day and sulk, she couldn't. She had shit to do, and it wasn't gonna get done within the confines of that apartment worrying about Zo. Porsha had to be downtown for a photo shoot for some brand of liquor she couldn't even remember the name of. At the end of the day, it didn't matter. It was a paycheck and another notch on her résumé, which was getting quite extensive. It started out as a side hustle just to put with the paycheck she got from her day job so she would be able to eat after paying rent, but over the past few weeks, she had been getting more and more calls. One photographer described her as having a look.

Porsha pulled on her robe and stepped outside her bedroom. When she touched the hallway, the aroma of bacon and eggs staggered her. It wasn't until she smelled the food that she realized she hadn't eaten since the day before and was starving. Following her nose and her stomach, Porsha made her way to the living room, where she found Frankie sitting on the sofa, hunched over the coffee table, stuffing her face.

"There's a plate for you on the stove," Frankie told her, without bothering to look up from her food. She was dressed in a pair of tight blue jeans, a graphic T-shirt, and a pair of white Nikes.

Porsha went into the kitchen to retrieve her plate, then returned to the living room and sat in the La-Z-Boy chair with her food. "You're up and dressed early," she said, taking a forkful of fluffy cheese eggs.

"Gotta run some errands," Frankie told her. "What're you doing out of bed before noon on your day off?"

"Ain't no such thing as days off when you're on your grind. I don't have to work today, but I have a photo shoot."

"Where's Zo?" Frankie asked. The last thing she remembered was him leaving to go to the store before she fell asleep.

"Fuck Zo-Pound," Porsha said with an attitude. She went on to tell Frankie about him disappearing and then calling with a lame excuse. "What kinda nigga creeps off in the middle of the night unless he's up to no good? He's probably got some hood rat bitch tucked away somewhere in the projects."

"Nah, I don't think Zo is creeping on you. He isn't the type," Frankie said.

"Any nigga with a dick is the type," Porsha countered. "And what makes you such an authority on Alonzo these days?"

Frankie put her fork down and looked at Porsha. "I overlooked it the first few times you said some slick shit, but I'm starting to feel disrespected. What the fuck is your problem?"

"I'm sorry, Frankie. I'm just stressed the fuck out, that's all. My life is hectic, and sometimes I hate it, but the one bright spot in all this craziness is Alonzo. Look, I'm not slow. I know what it is Zo does in the streets. I don't necessarily agree with it, but I don't knock him for it. I put up with the strange hours, not seeing him for days sometimes, and bitches throwing shade . . . all this, and I still feel like I'm number two in his life. That funny shit he pulled last night feels like the last straw."

"Porsha," Frankie began, "I may not be an authority on Alonzo, as you put it, but I know enough about him to know that his heart is in the right place when it comes to you. He's in love with your black ass, and anybody with eyes can see it. Granted, that was strange of him to slip out to the store and not come back, but there had to be a reason. Maybe it was an emergency? Something could've gone down on the streets."

"It couldn't have been that serious, because he left his gun," Porsha said.

"Zo hit the streets without his gun?" Frankie was shocked. "This definitely doesn't make sense. Dig, when I go out, I'm gonna hit the hood and see if I can track him down." Frankie threw her paper plate into the trash and headed for the door. She grabbed her Yankees fitted and pulled it down over her head, letting her hair hang out.

"Maybe I should go with you," Porsha suggested.

"Nah, you go to your photo shoot and get that money. I'll hit you if I find anything out," Frankie assured her, and left.

Porsha tried to finish her food, but she'd lost her appetite. She thought on how she had made Zo leave his pistol in the house and wondered if that had been a blessing or a curse. She thought about trying to call him again, but if he didn't answer, it was only going to make her nerves worse. After sticking the plate in the fridge for later, Porsha showered and dressed for her photo shoot, trying her best not to think about Zo-Pound and what he might be up to.

Frankie opted to take the subway to the projects instead of a taxi. She needed time to think, and the ride would give her just that. She was calm and collected in front of Porsha, but she was really terrified. All she could think about was Rick Jenkins and Alonzo possibly having thrown his life away for her bullshit. She couldn't rest until she made sure Zo was out of harm's way, and that's what brought her to the projects.

Frankie strolled up the block, tugging at the black bandanna around her neck like a designer scarf. It was irritating her scar. She scanned the faces of the young men on the avenue. None of them was Zo-Pound, but one came frighteningly close. Lakim was leaning against a black iron gate, talking to King James, while a few younger dudes milled around them like sentries. Frankie angled toward them, making sure to keep her hands in plain sight as she approached. One of the young dudes noticed her and came to stand between her and the group. He couldn't have been more than a teenager, with long braids and a scar on the right side of his face.

"You lost, baby?" Cain asked. His tone was pleasant and even, but his presence radiated menace.

"Nah, I'm not lost," Frankie told Cain, and tried to step around him, only to have Abel block her path.

"Says who? Says you? You must be lost, crossing this block with that bandanna around your neck. You need a pass to fly any color but the correct one on this block." Abel fanned the red silk scarf that was looped around his belt. "If you wanna walk through here, I'm gonna need you to drop that flag."

"I'm not into gang-banging, so that don't apply to me," Frankie told him. She let her hand drift to her shoulder bag, where she had her .380 tucked.

"I wonder what she's got in the bag?" Cain asked, letting his eyes roam to the purse.

"Maybe we should take it and see," Abel suggested. They were toying with Frankie.

Lightning-quick, Frankie's hand dipped into her purse. She didn't draw the gun, but she had it clutched firmly in her hand, ready to fire it through the bag at a moment's notice. "You reach for this bag, and you ain't gonna have to wonder what's in it, because I'm gonna show you."

"So pretty lady wants to play . . ." Cain began.

". . . We like games," Abel finished.

"Yo, stop harassing that girl and let her through!" King's voice boomed. The twins parted like the Red Sea, allowing Frankie to pass.

"Maybe later on, I can get you to show me what's in the bag," Cain whispered to her.

Frankie stopped and looked over her shoulder. "If that's your version of being flirtatious, you have a lot to learn."

"I'm a quick study *under* the right teacher. We can ride that course all the way to an A plus." Cain smirked.

Frankie looked Cain up and down. He wasn't the prettiest thing she'd ever seen, but his swag was cute. "Come see me in about two or three years, shorty," she capped, and kept walking.

Cain stood there smiling dumbly until Abel punched him in the arm and pulled him out of his moment.

"Close your mouth. You're drooling," Abel teased him.

"Fuck you, you're just mad she was feeling me," Cain said.

"She wasn't feeling you. Look at how she's dressed, she probably don't even like dick," Abel shot back. He wasn't used to girls picking Cain over him, and it stung.

"Frankie Angels, what brings you to the slums?" King embraced her. He and Frankie knew each other through a girl named Sahara whom King had dated a while back. It had been King who bailed them out of jail when they got locked up for fighting a girl named Debbie whom they were subleasing an apartment from.

"Not much, just looking for a friend of mine. Y'all seen Zo today?" Frankie asked.

"What you want with my brother?" Lakim asked in a less-than-friendly tone. He also knew Frankie but in a different way. Back in the days when Frankie had been running with a crew of girls who called themselves the Twenty-Gang, they had robbed Lakim. Frankie couldn't have been more than a teenager at the time, but even back then, she was playing grown folks' games. The beef was years old and had long been squashed, but Lakim always paid extra-special attention to her, because he knew what she was capable of.

"His girl, who happens to be my best friend, is worried

about him. Zo slid out the crib last night to go to the store and never came back," Frankie told him. From the look that flashed across Lakim's face, she knew that he knew something, but he didn't seem to be willing to tell it.

"Zo got himself into a pinch last night," King told her.

"What kind of pinch? Is he OK?" Frankie asked in a concerned tone.

"He got knocked last night, but I got my lawyer on the case. The charge is bullshit, fabricated by two thirsty-ass cops," King informed her.

"I hate a cocksucking-ass pig. They know Zo ain't killed nobody," Frankie said heatedly.

"How did you know they picked him up for murder?" Lakim asked with a raised eyebrow.

Frankie hesitated before answering. "Oh, because King just said—"

"I only said he got locked up. I never said what for," King said, cutting her off. "Something you wanna tell me, Frankie Angels?"

Frankie felt like every eye in the hood turned to her, waiting to see how she would answer the question. She considered lying, but something about the way King was looking at her made her hesitant. Frankie Angels could stare down most men without flinching, but his gaze made her cringe. She felt like if her words weren't chosen very carefully, they could very well be her last.

"Look," she began, "when Zo came by last night, he told me that his name was on the wire over this kid who got clapped. Outside of that, I really don't know the details." What she said wasn't completely true, but it wasn't a lie, either.

"If Zo was in trouble, why the fuck would he come to you before coming to me, and I'm his brother?" Lakim asked suspiciously.

"How the hell should I know? When he came by Porsha's house last night, he told me what was up, but he didn't seem too concerned, so I left it alone," Frankie lied.

Lakim shook his head. "I keep telling that nigga these bitches ain't no good."

"That bitch, as you call her, is my best friend, so I'd appreciate it if you watched your mouth when you speak about her in front of me," Frankie told Lakim.

"Put ya fangs away, shorty. It ain't that serious," King interjected. "The immediate situation is getting Zo out of the slammer. Did he tell you anything else?"

"Not really, you know how Zo is," Frankie said.

King nodded. "Indeed, he always plays his hand to his chest."

"This is some bullshit! My brother is about that action, but he ain't no killer. He ain't like us, King," Lakim said emotionally. The thought of his baby brother spending the rest of his life in a cage made him weak.

"What is or isn't in that man's heart isn't for us to say, and it ain't what's important. Zo-Pound is family, and we look out for family, you hear me?" King asked Lakim.

"I hear you, God, but thinking about baby bro laying up in the system is fucking with me," Lakim told him.

"La, Zo ain't no stranger to time. Zo did a nickel and never asked a nigga for a crumb, so I'm sure he'll keep for a few days until we can get him out," King said.

"I know bro can handle it, but that ain't stopping me from

feeling helpless. We getting money, so the rules shouldn't apply to us," Lakim reasoned.

"That's where you're wrong, La. When it comes to murder, the same rules apply to rich niggaz and poor niggaz," King told him. "On the legal side, I'll wait until I hear back from the lawyer, but on some G shit, I'm gonna launch my own investigation. Nine times outta ten, the police are reaching by sweating Alonzo for the body. I know Zo-Pound, and if he put a nigga to sleep, he damn sure didn't leave any evidence behind. He's too careful for that, so there has to be a leak in the pipes somewhere. We gonna find that leak and plug it." He patted his waist, where he had the big Desert Eagle tucked.

Frankie felt like a look passed between her and King when he made the gesture. "If there's anything I can do, just hit me up," Frankie told him. She was anxious to get up out of there, because the more they spoke, the worse she felt.

"Yeah, we'll definitely be in touch," King assured her. There was something about the way he looked at Frankie that made her uneasy.

Frankie gave a rushed good-bye, then hot-footed it out of the projects as fast as she could. Lakim's eyes stayed glued to her until she had disappeared from sight.

Frankie couldn't get away from the projects fast enough. The whole time she'd been talking to King, she feared that he'd see through her half-truth and tear her head off. He never came out and said it, but Frankie had a feeling that he knew she wasn't being totally honest, and the question remained, why he didn't expose her for it? Whatever his reasons were for toying with Frankie, she couldn't be sure, but that wasn't the immediate issue. She had to get Zo out of the jam he'd gotten himself into.

She didn't have the money to drop on a high-powered lawyer to help him, but that didn't mean she was totally without resources. Frankie ducked into the corner bodega and purchased a long-distance calling card, then began the tedious process of trying to find a pay phone. The fossils had become nearly extinct since the invention of cellular phones, but after walking about eight or nine blocks, she was able to find one. She could've made the call on her cell phone, but wireless lines weren't secure, and she couldn't risk the call being traced.

Frankie followed the directions on the back of the calling card and punched in an overseas number she had committed to memory many years ago. When it was given to her, she was instructed to only use it under the direst of circumstances, and helping Zo qualified as just such circumstances. She listened intently, praying that the number still worked. On the fourth ring, her prayers were answered, and someone picked up, but they didn't speak.

"It's me, Fran—it's Angels."

Still silent.

"Listen, I know what you said, and I swear to Christ, I wouldn't even call you if it wasn't important," Frankie said.

More silence.

"OK, you want me to beg? I'm begging!" Frankie was emotional. "Please, you're the only one I can turn to. You don't have to talk, just listen." And with that, Frankie began pouring out the details of her tragic life over the past few years and hoped it was enough to melt an icy heart.

"I don't trust that bitch," Lakim said venomously after Frankie had gone.

"You don't trust nobody. Frankie Angels is solid," King told Lakim.

"Why do they call her Frankie Angels?" Cain asked. He'd been so quiet neither King nor Lakim had noticed him standing there.

King looked at Cain and caught the telltale glint of infatuation in his eyes. "Frankie is *skilled* at eluding the Reaper," King told him. "She's died and come back twice, and those are just the times that I know of. That girl has been through more shit than a little bit and is still standing. If that ain't angels protecting her, I don't know what to call it."

"She's a little *too* lucky for my tastes," Lakim said coldly. Something in his gut told him that Frankie knew more than she let on about his brother's case.

King draped one of his muscular arms around Lakim and pulled his friend to him. "La, you need to relax. I know you stressed about what's going on with Zo, but you pointing that anger in the wrong direction. I got something you can focus that on, though," he said sinisterly. "Y'all took care of that for me?" he asked the twins.

"You know it," Cain told him. With a wave of his hand, he motioned for everyone to follow him to the green Honda sitting at the curb. He gave his brother the signal, and Abel gleefully popped the trunk. Tucked neatly inside was a man, bound and naked. His eyes held the look of a terrified rabbit.

"Who the fuck is that?" Lakim asked, not really sure what to make of it.

"This is one of the niggaz who had a hand in that shit that happened with Shorty," King told him.

"His name is Big Money Savage." Cain filled him in, prodding Big Money with his finger.

The name immediately rang off in Lakim's head. "You mean to tell me you've got a member of the Savage family tied up in the trunk?" He was shocked.

"You say it like these niggaz are connected or something," King said.

"Nah, they ain't connected, but the name Savage is ringing in the streets," Lakim told him. "There's a bunch of those crazy muthafuckas. They're like Bebe's kids, only packing uzis."

"Well, I didn't find no uzi on this piece of shit, but he did have a punk-ass twenty-five on him when we swooped down," Abel joked.

"Shut up, stupid," Lakim snapped. "King, I don't know how you, of all people, don't know the Savages when you were locked up with their brother Mad Dog."

King flashed through his mental Rolodex and put a face with the name Mad Dog. He had met a kid who went by that moniker while passing through Sing Sing state prison. Mad Dog was very passive and mostly kept to himself, reading or working out, but there was a monster lurking beneath that calm exterior, and King had seen it firsthand. He had been on a visit at the same time as Mad Dog when an inmate who was also on the visiting-room floor said something crazy to Mad Dog's sister. Without wasting a second, Mad Dog was on the inmate, punching him and slamming his head repeatedly against the ground. The COs tasered and pepper-sprayed Mad Dog, but he kept fighting as if they were merely spitting on him. The COs ended up having to beat Mad Dog unconscious with their batons to stop his attack, but not before he knocked two of them out, too. Mad Dog spent a month in the infirmary. When they released him back to the cell block, he went back to being tucked away and reading peacefully, as if the brutal attack had never happened. Ironically, King could remember joking with a few of the other inmates about how he would hate to ever have to go against Mad Dog in the streets.

King found himself faced with a dilemma. It had been the Savages who were responsible for Shorty's death, obviously trying to assassinate King. If he let Mad Dog live after having spilled innocent blood in a neighborhood he had sworn to protect, he would appear weak. But if he killed him, it could spark a war with the notorious family, while he was still trying to make heads or tails of his war with the Clarks.

"You sure about this?" Lakim asked, noticing the look of uncertainty on King's face.

King approached the trunk of the car and looked down at Big Money. Unexpectedly, he ripped the duct tape away from his mouth. "So you're kin to Mad Dog Savage?"

"That's my cousin! If you know I'm related to him, then you know what'll happen if I'm returned to my people in anything more than one piece," Big Money blurted out, hoping his relation to Mad Dog might save him from whatever they were planning.

"Why should I show you the courtesy, and you didn't do the same for my little homie?" King asked him. "He was just a kid, barely old enough to have gotten his dick wet, but you sent him to his mother in pieces, so why shouldn't I send you to yours in pieces?"

Big Money shook his head sadly. "That wasn't for him," he said sincerely, "but there's casualties in every war."

"Spoken like a man with the heart for this shit," King said approvingly. "Cain." He turned to the scarred twin. "Since Big Money's got so much heart, make sure his heart is the first thing you cut out when you kill this bitch." He turned and walked away.

"Wait, wait . . . I can—" Big Money began, but his words were cut off when Cain slammed the trunk shut.

Lakim caught up with King. "King, I know you tight, but let's think about this. He's related to the Savages, which means he's protected. Killing him will mark us."

"Yeah, so you keep saying, but let me ask you this. What makes his life more valuable than Shorty's, his name?" King asked. "Shorty had a name, too, and I'm going to make sure everyone remembers it." Without another word, King walked off and left his soldiers to carry out his sentence.

TWENTY-NINE

SLEEP DIDN'T COME EASY FOR ASHANTI THAT night. There was too much going on. Every time he heard a noise, he grabbed his gun from under the pillow, thinking the police were going to kick his door in and try to arrest him for his part in the deadly shootout in the Bronx. Animal seemed to think that the police hadn't gotten a good enough look at Ashanti to place him at the scene of the crime, but he figured why take chances. If they came to his house looking for someone to pin a case on, all they would find was hot lead and death.

In addition to everything else he was going through, Ashanti was having a hard time wrapping his mind around being dumped by Fatima. Part of him wanted to be mad at her for bailing on him, but he couldn't say that he blamed her. She was a young girl who had her whole life ahead of her and had already been through so much. She deserved better than a boyfriend behind a wall or in the ground, and Ashanti was likely headed for one or the other, if not both. Still, it hurt him to the core to think about it. He loved Fatima, and a life without her was too painful for him to dwell on without getting emotional.

Ashanti continued to lie in his bed, staring at the ceiling until the first rays of the sun came peeking through his apartment window. When it became obvious that he wasn't going to get any rest before he was to meet the others back at the church that morning, he decided to tend to his other bodily need: food. With everything going on, he hadn't eaten in almost two days and was ravenous. He jumped into the shower and dressed in sweatpants and a T-shirt so he could run to the corner store and get a hero sandwich. He got to the door, and as an afterthought, he went back and snatched his Beretta from under his pillow. He gave the silencer fitted at the end of the barrel a good twist to make sure it was secure before stuffing the weapon down the back of his pants. As was his ritual every time he left his apartment, he stopped in front of the framed picture hanging to the right of the door. The picture was of him, Animal, Brasco, and Nef, sitting on a project bench. Animal was holding up the magazine cover with himself on it. He wished Brasco and Nef had been there with him to stand with Animal, but they weren't. Brasco was still locked up, and he didn't speak to Nef much those days.

"Looks like it's just you and me, big homie." Ashanti kissed his fingers and patted the picture before leaving the apartment. On his way out, he made sure to lock both the top and bottom locks. He lived in a nice building, but it was still in the hood, and he knew some of the tenants were suspect, including himself.

Ashanti stepped out onto the stoop of his apartment building and gave a cautious glance up and down the block, searching for anything that might've seemed out of place. He was ducking the police, Shai's shooters, and God only knew who else who might've wanted a piece of him. Thinking of Shai turned his thoughts to Swann and the bit of information Percy had revealed to him, and all Ashanti could do was shake his head. On the streets, Swann was known as one of the realest dudes to ever shit between two pairs of shoes, but even the realest cats had secrets, some more detrimental than others. What Ashanti knew about Swann could've shattered his street credibility and possibly gotten him murdered if it ever got out. Ashanti would hold on to the secret as leverage against Swann should he ever find his back truly against the wall.

On his way to the store, Ashanti tried to hit Zo-Pound to see what time he wanted to link for the meeting, and his phone went straight to voicemail. He tried him three more times with the same results. Normally, he wouldn't stress it, but in light of Zo's suspect behavior lately, it made him uneasy.

For as long as Ashanti and Zo-Pound had been friends, they had always kept it one hundred with each other, until the situation with Rick Jenkins. Even after Ashanti had confronted Zo and told him what the police were saying, he still tried to spin Ashanti. Murder was a very sensitive subject, and Ashanti could understand Zo not wanting anybody to know, but Ashanti wasn't just *anybody*. They were brothers in arms. What Ashanti found even more disturbing than Zo keeping secrets was the fact that the murder seemed so random and totally out of Zo's character. Zo had bodies under his belt, but he wasn't a cold-blooded killer. For Zo to take a man's life, he had to have been pushed, but what could Rick have done to send him over the edge when they supposedly didn't know each other? There were so many questions that needed answering, and Ashanti just hoped that they had enough time to touch on all of them.

Ashanti slipped into the store and greeted the young Arab dudes who worked there. He didn't have to tell them what he wanted; they already knew, because he got the same thing every time: turkey, ham, and Swiss, with extra mayo, oil, and vinegar. He kept one eye on the dude making his sandwich and one cast out the bodega window. Outside, a blue-and-white police car pulled to the curb in front of the store. Ashanti felt the icy trails of sweat running down his back and pooling near the butt of the Beretta tucked into the back of his sweatpants. His heart thundered in his chest as one of the officers got out of the car and started walking toward the bodega. Ashanti's hand involuntarily slipped over the gun, finger trembling over the trigger. The cop stopped and listened as a call came in over the radio mounted on his shoulder. After responding to the radio call, the cop turned on his heels and went back to the squad car, which peeled off. Whatever had happened must've been more important than what he wanted in the store, and Ashanti was thankful for it.

"Yo, ack, hurry up with my sandwich!" Ashanti called behind the counter. He was overcome with the urge to get off the streets. When his sandwich was done, Ashanti grabbed his bag, threw a ten-dollar bill onto the counter, and skirted without bothering to wait for his change.

The whole walk back to his building, Ashanti kept looking over his shoulder, as if he expected someone to jump out behind him. He skipped the elevator and bounded up the few flights to his floor. Tucking the sandwich under one arm, he fished his key from his pocket, undid the bottom lock, and slipped inside. Only when his back was pressed firmly against his apartment wall did he breathe a sigh of safe relief. When he'd calmed, he realized something of great importance that he'd missed when he came in. When he left to go to the store, he'd secured both locks, but when he came back, only one was still in place.

Ashanti dropped his sandwich and reached for his gun; at the same time, the shadows in the apartment closed in on him. He pulled his gun and fired on the closest thing to him. From the scream in the darkness of the apartment, he knew he had hit his mark, but he would never get to see it fall, because a split second later, he was clubbed in the back of the head with something heavy, and everything went dark.

Ashanti was awakened by a glass of cold water being thrown in his face. He sprang up, only to be overcome with vertigo and plopped back down in the chair he was sitting in. The room was spinning, and all he could see was shapes and colors, but he knew he wasn't alone. As his vision cleared, he was able to make out a face hovering over him.

"Animal?"

"No, nigga, the boogey man," Animal said harshly.

"Does he always greet his guests by shooting them?" Kahllah asked from the sofa where she was sitting. She had her T-shirt raised, while Gucci examined the bruise on her stomach. Had it not been for the fact that she was wearing body armor when Ashanti shot her, the wound would've likely been fatal.

"When they show up at my crib uninvited," Ashanti replied. "What is this all about? I thought Priest said we were gonna meet at the church."

"Priest is gone, and so is the church," Animal said sadly. The sorrowful look on his face said what his mouth could not.

"I'm sorry," Ashanti said sincerely.

"No need to be. Death comes for us all eventually. Some sooner than others," Animal said, as if he were simply talking about a spilled glass of water instead of the loss of his father.

On the exterior, Animal was as composed and cool as ever, but Ashanti knew his friend well enough to tell when he was hurt. "So if Priest is dead, what are we supposed to do now? He was the key to us settling this thing with Shai."

"Just because Priest is dead doesn't mean the plan is." Animal showed him the SD card. "Do you have a computer?"

Animal, Ashanti, Kahllah, and Gucci sat huddled around Ashanti's desktop computer. All their eyes were locked on the screen as they pored over the information that was on the SD card. There were names, dates, crimes, and dollar amounts. In the right hands, the electronic files could topple New York's entire criminal underworld.

"Man, this is bigger than I thought," Ashanti said, in shock. "Animal, do you know what you can do with all this?"

"I didn't at first, but Priest did. He gave his life so that I could put it to use, and I intend to. This is the trump card we needed to end this feud with Shai Clark once and for all."

"So what now? Do we turn the information over to the police and let them go after Shai?" Gucci asked.

"Silly little girl, we don't talk to police," Kahllah told her. "And even if we did, they'd likely lock us up and take it from us. There's blood on all of our hands, including yours." She pointed at Gucci.

"OK, so if we aren't going to take it to the police, then who?" Gucci asked.

"We take it to Shai and use it to negotiate a reprieve from his executioners, exactly as my father planned it," Animal said.

"Yes, but his plan included him being the go-between. Now that Father is dead, we don't stand a chance of getting anywhere near Shai Clark without getting shot. We need to find some type of leverage, insurance to make sure he plays fair while we speak our piece. Unfortunately, I have no idea what, though," Kahllah said.

"Fuck it, without a buffer, it looks like the only choice we have is to bang until there's nobody left standing," Animal said heatedly.

"I'm fine with that. Since Father is gone, my spirit isn't long for this world anyhow. I'm ready to die if the cause is a just one, and you've proven that your cause is just that, Animal," Kahllah told him.

"Kahllah, you gangsta as hell, but I'm sure we can think of something else that doesn't involve sacrificing ourselves," Ashanti told her. "Animal, what you wanna do, big homie?"

Animal leaned against the wall, pinching the bridge of his nose in an attempt to alleviate some of the tension that had built up. He glanced around the room, taking in each of the faces that were upturned toward him, waiting for a sign or some direction. Being a leader wasn't something new to Animal; he'd held the same position in the Dog Pound, but that was different. Brasco, Nef, and the others had gotten into the race car to hell willingly; the rest were shanghaied. Animal was the glue that bound them all together, so it fell to him to make sure they survived the ordeal.

"I've got an idea." Gucci spoke up, and all eyes turned toward her.

THIRTY

PURPLE CITY GENTLEMAN'S CLUB WAS ONE OF the newest strip clubs to pop up in New York City, but in the short time it had been open, it had caused quite a buzz. It was part of a franchise, started by a hustler/killer named Diamonds who operated out of Miami. The New York location was the second one to open, and there was currently one under construction in Los Angeles. Diamonds was as much of an entrepreneur as he was a criminal.

It was still early in the evening, so the spot hadn't really kicked off yet, but there were a few dudes who had slipped in during happy hour and decided to linger until the main event to avoid paying the twenty-dollar cover charge. A few of the new girls were doing their best to entertain them and get all the paper they could before the show stoppers came out and snatched it all up. Purple City was known to have some of the most beautiful and skilled dancers on the circuit. They rotated their stable regularly, so you weren't likely to see the same girls from week to week.

Four girls danced around both sides of the large glass-top bar that divided the room. The extra-thirsty cats occupied the seats close to the bar. One dude in particular was feeling himself, thanks to the frosty bottle of Patrón in his hand. He probably spilled more liquor than he drank, while he threw dollars at the girls and tried his best to cop a cheap feel. He was one of those dudes who did the most for the least, draped in an imitation fur jacket with an oversized hood. The temperature outside had dropped but not enough to call for the coat. Behind black sunglasses, he did his best impersonation of a rapper.

Swann sat in the back of the club, nursing a bottle of champagne and taking slow tokes off a hookah. Dancing on the table in front of him was a light-skinned girl who was pretty but could stand to lose a few pounds and schedule an appointment with the dermatologist. Swann motioned for her to turn around, and she proceeded to touch her toes and wiggle her large ass in his face. Swann ran his hand down her ass and slipped two fingers into her pussy. She was warm and tight, and for a moment, he thought about taking her into the bathroom and monkey-fucking her. When he removed his fingers, a smell reached his nose that made him decided against it.

"Next," Swann said, dipping his finger into somebody's stray glass of vodka, hoping the potent alcohol was strong enough to kill whatever she had deposited on his hand.

Another girl took the first one's place. This one was tall and exotic-looking, with locks of deep raven that fell down her back. Her movements were sensual yet not fluid, so you could tell she hadn't been dancing long. She turned her back, dropped down, and popped her ass for Swann. When she flipped her hair, he could see the tattoo on the back of her neck. It was a dragon swallowing its tail. Bending over and arching her back, she shook her perfect ass in Swann's face.

Swann's brain screamed for him to mount her on the stage and take her from the back like the whore she was, but his heart wasn't in it. Under different circumstances, he would've probably sucked a fart out of the pretty girl's pussy in front of everyone in the room and not care how anyone felt about it, but he had so much weighing on him that even pussy couldn't take his mind off it.

Swann hadn't seen too much of his best friend, Shai, since Percy was murdered. Swann and Shai were thick as thieves, but lately, Swann had kept his distance. He was still handling his business as far as being underboss of the Clark family and field general, but most of his attention had been turned to his little personal war with Ashanti. The teenager was reckless, and there were no limits to how far he was willing to go. When it came to the streets, he was *all in*, and that meant he had to go. Swann had buried one Animal and wouldn't see another one born on his watch.

Swann had used a good deal of the Clarks' resources and lost some key men trying to take Ashanti out. Those kinds of losses didn't go unnoticed. Swann would have to answer for it sooner than later, and when that time came, he planned to present Ashanti's corpse to Shai and dress it up as if it was a victory in the war effort against King James. All Swann had to do to give the story an airtight seal was kill Ashanti, but that was proving to be a bit more difficult than he expected. Swann had to come up with some slightly more conventional methods of getting Ashanti out of the way.

A lanky, sand-colored young man with a boyish face, a head

full of thick black curls and eyes so brown that they looked copper, approached Swann. They called him the Turk, because he was the offshoot of a black prostitute mother and an alcoholic Turkish butcher, who freelanced as a career criminal. Turk had hooked up with the Clarks by being friends with Baby Doc. They went to school together, but Turk was more into the streets than he was into books. He started out as a runner and worked his way up to soldier. Swann had promoted him after Holiday got put on injured reserve and Ty got murked. Turk wasn't a cold-blooded killer like Holiday, but he was willing to clap his gun. That was the only opening Swann needed to plant his seeds of corruption. Under him, Turk would get his first taste of blood and start his slow walk to hell.

"Your guest has arrived," Turk said to Swann with a knowing smirk on his face.

Swann exhaled the hookah smoke. "Then by all means, invite the fly into the spider's parlor."

Turk waved his hand to get the attention of the two men who had been standing near the door waiting for his signal. The men said something to someone outside Turk's line of sight and began making their way through the club toward Swann. Muscled between them was a pretty light-skinned girl, dressed in tight jeans and a baseball cap with a leather jacket. Her shape was evident even through the jeans. Turk openly ogled her, but she didn't seem to notice him, stepping past the young man and standing before Swann.

"So you're Tima?" Swann asked.

"Fatima," she corrected him.

"Whatever, just have a seat." Swann motioned toward the empty space next to him.

Fatima looked over her shoulder at Swann's men, who were circling her like vultures. She began to think that what she planned to do was a bad idea and she should leave.

Swann put the hookah tube down and looked up at Fatima. "Shorty, you've already come too far to do anything about it if my intentions were to harm you. Why don't you sit down?"

"You can't blame me for being a little nervous. I've seen enough of people like you to know better than to keep my back unguarded.

"You don't have to worry, Fatima. I respect your father, and I gave him my word that I would let no harm come to you so long as you were under my roof. What happens to you when you leave here all depends on what you have to say. Please." He motioned toward the seat again.

Fatima sat down, hands folded over her purse, trying to watch Swann and his men at the same time. "How do you know my father?" she asked.

"Cutty is a man of respect on these streets. We all knew him growing up. Rio, Shamel, that whole crew. They were the ones we aspired to be like," Swann told her.

"And look at them now," Fatima countered.

"Anyway, what is it that you want from me?" Swann asked in a tone that said he had better things to do.

"A pass," Fatima said.

Swann burst out laughing. "You've gotta be fucking kidding me. Ma, don't act like you don't know what ya man and his crew been up to in these streets. King James is about to foul out of the game, and anybody else riding with him will be retired to the locker room, too."

"Swann, whatever is going on between King James and the

Clarks isn't my business. I'm just tied up in it because I'm with Ashanti, and he's with King, but this isn't really our beef. I'm not stupid. I know what kind of power Shai has. I just want to bow out gracefully with my man," Fatima explained.

Swann looked up at Turk, who simply shrugged and shook his head, before turning his attention back to Fatima. "Shorty, you must've fell and bumped your head. Do you know how much shit Ashanti has done, and you want me to give him a pass? Get the fuck outta here! If all you've got to bargain with for that man's life is a pretty smile and a sob story, then you've wasted my time. Get out before I have Turk throw you out." He dismissed her like a common beggar.

"I can tell you where to find Animal," she blurted out. It was the only card she had to play, so she did.

Swann's eyes narrowed to slits at the mention of Animal's name. "I know where to find him, too, buried in a shallow grave under a bunch of junked cars, right alongside his bitch."

"Are you willing to bet money on that?" Fatima asked, taking her cell phone from her purse. She scrolled for the image she was looking for, then handed the device to Swann.

Cautiously, Swann took the phone and looked down at the image. It was slightly blurry, as if she had been sneaking to take the picture, but Swann would know Animal anywhere. He'd been around him since he was a kid. Without warning, Swann lunged and grabbed Fatima by the neck. One of the bouncers moved to intervene, but Turk and the two men who had walked Fatima in formed a wall in front of him.

Turk lifted his shirt and showed the bouncer the butt of the gun in his pants. "Take a walk or take a nap."

The bouncer turned on his heels and went the other way.

They paid him to break up fights between drunks, not take bullets over things that had nothing to do with him.

"What kind of fucking games are you playing?" Swann snarled in Fatima's face.

"It's not a game. Animal is alive." Fatima gasped as Swann's fingernails bit into the flesh of her throat.

"Tell me what you know, and if even for a second it feels like you're lying, I'm gonna finish your pretty ass," Swann warned.

"I'm not lying. I've seen him. I was with him last night at this old church. He was there with a man named Priest." Fatima went on to tell him the story of the shootout at the warehouse and her abduction.

Swann searched her face while she spoke, looking for any traces of a lie, but she seemed to be telling the truth. It all made sense now, Priest's strange behavior since Shai had ordered him to execute the young couple and his refusal to produce proof of their deaths. Swann had tried to tell Shai that something didn't feel right about Priest's story, but Shai had taken the executioner's word as law and didn't press it.

"That fucking snake," Swann grumbled, thinking of Priest's betrayal of the Clarks. He had no idea why Priest would go against them for Animal, but he intended to make sure the old head didn't live long enough to regret it. "Write down the address." Swann slid her a napkin and a pen.

Fatima hurriedly scribbled down the address of the church. She felt horrible about what she was doing, but one lesson that life had taught her was that self-preservation was the golden rule. Fatima knew Animal was her boyfriend's best friend, but she didn't know him and owed him no loyalties. She reasoned that if Gucci was in her position, she would've done the same to save her man's life. "Swann, I don't know what's going on, and I don't want any part of it. I just want to be left out of this shit."

"Oh, I'm going to leave you out of it, all right." Swann addressed his protégé. "Turk, take this bitch in the alley and put her out of her misery."

Fatima's eyes grew wide with fear as Turk and the two men stalked toward her. "But you promised my father I would be safe," she reminded Swann.

"I told him that no harm would come to you *under my roof*, but I don't own Purple City." Swann smiled wickedly.

The two men who had walked her in snatched Fatima to her feet. When she looked at Swann, her eyes reflected the hurt and betrayal she felt. Much like how she had just betrayed Animal and, by extension, Ashanti. "You a foul nigga, Swann, real foul."

"I've been called worse by better, sweetie." Swann laughed.

"I got friends out there, Swann. You can't do me like this and think ain't nobody gonna come see you about it," Fatima threatened.

"Bitch, save that Mafia princess shit. Your father is a washed-up hustler who ain't never gonna see daylight again, and you ain't got no real connections on the street, because if you did, you wouldn't be in here selling your boyfriend and his people out begging for a pass. Ain't nobody gonna do shit if you turn up missing," Swann said, mocking her.

"I beg to differ," someone said. They turned and saw the corny dude with the fur and sunglasses who had been stunting at the bar.

"Who the fuck are you supposed to be?" Swann looked the clown up and down.

The clown removed his sunglasses so that Swann could see

his face clearly. "You mean to tell me you don't remember the faces of all your victims? I know I do."

"Animal!" Swann gasped.

"Back from the dead like I never left." Animal slid out of the fur coat and let it hit the floor. His Pretty Bitches hung under his arms in the harness. "You and me got unfinished business."

"Kill that muthafucka!" Swann roared, leaping over the booth he was sitting in and heading for the back door.

Animal snatched Fatima out of the way, just before Swann's men opened fire. Drawing one of his Pretty Bitches with one hand and keeping Fatima tucked with the other, Animal returned his enemy's fire. He knocked the top of one of Swann's boys' heads off, splattering the remaining two with his blood and giving them pause. The breath of a second was all Animal needed to throw Fatima to safety and draw his other gun. One of the bouncers, who happened to be passing by when the ruckus started, felt like he wanted to be a hero and tried to tackle Animal. Animal spun with the force, slamming the butts of both guns into the bouncer's skull, busting his head open to the white meat. The bouncer hit the floor, on his back, and Animal knelt, shoving the gun into his mouth, hand trembling with rage. He'd thought about sparing him, but since the bouncer wanted to be remembered, Animal would make sure it was so. He jerked his finger on the trigger and knocked out the back of the bouncer's throat.

Turk and the remaining henchmen tried to close in on Animal, but the stripper with the dragon tattoo jumped down off the table and blocked their paths. She stood there half-naked in heels and a thong, eyeing the men like a lioness about to pounce. "Leave while you still can," she told them.

"Get the fuck out the way." The henchman lunged forward, trying to knock her out. The stripper weaved with the skill of a professional boxer and came back with a vicious hook to the henchman's ribs. When he doubled over, she grabbed Swann's abandoned champagne bottle and broke it over the back of the henchman's head. Without pausing, she spun on Turk, slashing his arm with the bottle, causing him to drop his gun. She pinned him to the wall with her forearm, flipped the broken bottle over like a dagger, and placed it against Turk's throat. She had barely touched him, and there was already a trickle of blood running down his neck. He still had the tender flesh of a child.

She stared at Turk's face. His lip quivered, and she could see tears dancing in the corners of his eyes, but even in the face of his impending death, he would not break. He was prepared to leave the world, but it wasn't his time. "Too young to die and too stupid to live," she said, as if she were having a heart-to-heart talk with him.

"You ain't no stripper. Who are you?" Turk asked, not even sure why he cared.

She wasn't sure why she was compelled to answer him, but she did. "My name is Kahllah El-Amin, but my victims know me as the Black Lotus. Remember it and the fact that tonight I showed you mercy," she told him, before drawing her fist back and knocking him out.

Swann burst from the rear exit of the club, nearly tripping over his shoelaces and falling on his face. He spared a nervous glance over his shoulder, making sure the killer wasn't following him. He felt bad about leaving Turk behind but figured getting out alive would be the ultimate test of the youngster's resilience. If Turk made it, Swann would see that he was rewarded accordingly; if he didn't, then Swann would search for his replacement.

Swann barreled down the alley, desperately trying to reach the avenue where his car was parked. He had just emerged from the mouth of the alley when a fist slammed into his jaw unexpectedly. Swann stumbled and crashed to the sidewalk in a heap. When he looked up, he saw Ashanti sneering down on him.

"I heard you were looking for me, blood." Ashanti raised his foot and brought it down on Swann's face.

Animal came out of the back exit, with Fatima behind him and Kahllah on their heels. Animal had given her the bogus fur coat to cover her body, since she hadn't had time to get dressed before their exit. She looked crazy, but she'd have looked crazier running the streets half-naked. As soon as Ashanti and Fatima saw each other, they rushed into each other's arms. Fatima was frightened and on the verge of hysterics.

"It's OK, ma. You did good." Ashanti hugged her to try to stop her trembling.

"I was so scared, but I had to see it through. I told you I'd do anything for you, and I meant it." Fatima kissed him.

"That's my rider." Ashanti gave her another squeeze. He turned to his homie. "Animal, that was some ice-cold planning. How the hell did you manage to get Kahllah and the guns in the joint?"

"The owner of the franchise owed me a favor. Let's just say we have a history." Animal smirked, thinking back on

Diamonds and the work he had put in for him when he had passed through Miami. "I'll fill you in later, but for right now, we need to get the ladies to safety and take care of Sleeping Beauty." He motioned toward Swann's unconscious form.

"I know a basement we can take him to and work his ass over until he agrees to go along with the plan," Ashanti said.

"Nah, I think we're gonna go with a different approach. Help me get this nigga up and into the car."

THIRTY-ONE

A VICIOUS SLAP BROUGHT SWANN BACK TO consciousness. His eyes snapped open, and he looked around woozily. He was lying on his back, looking up at a blurry tree line. In his ears, he could hear the sounds of dusk. Slowly, the pieces began to fall back into place, and he remembered the events that had led up to that moment.

"Should I slap him again, just to make sure he's awake?" Ashanti drew his hand back.

"Nah, I think old Swann is back with us. You with us?" Animal asked.

"Don't you know how to stay dead?" Swann sat up on his elbows.

"Despite your best efforts to send me on my way, it would seem that the afterlife isn't quite ready to receive me," Animal told him. He extended his hand to help Swann up, but Swann was hesitant to take it. "Swann, you should know better than anyone else that if I wanted to hurt you, I'd have done it already. I don't play with my food, I eat it."

Swann allowed Animal to help him to his feet. He wasn't restrained, nor was he going anywhere. Animal stood to one side of him, Ashanti on the other. Lingering a few feet away, watching out for police or nosy joggers, was the stripper who had been dancing for him. She was now fully dressed in leggings, combat boots, and a leather jacket. Dangling at the side of her leg, in a gloved hand, was a Desert Eagle. Swann didn't recognize where they were at first, but when he saw the park bench, realization hit him. All he could do was laugh at the irony of where the young killer had chosen to bring him to execute him. They were in the same park where he had murdered Tech, his friend and Animal's mentor.

"OK, you got the drop on me fair and square. So what now, you gonna gun me down in the park like I did Tech and finally have your revenge? Fuck it, let's get it over with." Swann spread his arms, daring Animal to shoot him.

"Put your arms down, simple-minded nigga. You think I'd be dumb enough to shoot you out in the open like this? I just thought the nostalgia of this place would be good to set the mood and, being that it's all public, put your scary ass at ease until you heard me out," Animal told him.

"I thought the only talking we had to do was over gun smoke," Swann cracked.

"Indeed, and I'm sure before either of us departs this world, we'll dance, but the party is gonna have to be put on hold for a while. I need a meeting with your boss," Animal told him.

Swann's eyes widened in shock. "Nigga, is you on the pipe? Shai would never sit at the same table with you, unless it was to watch you die!"

"This is what I already know, which is why I brought you

in as my trump card. You're gonna put the meeting together and make sure Shai plays nice while I speak my piece. I think your boss will be very interested in what I have to say," Animal assured him.

"And what if I tell you to eat a dick instead?" Swann challenged.

Animal drew both of his Pretty Bitches and leveled them with Swann's face. "Then I'd say I don't give a fuck where we at, and I'd blow your head off your shoulders."

Ashanti stepped between them. "Thankfully, we ain't gonna have to do all that. Swann is gonna put this little meeting together for us, and he's gonna do it with a smile."

"And why the fuck would I do that?" Swann asked.

"Because I know why you really took Percy's death so hard," Ashanti told him.

"Percy was my lil' man. I'd be at you for killing any of my homies," Swann told him.

"But not like you were at me over Percy. Your connection was *special*," Ashanti countered. "I'll bet you cried like a baby when you found out how my boy tore that pretty face of his up." He traced a cut around his face, mocking what Cain had done to Percy.

"You little muthafucka." Swann lunged at Ashanti, but he was restrained by Animal and Kahllah. "Percy was harmless! I kept him in that position so he could stay out of this shit."

"I guess if he was my kid, I'd be doing the same, trying to keep him out of harm's way. What do you think your boss will say when he finds out about your wayward seed and who the mother is?" Ashanti asked.

The question hit Swann like a slap. "Shai would kill you

quicker than he'd kill me if you put that lie out there. You better be careful where you're about to tread," Swann warned.

"I might be young, but I'm not dumb. I would never try to throw a rock that big unless I was sure I could lift it." Ashanti pulled an envelope from his back pocket and handed it to Swann.

With trembling hands, Swann opened the envelope and removed the contents. It was an old birth certificate, bearing his signature. The child in question was several years old when Swann signed off on the certificate, and even then, he had did so under duress. The mother insisted that it wasn't proper for the baby not to have a father's signature on the birth certificate, too, even if he would never be able to publicly claim him.

"Where did you get this?" Swann asked, barely able to mask the cracking in his voice.

"Percy spilled all his secrets before he died," Ashanti told him. "What kind of scandal do you think this would create if it got out? You think Shai would forgive you for embarrassing him and making a mockery of his father's legacy?"

Swann had no answer. All he could do was continue to stare at the birth certificate in disbelief. The child named on it was Percy, the mother June Higgins. She'd signed it under her maiden name to avoid the scandal that would come with the ex-wife of a crime boss having a child with one of his workers. Twenty years after the fact, Swann's darkest secret had come back to haunt him.

Back then, Swann had been a boy of thirteen or so. He was just another snot-nosed kid trying to work his way up through the ranks of the organization. June had already begun her fall from grace, but her body was still holding up, and she didn't hesitate to use it to get what she wanted. Most of the crew knew better than to go anywhere near her, for fear of death if Poppa or Tommy ever found out, but you had the few young and foolish who were willing to gamble their lives to get inside June Clark's legendary walls, including Swann. She had caught the teenager one late night when no one was around, drunk off E&J mixed with malt liquor. She was thirsty for a hit and short on cash, which is when June was most dangerous. Swann tried to resist, but he was no match for the old seductress. June put her mouth and her pussy on Swann in ways none of the girls his age he'd been with ever had. He was so turned out off her airtight snatch that he wasn't even thinking about a condom when he blew his load inside her.

Years went by without anyone hearing from June, until one random night, she showed up on Swann's doorstep looking like death warmed over, with a kid who wasn't a Clark and a story to tell. By then, Swann was already a part of Tommy's inner circle and Shai's best friend, so there was no way he was going to let it get out. He gave June some money and dismissed her, praying that he'd never see her or the child again. This held true until a few months ago, when the boy Swann had produced with his best friend's mother had resurfaced as a low-level homosexual pimp, looking for permission to get money on the streets that the Clarks claimed as their own. Swann had taken Percy under his wing, upgrading his stable and his game plan. It was the least he could do for the son he'd abandoned.

Animal shook his head. "Something like that getting out would be a black eye to the Clark family. I can only imagine how Shai would take it. He might be hurt enough to have you killed."

"What's it gonna take to keep this quiet?" Swann asked, barely above a whisper.

Animal took Swann's hand and placed a cell phone in it. "A simple phone call."

THIRTY-TWO

THE MEETING WAS SET TO TAKE PLACE at Daddy's House, the restaurant Shai had recently opened in honor of his late father. Shai was surprised when Swann called him and said that King James's men wanted to meet to discuss a truce. Had it been anyone but Swann calling to arrange the meeting, Shai would've assumed that it was a setup, but he trusted Swann. He had expected to be meeting with King James himself or possibly his second in command, Lakim, but was shocked to find Ashanti, a woman he had never met, and a man who was supposed to be dead. For a few long moments, all Shai could do was stare at Animal in disbelief.

Angelo and the soldiers who had come along as members of Shai's security detail immediately reached for their weapons, causing Animal and Ashanti to do the same. It was Swann who stepped between them.

"Swann, have you lost your fucking mind, siding with the enemy over your family?" Shai snapped.

"Shai, the Clarks have been better to me than my biological family since I was a kid. I'd never take the side of another man over you. All I'm asking is that you hear them out, please." Swann motioned for Shai to take the empty seat at the head of the dining table. Shai was clearly upset with Swann, but he took the seat.

Angelo leaned in and whispered to Swann. "Swann, I've known you a long time and have always given you credit for being smart, until now."

"Angie, I know what it looks like, but it's not what you think," Swann told him. "Just listen before you go flying off the handle."

"I'm listening, but I'm also watching you. I don't know what the fuck you think you're doing by setting this little meet-up, but when it goes to the left and Shai gives the order to kill you, it'll be my bullets you feel first," Angelo promised.

For a while, there was just quiet, with Shai and Animal staring at each other from across the table. The tension between them was so thick you could've cut it with a knife. Shai stared at Animal curiously, wondering if he was stupid or brave for coming there. Part of him wanted to order Angelo to kill Animal and Swann both, but there was also a part of him that was curious about why he would risk his life to come.

"In all the years Priest has been with my family, he has never disobeyed a direct order given by a Clark, yet I ordered him to kill you, and here you sit," Shai said after a long silence.

"Sometimes a man has to choose between doing his duty and doing the right thing," Animal said, thumbing Priest's gold rosary around in his hand.

Shai looked down at the gold beads. "I know that only death could've parted Priest from that old thing, and the fact that you have it means the rumors of his demise are true. Did you kill him?"

"I was there when he died, but it wasn't by my hands. Priest gave his life so that I could be here at this meeting," Animal said.

"Bullshit. What the hell makes you so special to where Priest would even piss on you if you were on fire, let alone give his life for you?" Shai asked.

"That piece of business is between Priest and me. Just know that it was important to him that we sat down and tried to put our old grievances to bed," Animal said.

"And what makes you think that I'm ready to turn the other cheek after all the grief you've given me?" Shai asked him.

"Because you're a businessman, not a warlord," Animal said. "I'm willing to bet you're just as tired of fighting as I am."

Shai shrugged. "I may have a few more rounds left in me."

"More than likely, you do, but like I said, you're a businessman. There's no money to be made in war, especially when you have nothing to gain from the death of your enemy other than saving face and slaking your thirst for revenge," Animal said.

"And you're quite the authority on revenge," Shai shot back.

"Yes, it has been the motivating factor in my life for more years than I can remember. Most of the things I've done have been motivated by revenge, including going to war with you over what happened to Gucci."

Shai nodded. "Not that I owe you any explanation, but I never meant for that girl to get hurt. My men were reckless, and she happened to be in the wrong place at the wrong time."

"Maybe, maybe not, it doesn't change the fact of what

belongs to me was touched, and I acted accordingly, as any man would've done. Could you say that you would've done any less had it been Honey who was shot instead of Gucci?"

"No," Shai answered honestly.

"Then you understand my position. Both of us are men willing to do whatever it takes to protect those we love, even if it means bowing out gracefully," Animal said.

"So you're throwing in the towel?" Shai asked in disbelief. Men like Animal would rather face death than concede defeat.

"No, just taking the high road on this one. Gucci is alive, and so are my friends, and I'd like to keep it that way. You give me your word that this is over, and I'll give you my word that I won't come after your family and make you watch them die," Animal said.

"You threatening me?"

"No, Shai. I'm not threatening you. I'm just telling you how far I'm willing to go with this," Animal said.

"And what's to stop me from having all of you slaughtered right here and ending it?" Shai asked.

Animal motioned to Kahllah, who stepped forward and handed him an iPad. Animal tapped the button, burning the screen to life, and slid it across the table to Shai so that he could see what was on it.

Shai looked down at the information displayed on the iPad, and his eyes widened. Curious, Angelo looked over Shai's shoulder to see what was on the screen, and he, too, found himself shocked. "What the fuck is this?" Shai asked.

"The information the Little Guy had on all the crime families, including the Clarks. This is the reason you'll go along with my terms and agree to end this," Animal told him.

"I take it this isn't your only copy?" Shai asked.

Animal smiled. "Of course not. Right now, I have people on the streets with orders to take hard copies and discs with this information to every major newspaper and the FBI if we don't walk out of here the same way we came in within one hour. Give me your word that this is over, and this information goes no further than us."

Shai thought on it. "OK, let's say that I did decide to give you a pass. It's only good for one free ride. Your boys are still on the hook." Shai motioned toward Ashanti.

"No dice. It's a package deal or nothing," Animal told him.

"Then I guess it's nothing. Ashanti and his pal King James have been running around pissing on my name. Do you think I'm gonna give him a pass so they can keep killing my men and trying to muscle in on my turf?"

"The truce extends to all of us, King James included. You let them keep whatever territories they took over, and they won't take any more. You'll even be paid a restitution of five hundred thousand dollars for the pain and suffering you've been caused," Animal suggested.

"And you can speak for King James?" Shai asked.

"No, but I can," Ashanti said, speaking up. He knew that King wouldn't like the fact that he'd negotiated behind his back but figured he'd get over it when he found out that they could finally get back to making money without being killed off.

Shai excused himself from the table and huddled with Angelo in the corner, whispering. Every so often, they'd cast a glance over at Animal, who was sitting at the table as if he didn't have a care in the world, and Swann, who stood by the door nervously. He looked like he was ready to bolt, but Shai had two shooters positioned by the entrance to ensure that nobody came in or out unless he said so.

"Big homie, we ain't got five hundred stacks to give this dude, and even if we did, I don't think King James would be willing to part with it," Ashanti whispered to Animal.

"Don't worry about it. I was a millionaire before my little disappearing act, remember." Animal gave him a wink.

After a few minutes, Shai came back to the table. "Animal, I don't like you, can't say that I ever have, but I respect you. You've always been a man of your word, and I trust that your word is strong enough to consecrate this truce and make sure all parties stick to it." Shai extended his hand.

"I'll do my part." Animal shook his hand.

Angelo shook his head in total disbelief at what he had just witnessed. "You know what, kid, if life had dealt you a different hand, you'd have probably had a hell of a career as an agent. You just brokered a hell of a deal."

"So tell me, is there anything else that I can do for you while you're in here bartering favors?" Shai asked sarcastically.

"Actually, there is. I want my life back," Animal told him.

THIRTY-THREE

"IT WAS THE STORY THAT ROCKED THE tri-state area. Every news channel was reporting the story of murder, extortion, and corruption that had stretched from New York City to Puerto Rico. It was a story so twisted that some said it was straight out of a crime novel," the reporter on the television screen began.

"Many of you may remember the story of the former street hustler, turned platinum-selling rapper, turned baby-faced killer and eventual fugitive Tayshawn Torres, who went by the street name Animal. He was arrested and convicted of the slaying of a Brooklyn man outside a Manhattan recording studio in what was deemed a robbery attempt gone wrong. During transport from the courthouse, an already strange case took an even stranger twist when Torres mysteriously vanished after a daring broad-daylight shooting that led to the deaths of several people, including a police officer, and almost claimed the lives of two homicide detectives. It sparked what was called one of the biggest manhunts since Larry Davis, but it eventually came to a bloody end when the bodies of Torres and his girlfriend,

Gucci Butler, were found in the trunk of an abandoned car. The couple had been killed, gangland-execution style . . . or so we were led to believe. As it turns out, it was all a part of an elaborate hoax, orchestrated by a vicious drug cartel, based out of Puerto Rico and operating in New York City, and foiled by a member of the NYPD whom some are calling a hero and others a rogue.

"Torres found himself at the center of a plot to extort millions of dollars out of his record label, the notorious Big Dawg Entertainment. At the center of this plot was the former head of the San Juan, Puerto Rico, drug task force, Captain Herman Cruz. When Torres refused to participate, Cruz tried to have him assassinated, but the would-be assassin was shot dead, and Torres would later be charged with his murder. Fearful that Torres would expose the plot to the police, Cruz sent men to kidnap the young rapper en route to Riker's Island so that he could execute Torres. The rapper was able to escape before the death sentence was carried out, but he still wasn't out of the woods. He was a wanted man and a falsely accused cop killer.

"Fearful for his life if he turned himself in, Torres turned to an unlikely source for help, ten-year police veteran Tasha Grady. Officer Grady knew Torres from the multiple times she'd arrested him as a juvenile, and she was also one of his biggest supporters when he turned his life around for the better. In exchange for surrendering to her, Animal asked Grady to look into his claims. When she did, what she found was something out of a gangster movie. Knowing she had to keep Torres and his loved ones out of harm's way until she could crack the case and have them testify in court to their claims,

Grady staged the fake execution and leaked the report about the corpses of Torres and Butler that were found in the car trunk.

"By the end of Officer Grady's investigation, nearly two dozen indictments had been handed down, and more were still coming. Among them were several political figures in Puerto Rico and a handful of New York police officers who had acted as muscle for the cartel in New York. There was no sign of Herman Cruz, who had disappeared at the height of the investigation and hadn't been heard from since, but law-enforcement agencies vowed to keep looking."

Animal's name had been cleared of the additional murders that had been tied to him during his time as a fugitive, along with the escape charge, but he still had to answer for the shooting outside the recording studio. Because of the circumstances, he was granted a new trial. Animal's lawyer, Keith Savage, spun a tale of impoverished circumstances, cruel society, and doomed love that tugged at the heartstrings of everyone, including the judge. When he was done, there wasn't a dry eye in the courtroom. In light of the extenuating circumstances and in exchange for Animal not suing the police department, the judge reduced the murder charge to involuntary manslaughter and sentenced Animal to the minimum, one to three years, of which he would likely serve less than a year and come home on parole.

It was a quiet win for the streets.

"Yo, that's the kid who gave me the CD that time," Nickels Clark said. He and Turk had been sitting on the sofa in Shai's office, watching the news broadcast with him. Swann had taken a leave of absence, so Shai had been keeping Turk close to him. He'd heard about what happened at Purple City, and his respect level for the young Turk went up. He pulled him off the streets and let him hang around with Baby Doc and Nickels. The boys had gotten so close Shai's nickname for them was the Three Stooges. They were always getting into mischief, but it was mostly innocent things that boys did. Some joked that they were going to be the next generation to run the Clark family, but Shai hoped that he could keep them innocent for a time longer.

"Yes, that was the notorious Animal," Shai told him.

"I never would've known that he was actually doing the stuff he was rapping about in his music," Nickels said.

"I seen him in action. The boy is about that life," Turk told Nickels.

"Listen to you two praising him like he's Superman or some shit." Angelo shook his head in disappointment. "This is the biggest crock of shit I've ever seen." He turned off the television. Animal's story had been playing on TV all week long, and he was sick of hearing about it.

"You know it, and I know it, but the people believe whatever the media tells them," Shai said. He was standing near the window in his office, staring down at a table that held a display of dominoes stacked in the shape of his initials, SC. Nickels had done it for him. "Let it rest, Angie."

"I still feel like a sucka for giving that bitch-ass nigga a pass. We should've earthed him and his faggot-ass team," Angelo fumed. He felt like Shai had let Animal off too easily, and it could be seen as a sign of weakness.

"That's because you're a pessimist. You always see the

glass as half empty." Shai poured himself a glass of scotch. "Orchestrating this little circus of lies was a double win for the Clark family. Not only did I get the SD card with the Little Guy's list of names and dirty deeds, but I finally got rid of the biggest headache I've ever had. With that bit of information on all the crime families, we've shifted the balance of power in favor of the Clarks. I may not be thrilled by the way it played out, but I'm satisfied."

Angelo shook his head. "I still don't see how you did it. Twisting this shit up so Animal walked away with a slap on the wrist and everybody else burned was the greatest magic trick I've ever seen. How the hell did you pull it off?"

Shai held up the SD card. "Technology, my friend. Most of the people who took the fall were on the Little Guy's list. They were all shit birds who were already under the microscope and just didn't know it. They were going to fall eventually, so I just gave a little push." He plucked one of the dominoes, causing them all to topple. "And everything else fell into place on its own."

"And the cop, Grady?" Angelo asked. "What's her stake in all this?"

"She was the easiest of them all to get on board. Animal had been knocking the bottom out her pussy since he was sixteen years old. She had a soft spot for him. When I presented her with the options of either going along with the plan or being exposed as a pedophile and losing her pension and possibly facing jail time, it wasn't a hard choice," Shai said coolly.

"You're a slick fuck, Shai. Real slick." Angelo laughed. "I think the biggest question of all is how'd you play the Puerto Rico angle? How did you know about the stuff going on with

Herman Cruz, let alone compile enough dirt on his organization so that a dead man took the fall for all this?"

Shai sipped his scotch. "For that, I had to make a deal with the devil. Isn't that right?" He addressed the man who had been sitting quietly in a chair across from him the whole time. He was as black as a moonless night, with jade-green eyes.

"It sure is." K-Dawg raised his glass and smiled wickedly.

"Man, why don't you turn that off? It's making me sick listening to it," Detective Brown told his partner. They were parked on a street corner in their brown Buick.

"Yeah." Detective Alvarez turned off the radio. "It's a hard pill for me to swallow, too. After all the shit this little fucker has done, he gets a pass, that bitch Grady gets a promotion, and we get dick!"

Brown shook his head sadly. "The stories of our careers. I guess it isn't all bad, though. Animal is off the streets for a while, and his buddy Zo-Pound will be joining him shortly. We can get at least fifteen years out of him for the Rick Jenkins murder."

Alvarez's face darkened. "Yeah, about that . . ."

Brown turned around in his seat and looked his partner in the eyes. He knew without him saying from the expression on his face. "Tell me you're shitting me?"

Alvarez shook his head sadly. "Houdini."

When Zo stepped out of the courthouse, the first thing he did was take a deep breath. He turned his face to the sky and let the sun shine on it for a few moments. He had only been locked up for a week, but it felt like a lifetime.

When he got knocked for the Rick Jenkins killing, he just knew it was a wrap. He had been careless and left clues that led back to him. That, coupled with the chick from the motel running her mouth, was the nail in the coffin. When he'd reached out to the lawyer King James kept on standby for them, he was told, "If they offer you anything under ten years, jump on it and say thank you." Thing were looking grim for Zo-Pound, but then his luck mysteriously turned. The girl, Linda, had vanished without a trace, so they no longer had an eyewitness. In a stranger turn, some dude Zo didn't know from a can of paint came forward, confessing to the murder, and he had the murder weapon in his possession to prove it. The gun and the confession were all Zo needed for his lawyer to get the charges dropped. Zo would always remember the day he got that bit of news as the first time he'd ever witnessed a miracle.

At the bottom of the courthouse stairs, Porsha awaited him, hand on her hip and lips twisted up. She was a welcome sight. Zo jumped down the stairs two at a time and scooped her up in his arms, twirling her like they were the stars of a Broadway musical. People stared and pointed, but neither Zo nor Porsha even noticed them. At that moment, they were the only two people in the world.

"Damn, I missed you." Zo kissed her passionately on the lips.

"Not more than I missed you," Porsha said. "When all that shit hit the fan, I thought I would never see you again."

"You almost didn't. Baby, how did they get the gun?" Zo asked.

"I gave it to them. You left it at my house the night you went to the store and never came the fuck back." Porsha slapped him on the arm. "You know better than to be carrying around a dirty gun, Zo."

"You're one hundred percent right, and it's a mistake I won't make again. But it ended up working out. I knew you were crafty, ma, but not this slick with it. You're my guardian angel." He hugged her.

"You got an angel watching over you, but it ain't me." Porsha nodded at Frankie Angels, who was sitting on the hood of Zo's Audi, idling at the curb. "It was all Frankie's planning that got you out."

Zo walked over to the car and wrapped Frankie in a tight hug. "You little fucking gangster, I never thought I'd be so happy to see your face!"

"Eww, get off me, old stink-ass jail nigga." Frankie pushed him away. "When is the last time you had a shower?"

Zo lifted his arm and smelled himself. "Yeah, I am a lil' tart, ain't I? But fuck all that, Frankie, I owe you a huge debt. I would've rotted in there if you hadn't swung this, ma."

"Zo, when my back was against the wall, you did the same for me. I owe this to you," Frankie said. "But I can't take all the credit. I got a little pull in the hood but not enough to make a man trade in his freedom. I had to reach out to an old friend for that."

"Well, when you speak to this friend of yours, tell them I am eternally grateful," Zo said.

"You can tell them yourself." Frankie knocked on the back window of the Audi. The car door opened, and out stepped a beautiful light-skinned woman, with short-cropped red hair and alluring hazel eyes. "Zo," Frankie continued, "this is my home girl, Evelyn."

Evelyn extended her hand. "Nice to meet you, Zo, but you can dead the Evelyn. My friends call me Eve."

King James wasn't pleased about the fact that Ashanti had gone behind his back and played boss negotiating with the Clarks. He was a man of great pride, and if looked at wrong, the move could've been seen as a sign of weakness. To his surprise, the soldiers were actually relieved that the war with the Clarks was over and they could get back to the money. They praised King as a great leader for stopping the fighting, never knowing that it was actually little Ashanti who had brokered the peace. It was a secret they decided it would be best to keep among themselves. Everyone was happy, except, of course, Lakim.

"Yo, God, I told you that little nigga was getting too big for his britches. Who the fuck does he think he is?" Lakim asked heatedly.

"I'd say he was the man who saved our organization. La, you and I both know it would've only been a matter of time before Shai crushed us," King said honestly.

"Fuck that, God. I was ready to go to the end with it," Lakim said.

"I'm sure you were, my G. Don't worry, though, I'm sure once word gets out what we did to ol' boy, we'll have our hands full with new enemies, and you can kill until your heart is content."

"I'm coming, I'm coming!" Ma Savage yelled, as she shuffled in her house shoes to the front door. When she opened it, there was man standing on the other side, wearing a brown UPS uniform and a hat. The hat was pulled down low, covering most of his face, but she could still see the nasty scar near his eye.

"What the fuck do you want?" Ma Savage barked.

"Package for the Savages, ma'am." He nodded toward the box on the doorstep. "I just need your signature right here." He handed her the clipboard.

Ma Savage snatched the clipboard, scribbled her name on it, and slammed it back into the delivery man's chest. "Here, now, get the hell off of my property before I put a hole in you, ugly!"

The delivery man tipped his hat. "You have a good one, ma'am." He smiled and left.

Ma Savage picked up the box and noticed that it was a lot lighter than she expected it to be based on its size. She carried it into the living room, where Fire Bug was sitting on the couch watching BET.

"What's that, Mom?" Bug asked.

"How the hell should I know? Probably some shit Maxine ordered off the Home Shopping Channel. That child is always buying things she doesn't need," Ma Savage said, looking for something sharp to open the box with.

"Let me get that for you," Bug offered, taking a box cutter from his pocket. He was nosy as hell and wanted to see what the package was. When he cut it open, he almost vomited.

"What the hell?" Ma Savage peered into the box. When she saw Big Money Savage's eyes staring up at her from his severed head, she let out a scream that could be heard throughout the neighborhood.

EPILOGUE

EIGHTEEN MONTHS LATER.

ANIMAL SAT ON THE DECK OF HIS beachfront Malibu home, looking out at the water. He giggled like a tickled child every time he thought of how far he had come from the slums of Harlem.

When he'd resurfaced from the dead, again, and the scandal hit the fan, Animal became a bigger celebrity than he already was. People were coming at him left and right with film and book offers. More important, his album sales had quadrupled when his story hit the media. Upon an audit of Don B.'s accounts, it had been discovered that Animal was owed quite a hefty sum for years of unpaid royalties. The Don was skimming Animal's estate and figured he could get away with it, because a dead man couldn't complain about fudged numbers. The unpaid royalties, coupled with the current royalties owed from Animal's recent spike in sales, put Big Dawg in debt to him for several million dollars. He would never have to rob, hustle, or kill ever again.

The past few years had been a roller-coaster ride through hell and back, but he was still around to reflect on it. His mind went to the father he'd barely had a chance to know, and he found himself sorrowful. Priest had been a less-than-stellar father, but when Animal needed him most, he was there. Had it not been for his sacrifice, Animal would be six feet under instead of on top of the world. Animal had decided while he was in prison that he would lay the demons of his childhood to rest and focus on the future. If Priest had taught him anything, he had taught him what *not* to do with his own children.

As if on cue, T.J. came toddling out onto the deck. He was a beautiful chocolate little boy, with a mop of curly black hair and pretty lips. The spitting image of his father. T.J. was dressed in only a Pamper, a pair of Jordans, and Priest's gold rosary.

"Come here." Animal scooped T.J. onto his lap. "Where did you get this?" He removed the chain, And T.J. started crying. "No, this isn't for you. You ain't gonna be nothing like your daddy or grandpa, you hear me?"

In response, T.J. leaned in and hugged Animal. It was as if he knew his father was slipping back to his dark place, and he wanted to help pull him out of it.

"You're a good boy, T.J. You ain't gonna get caught up in none of this bullshit." Animal rubbed his back.

"He sure isn't." Gucci stepped out onto the deck. Her hair was micro-braided and pulled back into a ponytail. The long sundress she wore blew in the warm breeze. She took T.J. off Animal's lap and took his place, holding T.J. in her arms. "What you doing out here?"

"Just thinking," Animal said, running his hand down her thigh. After giving birth to T.J., Gucci had gotten thick, and it was all in the right places. "Baby, me and you have been through some shit, and more than a few times it didn't look good, for our relationship or our lives, but look at us now." He motioned toward the view.

"Tayshawn, love is stronger than anything, including bullets." Gucci kissed him.

Animal's cell phone vibrated on the table, breaking their embrace. He picked up the phone and looked at the screen. It was an unknown number. "Speak on it," he answered.

"What's up, bro," Kahllah said, greeting him from the other end.

"Black Lotus, what's popping?" Animal's face lit up. While he was in prison, Animal and Kahllah had gotten very close. She wrote him all the time and came to visit almost as much as Gucci.

"I'm in Cali, landed in LAX about an hour ago," Kahllah told him.

"Kahllah, why didn't you call me? I'd have come and picked you up from the airport. I'm sure your nephew would've been happy to see you," Animal said.

"I appreciate that, Animal, but this isn't a social visit. I'm in California on business."

Animal got quiet. He gently slid Gucci off his lap and walked over near the edge of the deck, out of earshot. "Where are you?"

"About twenty minutes from your house. You feel like taking a ride for old time's sake?"

"Kahllah, you know I ain't 'bout that life no more," Animal whispered.

"Stop acting like that, Animal. This is easy money, and the mark is a piece of shit. He fondled the wrong person's kid, and they want him gobbled up. There's a quarter-million on his face, and I'd be willing to break bread with you for riding along. I'll give you fifty-thousand of my take and all you gotta do is keep me company. No wet work."

"No wet work?" Animal asked suspiciously.

There was a commotion in the background, like Kahllah was arguing with someone. The next voice Animal heard on the line wasn't Kahllah's, but it was an equally welcome one.

"My nigga, take the apron off and shake out real quick," Ashanti teased.

Animal's lips parted into a wide grin at the sound of his friend's voice. "Oh, shit, what you doing riding shotgun with Kahllah?"

"Well, you stayed on my ass about getting off the streets and stop selling drugs, so I did. I'm trying my hand at something new," Ashanti said in a mischievous tone.

"Same old Ashanti."

"Ain't shit changed with me, blood. Now, throw some clothes on. We're a few exits away from your pad, so we should be there in a few minutes," Ashanti said, and ended the call.

Animal stood on the deck for a few long moments, gazing at the water silently. He looked down at the rosary dangling from his hand, watching the cross swing back and forth. When Gucci saw him slip the chain around his neck, she knew what time it was.

"Animal, you can't be serious," Gucci said in disappointment.

"My father once told me that no matter how much a man changes, his true nature would always be there lurking under the surface." He kissed Gucci on the forehead and went into the house to arm up.

Gucci didn't even bother to turn around when she heard him go out the door. She just sat there on the deck, cradling T.J. and trying not to cry. She loved Animal more than anything or anyone except T.J., but deep down, she knew that she would always have to share her heart. It would always be him, her, and the streets.

When the doorbell rang, Gucci perked up. Maybe Animal had changed his mind, she said to herself, making hurried steps toward the door, carrying T.J. on her hip. "You're always leaving your key," she said, opening the door. She was surprised to find that it wasn't Animal on the other side.

The woman was tall, taller than Gucci, and had an athletic build and fire-engine red hair. She was wearing a tight-fitting white tank top and denim shorts that stopped just below her ass. She removed the designer sunglasses from her face and gave Gucci the once-over with steel-gray eyes.

"Can I help you?"

"I don't know yet. You Gucci Butler?" the redhead asked with an attitude.

"It's actually Gucci *Torres* now." She held up her hand, showing off her diamond wedding ring. "And I don't think we know each other."

"No, we don't know each other, but we've got someone in common. My name is Sonja, Red Sonja. Maybe you've heard of me?"

Gucci flushed with anger when she heard the name. She couldn't believe Animal's mistress had the nerve to show up at her house. "Yeah, I've heard of you. What the fuck are you doing at my house? I don't know and don't care what went on between you and Animal in Puerto Rico, but that shit is long dead and over with. He's mine now!"

Sonja laughed. "Calm down, hood rat. I didn't come here for your man. If I wanted him, he would've never left Puerto Rico. So pump your brakes."

"Then what the fuck do you want?" Gucci snapped.

"Just a little conversation, but I'm going to need you to watch that gutter-ass mouth of yours in front of these kids," Sonja said seriously.

"*Kids*?" Gucci was confused.

"I'm sorry, where are my manners? Come here, Celeste," Sonja said, calling to someone who had been standing off to the side.

A little girl appeared. She looked to be about two or three years old, with reddish-brown hair and almond-colored skin. She clung to Sonja's leg and looked up at Gucci quizzically with dark eyes . . . eyes that Gucci was all too familiar with, because she had been gazing into them for years. Gucci's mouth went dry, and she was suddenly nauseated. Had it not been for the fact that she was holding T.J., she would've fainted.

With a mocking smirk on her face, Sonja told the child, "Celeste, say hello to your baby brother."

OTHER WORKS BY K'WAN

Gangsta
Road Dawgz
Street Dreams
Hoodlum
Eve
Gutter (Gangsta Sequel)

THE HOOD RAT SERIES:
Hood Rat
Still Hood
Section 8
Welfare Wifeys
Eviction Notice
No Shade

ANIMAL SAGA:
Animal
Animal II: The Omen

SHORTS/NOVELLAS
The Game
Blow
Flirt
Flexin & Sexin (Vol 1)
From The Streets to the Sheets
From Harlem With Love
Love & Gunplay (Animal Story)
Ghetto Bastard (Animal Story)
The Leak (Animal Story)
Purple Reign (Vol 1: Purple City Tales)
Little Nikki Grind (Vol 2: Purple City Tales)
The Life & Times of Slim Goodie (Season 1)
First & Fifteenth (A Hood Rat Short)